NO LONGER PROPERTY OF
SEATTLE PUBLIC LIBRARY

Tales for THE DREAMER

by

RITA WIRKALA

Illustrations by

Mónica Acosta Gutiérrez

Maps by Elwin Wirkala

HOOPOE BOOKS
www.hoopoebooks.com

Published by Hoopoe Books
A division of the Institute for the Study of Human Knowledge

Text copyright © 2018 by Rita Wirkala
Interior illustrations copyright © 2018
by Mónica Acosta Gutiérrez

ALL RIGHTS RESERVED

No part of this publication may be reproduced or transmitted in any form or by any means, electronic or mechanical, including photocopying and recording, or by any information storage or retrieval system, except as may be expressly permitted by the 1976 Copyright Act or in writing from the publisher. Requests for permission should be addressed in writing to:
Hoopoe Books, 171 Main St. #140, Los Altos, CA 94022

www.hoopoebooks.com

ISBN: 978-1-944493-90-5

Contents

1: Cádiz, Spain

Late Summer, 2036

Omar scanned the sunset sky from the apartment's fifteenth-floor balcony.

"Looking for astronauts, Dad?" his son joked.

"China's space station is on the moon's other side, Jamal. We can't see it."

"Oh yeah. They don't want to be spied on!"

"Nowadays everyone spies on everyone, Jamal. Instead of solving serious problems, countries play hide-and-seek."

A flying taxi crossed his field of vision. It was rush hour, and the members of Cádiz's privileged class were merrily passing over the traffic that was clogging the streets below. Omar handed the telescope to his son. Jamal didn't miss the worried expression clouding his father's eyes. Omar had been stressed for days.

"Look, Dad, the moon has a red halo," said Jamal. "Think it'll rain?"

"I wish," Omar replied. "But the radio said no."

"What do *they* know?! Hey, look over there!"

Just then, a gust of ash-laden wind brought the dreaded smell of burning chaff. Omar pointed the telescope south toward Conil de la Frontera and saw an orange line snaking across the horizon. The fields were burning. A huge cloud of smoke billowed out and upward toward the sky. For a minute, father and son stood in silence, mesmerized by the eerily beautiful yellow-and-red tones. This was the third wildfire in the fields of Cádiz that summer.

Omar thought about the world of contradictions his son would inherit. Heat melting the polar ice caps, causing torrents of water to pour into the sea, flooding coastal cities and salting the aquifers. Rains, heavy and unpredictable, either submerging the fields or else not coming at all for months on end. Crops lying scorched under the sun before being harvested, and voracious insects eating still-ripening fruit right off the trees. Glaciers disappearing, and rivers running dry.

"The scientists sure are busy," Omar thought sarcastically, "but on Mars and the dark side of the moon! Time to come back down to Earth, guys!"

He took another look out the window. It had been a terrible summer. Down the street, a family was rummaging through garbage cans, looking for food.

"Put your shoes on, Jamal," said Omar. "Let's go for a walk."

Father and son, carrying bottled water, headed to the nearby beach. From the window, Mirta watched them cross the street. They looked like brothers from behind, she thought. Jamal, still a boy, wasn't as tall as his father, but both had the same gait, with long, purposeful strides.

A hot, hostile wind moved the wilted leaves of an old *ceiba* tree. Before they had even arrived at the water's edge, they were greeted by a foul smell. In the twilight they could see a carpet of dead fish covering the narrow strip of sand that was all that remained since the water levels had begun to rise in the Atlantic. Nothing here resembled the clean and spacious beach Omar remembered from his childhood twenty-five years earlier, after his family—fleeing Syria—had first arrived on these Spanish shores.

"Let's get out of here, Dad. I can't breathe!" said Jamal.

They walked along the waterfront against a wind that carried the stench of death.

Jamal spoke enthusiastically about their upcoming move. Ever since his father, a ship's captain and oceanographer, had been offered a position with the Hawaii Adventures and Exploration Cruise Company, Jamal had been dreaming about the islands. He imagined himself surfing, climbing Mauna Kea, exploring the rainforest in Maui, hang gliding off the high cliffs and watching a river of lava flowing from a volcano to the sea. He'd make new friends at school, and they'd take him to great, remote beaches. The fun in Hawaii was endless, he'd heard. He felt lucky.

Two teenagers blew past them on their flying skateboards. Only fourteen, Jamal would have to wait two years to get his license.

While Jamal watched the skateboarders with envy, Omar was lost in thought. The other job offer he'd received, which had come just a few days before, would disrupt all of his son's glorious plans—and his wife's, too. Mirta was delighted to be moving to Hawaii. It was a safe place to live and offered a nice house, high wages and beautiful surroundings. The chaos sweeping over much of the world didn't threaten the islands, whose stable microclimate and ample biodiversity had cushioned them from climatic disruption, at least so far. The only immediate danger was the rising sea levels, which had already been addressed by erecting massive, state-of-the-art sea walls. The volcanoes had been dormant for more than a decade.

It was his duty to ensure the welfare and happiness of his family, Omar thought, and going ahead with the Hawaii plan would be perfect in that respect. But now he was being pulled toward something different: to work for the common good—not in a tropical paradise, but on a cold, bleak island at the end of the world.

The article that accompanied the new job offer made it clear. Entire islands—whole nations—in the Pacific were already under water. In countries such as Bangladesh and Indonesia, people were fleeing en masse from flooded cities and fields too salt-ridden for agriculture. Or, as in many parts of Africa, they were fleeing from desertification. But something could be done to prevent such suffering, and he, Omar Homsi—because of his experience at sea and his scientific background—had been selected to coordinate a project that would help millions of these people.

He remembered that decades before, his own father had also faced a moral dilemma, when the civil war had begun in Syria in 2010. His father had had to choose between accepting a position in a government he didn't support, which guaranteed protection for him and his family, and taking the path of exile. He had chosen the latter—and a clear conscience. They had gone through hell before Spain had admitted them as refugees, but it had been the right decision.

Now it was Omar who needed to make a choice between the welfare of his family and his duty to the world. And having to make that decision overwhelmed him.

It was late when they arrived home. Omar took another look out the open window, as if seeking an answer to his questions. The stars twinkled but remained silent.

That night he had a dream.

The Lame Fox

He was at the beach, and someone sitting nearby on a rock said, "Omar, do you remember the story of the man who went into the forest and saw a crippled fox eating the leftovers from a lion's meal? A voice said to the man: 'Don't be like a crippled fox living on what others leave behind; be like the lion that provides for itself and leaves something for others!'"

Omar woke up with a start and a tremendous urge to hold on to the image, but it had already faded away. The dream had been vivid and powerful. The story it referred to was in a collection someone had given him years before, when printed books were still produced, but he had forgotten all about it until now. He got the distinct impression that his mind had retrieved this tale from some fold in his memory and had given it back to him in the dream for a reason.

The next morning, at breakfast, he recounted the dream to his wife.

"Mirta, don't you think we should be like the lion in the story?"

"What do you mean, Omar?" she asked, although she knew exactly what he was talking about.

"I was thinking ... this ... well … I think, Mirta, that we should accept the MBG Foundation's invitation and forget about Hawaii."

Mirta was silent for a while. Omar poured them both more coffee.

"Omar, I know the Foundation's project is important. But five years in a frozen wasteland?"

"It's not always frozen, Mirta. That was before the Great Meltdown."

"Have you thought about Jamal being isolated from the world, and from kids his age, for the next five years—maybe even longer?" Mirta asked. "If it were only you and me, it would be different. But gambling with our son's happiness.... I don't know what to tell you, Omar."

"Of course I've thought about Jamal! It would be a wonderful experience for him. Imagine learning how to use renewable energy and how to take advantage of the sun, the wind and the tides. How to produce food locally and create fuel from waste! If that wouldn't be great for a teenager, I don't know what would be! The MBG Foundation sees this project as a unique educational opportunity for all of the children who'll be going with us, and I agree with them—don't you?"

Omar spoke with conviction. He knew he was asking a lot, but he hoped he could win Mirta over.

"One of the scientists already proposed using the guano of penguins and other birds, plus clay and pulverized rock, to create fertile soil for vertical farming," Omar said. "Instead of the Hanging Gardens of Babylon, we'll have the Ascending Gardens of Antarctica!"

"Did you say Antarctica?" Jamal asked as he entered the room and flopped down next to his mother.

"Yes, son. Your father is thinking of accepting a different job offer, with a project on an island inside the Antarctic Circle. It's sponsored by the MBG Foundation. You've heard of them," Mirta said with a wave of her hand. "They want him as the project's coordinator. For at least five years! He's first on a list of four candidates for the job."

Jamal's mouth fell open.

"But what's gonna happen when the poles are totally melted, Dad? The ocean will swallow the place, just like the Maldives!"

"No, Jamal," said Omar patiently. "This is a fairly high volcanic island. It won't be submerged. The people at the Foundation know what they're doing."

"But why so long?" Jamal asked.

"Well, the main purpose is to continue a study of water

temperatures and the greenhouse effect in the Ross Sea. That study began sixty years ago but was interrupted for … political reasons. We'll be able to make predictions and alert people to climate change before it actually happens. Do you see? We'll also get a chance to study new animal migrations and newly endangered species," Omar added. "They're all indications of changes in climate. And we'll get to study a lot of other things, too, such as ozone depletion."

"Oh, sure! That's right above Antarctica, that hole in the sky that gives you skin cancer! And you guys give me crap when I go outside here without sunscreen! What am I gonna do *there*? Walk around in a spacesuit?"

Mirta got the shivers just thinking about the danger of strong ultraviolet rays.

"… And we'll be measuring the eastward shift of the planet's spin axis," his father continued, ignoring Jamal's protests, "which seems to be affected by the massive movement of water from the loss of the ice sheets in Greenland and Antarctica."

At this, Jamal's face took on a more serious look. The future. *His* future! He had thought the disappearance of the polar ice caps would be the biggest—and final—climate-related catastrophe. After that, the planet would stabilize, and people would adjust to the new reality. But now he realized there was more to it than that.

"Can water really do that—I mean, affect the Earth's axis?" he asked his father. "How's this gonna affect everyone?"

"We don't know yet," replied Omar. He paused, waiting for the information to sink in. For a while, nobody spoke.

Mirta sipped her coffee. Jamal rubbed his chin, hoping to find stubble that didn't yet exist.

"Are there gonna be other kids, Dad?" he said after a while. "If not, I'll be bored stiff."

"You bet! What makes this project different from the other eighty scientific bases in Antarctica is that this is going to be for families, a real community. I don't know everyone's ages, but you won't be alone. And you'll continue your studies in the Cyber, just like the other kids."

"See ya, Hawaii!" Jamal thought, having resigned himself to the change in plans.

"And what if I don't like it there?" he asked. "Could I fly back to live with Uncle Ramon or Aunt Leila?"

"There's no airport," Omar replied. "We'd go by boat with the whole group—about thirty, counting all the scientists and their families."

"You mean nobody can leave?"

"Only in case of an emergency. They'd send a long-range helicopter. Otherwise, there'll be a ship coming twice a year for resupply."

"So it's a jail."

"It's not a jail, Jamal. It's a project to see if we can save the world. We're privileged to have been chosen to participate. That is, if your mother agrees…"

Jamal had to admit to himself that his father was right. In the end, they were talking about the world of the future—his world. Because he'd probably live another hundred years—that is, if a global catastrophe didn't wipe everyone out first.

What would happen to the world if they didn't fix it now, before it was too late?

Or was it already too late? Jamal didn't ask; he knew that grownups often hid the hardest truths.

The silence in the kitchen was palpable. Even the dog under the table was still. Everyone was lost in their own thoughts—some confused and tangled, others clear as day.

Jamal took the hairband from his wrist and tied his dark hair in a ponytail. Mirta gazed at her reflection in the cup of coffee, feeling the weight of two pairs of eyes on her. After a minute she said, "I guess we won't be able to take Brutus."

Omar reached out and squeezed her hand, a smile spreading across his face. "No, the dog can't go," he said. "No invasive species allowed."

"Yeah, Brutus might eat the penguins! Right, buddy?" said Jamal, patting the dog.

"We need to act fast," Omar said. "So if you agree, I'll accept the job offer right away. They're in a hurry to get things going." Turning to his son, he added, "The Foundation won the public tender offered by the Ross Dependency, an organization that manages the area around the Ross Sea, since that land doesn't belong to any one country. As your mom said, they want us to agree to a minimum of five years, with their option to renew; so if what we're doing proves useful, it may well be a few years longer."

"What's a public tender?" Jamal asked.

"It's when a government or organization makes a proposal to buy something or hire people for a job, and then chooses one of the bidders based on price and quality. But thc condition in this case was that the winner would start the project within three months. Otherwise, they'll pass the license to the next bidder on the list."

The Foundation wasn't the only entity interested in that particular island in the Southern Ocean. Wick Palvo—"The Chief," as his closest collaborators called him—was a businessman who had discovered, thanks to a private mineralogical study he'd commissioned, that beneath the island's rocky soil lay a priceless deposit of tantalum. An increasingly rare mineral, tantalum played a key role in the manufacturing of electronic circuits, and Palvo had planned to make a fortune once he gained access to the last remaining mines by creating a bogus scientific foundation that claimed to be studying microscopic life on the island's rocks. When he learned from his office in Luxembourg that the MBG Foundation had won the bid and that he'd lost the chance of making an enormous profit, he wasn't happy.

"If we can't get it by legal means," he told Mike Dement and Bruno Beremolto, two of his henchmen, "think of another way. What are our options?"

They didn't know yet but promised a plan of action within forty-eight hours.

"I want to avoid violence. At least, *visible* violence.

Understood?" Palvo said, shoving chocolates into his mouth.

"Stop! Sugar content! Stop! Sugar content!" his HWatch warned him suddenly. Palvo took it off, put it in his pocket and swallowed another handful of chocolates.

"Welcome, everyone. I'm Omar Homsi," said Omar to the other holoconference participants. "First of all, I'd like to thank the board of the MBG Foundation for the extraordinary opportunity they've given us. I'll be the project coordinator as well as your captain during our voyage. This is my wife, Mirta, who'll be responsible for drafting the reports for the Foundation. And this is our son, Jamal, in charge of..."

Jamal interrupted. "Counting how many eggs penguins lay per year," he said.

The participants smiled at this, because they couldn't tell whether or not Jamal was joking. They'd soon learn that this was his style.

"My name is John Wood, and I'll be chief officer and second-in-command," said a man with an Australian accent. "The boat was donated by the British Royal Navy, so it's built to withstand any storm. It's been modified to accommodate families, so you'll all be comfortable. Its nautical instruments are the best that technology has to offer, plus it's got something very special, my friends: a quantum computer!"

This produced a stir of excitement. No one in the group

had one yet, and they were all eager to use the most advanced computer there was.

The scientists introduced themselves next. They came—some with their families—from various parts of the world. There were specialists in climatology; biology; oceanography; solar, marine and wind energy; geology; and various branches of engineering. There was also an astronomer who had just returned from orbiting Mars, as well as an agronomist (the one who had proposed the Ascending Gardens, recalled Omar), a doctor, a psychologist and a nurse. Each of them talked a little bit about their own responsibilities. The island's housing and research centers were already built, so the scientists would be able to start their projects as soon as they arrived.

They had been selected by the Foundation because of their talents, their personal values and their knowledge of English, which would be the community's lingua franca. Several had a second specialty, such as music or one of the visual arts, which made for a well-rounded community rather than just a collection of scientists. A few of them also had nautical experience and could oversee the ship's engines, as well as the electrical and communications systems, during the voyage.

"Very well, we'll be twenty-nine, including the four scientists we're going to pick up during the trip, and the eight children, who range in age from eight to fourteen. Jamal, you'll need to be a role model for these kids," Omar said, addressing his son.

"I've already packed the whip," Jamal joked.

The truth was that he was annoyed. There wasn't a single

boy—let alone a girl—his age. The second-oldest was that twelve-year-old Finnish boy. Boring!

"There's more good news," Omar said toward the end of the virtual meeting. "We're allowed to add another person of our choice, from any specialty. Any suggestions?"

The group discussed various professions without reaching an agreement, so they left the decision until the next meeting. There were other, more important, things to deal with.

"And what's the ship's name?" somebody asked John, the chief officer.

"*The Dreamer*," he answered.

Jamal waited for the holoconference to finish before asking his parents the question that was worrying him the most.

"So we can take Zeina, right? There's still room for someone else."

Mirta and Omar exchanged guilty looks. They had already thought of the girl, and how hard it would be to tell her that they'd be leaving the area and wouldn't see her for years. Zeina was the daughter of a widow who had emigrated to Spain from the poorest region of Mauritania, and who had worked for the Homsi family as a housecleaner. As a young child, Zeina would accompany her mother to work, and the Homsis had grown very fond of her. When her mother had died in an Ebola outbreak, Zeina—who by then was a teenager—began working as a nanny for other families while continuing her studies courtesy of a government program for orphans. But she had remained in touch with the Homsis.

"Zeina's working for a Spanish family in Tangier, and they pay her well," Mirta said.

"Mom, what are you talking about?! You know she doesn't like those people—she told us!" Jamal cried out. "They're total racists. They only hired her because she speaks Spanish and Arabic."

Zeina was a beautiful girl. She had inherited her luxuriant, flowing hair and large, almond-shaped eyes from the Berbers, and her dark skin from the Haratin Moors.

"But she's a minor," said Mirta, "and the court has assigned her a guardian. We can't just take her."

"Yes, we can," said Jamal. "She's turned sixteen already, and she's in the process of legally becoming an adult, or independent—or whatever—because she's an orphan and is studying, working and supporting herself. It's the law now. She'll get the papers in a month, Mom. She already told me."

"I'm happy for her, son, but listen," said Omar. "Zeina has no useful profession for a group of scientists, and we can't claim that she's family."

"Maybe we can make her the … the cook!" said Jamal. "She's taking a cooking course at night, so it's not even a lie."

"We already have Mrs. Piscarelli, the nurse. She'll be our main cook during the trip."

"Then could she be a babysitter?"

"Jamal, parents won't exactly be going out to the theater on the island. Or going dancing. And besides, who told you she even wants to come? The idea of living on a cold, remote island, without an easy way to return, might not appeal to her," said Omar, "especially now that she's won the national contest for ... what was that sport she taught you?"

"Broad jump. And pole vault. But we should at least ask her!" Jamal insisted. "How many times has she called us her only family?"

Mirta felt a lump in her throat. It was true, she thought; she, Omar and Jamal were the girl's only family. She looked at Omar and saw that he'd had the same thought.

"I understand, Jamal. But it's complicated," Omar said.

Jamal walked out, slamming the door behind him.

2: Tangier, Morocco

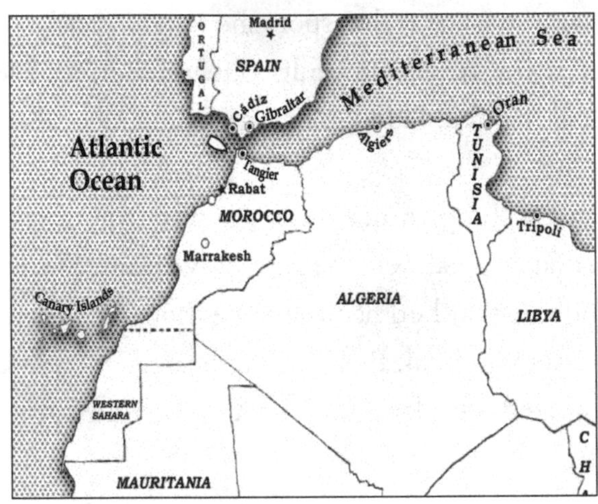

"The MBG Foundation group will never reach the island," Dement said to Palvo reassuringly. "They're gonna come down with a rare illness during the voyage, which will force them to return. Bruno's already spoken with a genius toxicologist."

"Right," said Beremolto. "The disease is fatal. They can forget about their little project. And don't worry, we've got the toxicologist in our pocket. We can trust him."

"And of course, that will terminate the contract," continued Dement, "which will then go to us, since we're next in line. It'll all be legal."

"We already know their itinerary," Beremolto added. "They're leaving from Cádiz. The project manager is a guy named Omar Homsi, an oceanographer and sea captain. He's a Syrian, or at least of Syrian descent. We're following his movements."

Palvo looked at them and silently congratulated himself. "What do you need to make it happen?" he asked.

"For now, fifty ounces of platinum—that is, a kilo-and-a-half or so—to pay the electrician who worked on the ship while it was being modified in Liverpool. He's ready to sell us the ship's blueprint," said Beremolto, "but he doesn't accept wire transfers, of course."

"We also need a boat, and a crew that doesn't ask questions," Dement added.

Palvo leaned back in his tiger-skin chair. A drone-cat purred in the crook of his arm. At its master's spoken command, the mechanical pet flew over to a table and brought back an e-cigar, as Palvo picked up the phone and made a few calls, motioning his henchmen to take a seat.

"You'll have everything in a couple of days," Palvo said into the phone, before putting it down and taking another hit from the glowing cigar. "You'll find *The Concordia* docked in Monte Carlo. Ask for Picapetra at the bar *Il Marginale.* He'll arrange everything and give you the platinum and crew list. And he'll help you register the boat so it can't be traced back to us."

Beremolto took note, speaking softly into his H-watch. Dement, however, took a capsule from his pillbox and swallowed it. Since he'd begun using the memory-activating drug Neurocrop, he didn't need those more-archaic methods.

While he was on the drug, his head throbbed with new ideas.

"And under which flag should we register the ship, sir?"

"Whichever you like," Palvo said, shrugging. "Ask Picapetra."

With their departure set for late fall, Omar worked tirelessly to complete the preparations for the voyage. They would sail through the Mediterranean to the Red Sea, then through the Persian Gulf and Arabian Sea, and along the coasts of India, Indonesia and Australia, to the South Pacific. Cyclones and tornadoes had become extremely violent, so it was advisable to keep close to the coast in case they needed to take refuge. Hobart in Tasmania would be their last port of call before reaching the islands inside the Antarctic Circle.

Except for the few who would be picked up along the way, the scientists and their families arrived in Cádiz a few weeks before departure. Omar invited them to a reception at his home. The informal gathering was a good way to start getting to know one another.

Mirta stood in the corner of the living room in front of a machine, with an old notebook in her hand. The machine pinged, and a green button lit up as the top tray slid open silently. Mirta then dropped the old notebook onto the tray and pressed the green button. The top tray closed and, a few minutes later, a lower tray slid open, revealing twenty clean, white sheets of paper.

“Here’s some new paper, kids, and the pencils are just over there,” she said, pointing to a table where they could sit and draw. Then she turned to greet the guests who had just arrived.

While Mirta made everyone feel at home, Omar started up the holoprojector, and a globe suddenly floated in the middle of the room.

“What is that?” asked Taro Wang, an engineer from Shanghai, pointing to a brown-gray area in the planet’s northern hemisphere.

“It used to be an ice cap,” Omar said. “Now it’s only tundra.”

“And this,” said Urho Ullakko, the Finnish geologist, pointing to regions of Canada, Russia and Scandinavia, “was always forested—the famous boreal forests. Today, half of the forest has disappeared.”

“Fires,” said Jon Kim, the Korean climatologist.

“Yes, thanks to drought and lightning. But also a beetle that bred like crazy in the mild climate and destroyed the trees,” Urho said. “I was there recently. The whole area is nothing but charred trunks and branches—like a vast cemetery full of gigantic black candelabras.” He sighed. “At least the fires killed off the plague of beetles…”

The grim picture of dead forests and roasted bugs seemed to hang in the air. To lift the mood, John Wood took a pointer and traced their ship’s planned route on the hologlobe, describing the different ports they would visit during the voyage.

The adults spoke about what they would each be responsible for on the ship. Mr. Wang would be the chief engineer;

TomohikoTaniguchi, a Japanese astronaut, would serve as communications officer; others would have various duties on deck and in the ship's service departments.

Then everyone talked about the work they'd already done in preparation for the voyage. Igor, the Ukrainian agronomist, had put together a seed bank of food and medicinal plants. Once *The Dreamer's* passengers were on the island, they would have aquaponic farms where vegetables would grow in pools with fish swimming below, in a continuous and sustainable self-contained environment.

Lin Wang, an engineer just like her husband, had selected the solar panels and turbines for wind and tidal power. That equipment would be sent to the island directly from Australia, along with solar-powered snow scooters for the icy steppes.

Jon Kim was bringing instruments for measuring the temperature of the ocean between Cádiz and Antarctica. Mr. Taniguchi described what he had learned, on his recent research voyage around Mars, about the effect of solar storms on communications systems.

Omar showed everyone the books he had brought for their library. Since the worldwide logging ban, all new publications were electronic, and traditional paper books were a rarity. Entire collections had been digitized and the originals pulped for other purposes. But the people who ran the Foundation had decided that a certain number of paper books, mostly scientific, would be necessary, because energy shortages on the island were likely.

"And where are the storybooks for us?" asked Liyang, the

Wangs' daughter, who had climbed onto a stool to inspect the shelf's contents. "There aren't any books *we'd* like."

So far, most of the youngsters hadn't really been paying attention to what the adults were talking about, but they perked up when they heard Liyang's comment.

"This is all they sent us, kids," Omar apologized. "Printed storybooks just aren't available."

"My dad didn't let me pack my robot," said Kimiko Taniguchi, the youngest child.

"Mine neither," added Liyang.

"What robot?" Omar asked.

"Their storyteller robots," blurted Ada Roble, one of the Californian twins.

"Sorry, girls. We have a weight limit per person," Omar answered gently.

"But who's gonna tell us stories?" Kimiko insisted.

"We'll all tell stories," her father answered.

"I doubt it," said Ming-Jung, the Kims' son. "You're all gonna be way too busy building stuff."

"Well, you'll still have the Young Interlectorum," suggested Mirta, "or you can listen to stories on the Intertale."

Jamal didn't really care about the storyteller robot, but he wanted to stick up for the younger children, and he knew they'd need something to do on the island. "Mom, those Intertale stories are crap," he said.

His mother gave him a sharp look, but he continued.

"They're dumb stories. You've said so yourself. And they're constantly interrupted by lame commercials. Plus they never have any new material—they always repeat the same stories."

"Well, that's true," Mirta acknowledged. "It's difficult to find good stories on the UNet. Unless…" Mirta paused.

"Unless what?" Mrs. Kim asked.

"Unless you know what you're looking for."

"But do the robots really have a better selection?" interjected Tina Roble, the Californian psychologist. "I doubt it. We always struggled to find good material for the twins."

"But they're interactive," her husband said. "They more or less know how to respond to the children's questions. That's why they like them."

"Not me!" said Tapio, the Ullakkos' boy. "They're for babies!"

"Yeah, and robots turn kids into little robots," Jamal observed. "Why can't *people* tell stories anymore, like in the old days?"

This comment didn't go down well, especially coming from a teenager. The parents felt a twinge of guilt, because it was true. They'd all relied on machines to tell stories to their young ones.

Ada's twin sister, Leia, spoke up. "I have an idea! If we can't bring robots, and if the Intertale has dumb stories and stuff, and if our parents are going to be busy ... can we bring a *real* storyteller? Like the one we had at our last party?"

Some of the adults stifled a laugh, but Mirta said, "You know what? She could have a point." Mirta's eyes sparkled, as if she'd just made a discovery. "We could all use a storyteller. After all, we have room for one more person, and we still haven't decided who that might be. Maybe we should bring a storyteller."

The scientists and researchers exchanged looks of surprise.

"With all due respect, Mrs. Homsi," said Jon Kim, "what on earth do storytellers have to do with a mission as important as ours? I thought we were going to vote on a serious professional."

"Well, we're not only scientists, Jon, but a community of families. And stories are essential, because they teach..." Mirta paused, searching for the right words. "They teach us how to live, and how to understand each other."

The room fell silent.

"I don't mean just *any* stories," Mirta clarified, "but the traditional ones that some storytellers specialize in."

"*We'll* teach the children how to live, Mirta," interjected Urho Ullakko, the geologist.

"It's not the same," Mirta replied. "Stories can be lifesaving."

Once again the people looked at each other in disbelief, waiting for a rational explanation.

"Can you explain what you mean, Mirta?" Mrs. Wang said politely.

"Yes, can you give us an example?" Dr. Roble asked.

"Well, we all know the story of the *Arabian Nights*, right?" Mirta said.

"I don't," said Mrs. Taniguchi.

"It's the story of a king who hated women because he was betrayed by one," Urho said. "So he commanded that each night, a different virgin girl be brought to his palace. The king would spend the night with her, and on the following day she would be decapitated. Then this one girl—Scheherazade, I think her name was—arrived. She started telling him a story but stopped in the middle, just before dawn. So the king postponed her execution because he wanted to know how the story ended. And that went on day after day, until eventually he relented and married her. In the end, Scheherazade saved her own life and that of many other girls."

"That's a horrible story!" Mrs. Roble exclaimed. "God forbid we tell that kind of story to our girls!"

"It's not only what the words *say*," Mirta replied, "but what they *mean*. Scheherazade's story is a metaphor, a way of suggesting that stories can save you. But, of course, to say they can save you is another way of saying they can help you."

Omar observed his wife but didn't interrupt. He understood her perfectly.

"What I mean," Mirta continued, "is that these stories, like the ones in the *Arabian Nights* and other traditional tales, were designed to help us understand ourselves and the world around us."

"I agree with Mrs. Homsi," Igor said. "Tales of wisdom are like science, but instead of logic and deduction, they use metaphor and allegory. And today, to find that type of material on the UNet isn't easy, because it's all jumbled together. It's a problem I see my grandchildren and great-grandchildren having all the time."

"Great-grandchildren? How old are you, Igor?"

The Ukrainian agronomist was a tall, strong man with a reddish beard and intense blue eyes. He appeared to be in his fifties.

"Well, it depends on what part," he half-joked. "My kidneys

are quite young, about three years old. The esophagus, about ten. I smoked a lot when I was young, and it gave me cancer. So they put in a new one."

"And your heart?"

"Oh, that's mine, so it's eighty years old," he said, to the surprise of all the adults in the room. "But if I may ...," he continued, going back to the discussion. "I see it this way. We're all experts in something here: climatology, oceanography, biology, medicine. Why not also have an expert in the old wisdom stories—the traditional tales, or whatever you want to call them?"

"Exactly," Mirta said.

"But where are we going to find a person like that now?" asked Mrs. Kim.

"Well, I think we might know one," said Mirta. "Two years ago, Jamal was sick for months with that new avian flu. We thought we were going to lose him. Our housecleaner's daughter came every day to sit by his bed and tell him stories. She knew so many! She was only fourteen, but she took care of him tirelessly and kept him alive. The doctors were astonished at his recovery. She'd be *perfect*!"

Mirta looked around the room. Jamal, a little embarrassed, rubbed his chin. Still no stubble.

"And how does a girl that young know so many stories?" somebody asked.

"She's from a Mauritanian family, from that country's interior," Omar said, "from a region barely touched by the modern world, where they keep Eastern traditions alive. She's the daughter and granddaughter of storytellers. She even speaks Arabic."

"Yeah, much better than me," said Jamal, who had learned a little from his father and grandparents.

"Storytellers? So that's a profession?" someone asked.

"Yes, absolutely. But it's a rare and endangered profession," said Omar.

Silence filled the room. Even the youngest ones were paying attention by now.

"Then let's do our bit to preserve it," said someone else.

The group voted on who their extra member should be, and the vote went to Zeina, the storyteller.

In Luxembourg, Palvo and his cronies were celebrating something different: the arrival of a messenger with an important package.

"Here it is," said the man, who wore a pair of thick glasses. He opened what turned out to be a small cooler and showed the group a thermally insulated capsule. "It looks innocuous, but inside this little container are millions of live bacteria that have been genetically modified to cause a fatal illness." He chuckled, seeing concern flicker over the faces of his audience. "Don't worry, the bacteria are inactive, as long as they're kept cool. They don't become active unless they reach room temperature."

"How do you use this stuff?" asked Beremolto.

"There are two ways. One is to dissolve it in drinking

water. The other is to dissolve it in water that you sprinkle near a source of ventilation. When the liquid evaporates, the residue—that is, the bacteria—dries out and gets dispersed into the air. Then, in less than an hour, these little guys spread through the … where were you going to use it?"

"None of your business," said Beremolto.

"Of course. Well, you see there are several options. It all depends on having access to a water tank or an air duct."

"Are you sure it won't raise suspicions?"

"The bacteria have been genetically modified to cause an incurable variation of bubonic plague, which is transmitted by rats. So they'll get the blame, as long as you make sure to scatter infected rat feces in the vicinity."

"And these rat turds, are they part of the package?"

"Yes, actually. They're in here. Just, you know, use gloves and masks, and be careful," the man said as he drew a small container out of the cooler.

"Just put it away for now and seal it all back up," Beremolto said, before rinsing his mouth with a shot of whisky.

The next day, *The Concordia*, a fishing boat sailing under the Panamanian flag, furrowed the waters of the Mediterranean Sea. Palvo's men expected to intercept the Foundation's ship, *The Dreamer*, and neutralize it before it arrived at the Libyan port city of Tripoli, where, according to their spies, it would make its first stop. Everything would look like an unfortunate accident, Palvo had been assured.

But the *The Concordia* was sailing slowly, taking its time because—again according to the informants—*The Dreamer* would be delayed for at least two more days in Spain. Omar Homsi had bought a ticket to Tangier, they said, and was sending a representative to pick up another passenger before setting sail.

The informants were right: Jamal, Omar's representative, was riding the ferry across the Strait of Gibraltar. As he watched the Spanish coastline dwindle away and Africa draw closer, Brutus lay at his feet, barking at seagulls every now and then. They were on their way to Tangier to pick up Zeina.

Ramon, Mirta's brother, had agreed to wait for Jamal at the Moroccan port, or else the boy's parents would never have let him go on his own. It helped that Jamal had Brutus to accompany him, of course. Not many people wanted to mess with a giant dog. This would be Jamal's last trip with Brutus for a long, long time. The boy's uncle would take care of the dog while they were all away.

"Do you need cash?" was the first thing Ramon asked Jamal after greeting him.

"What for?"

"In case you want to buy something. Don't forget, you're not in Europe anymore. Everything there is done with fingerprints and the click of a button, right?"

"Yeah, Unc. Money is prehistoric. Antediluvian. Nobody uses it."

"Antediluvian!" Ramon smiled at the word his nephew used, making a mental note to add it to his own vocabulary. "Well, here a lot of places still insist on plastic credit cards or cold, hard cash—especially in the *medina,* where your friend lives. You remember from your last visit? And keep that dog on a tight leash," Ramon said, shooing Brutus' big nose away. Although Ramon pretended he didn't like dogs, Jamal saw right through this pose and knew his uncle would love Brutus almost as much as he did.

Although autumn had officially started, Morocco seemed to have missed the news. A pitiless sun scorched the air as the two of them walked to the nearest cash machine. Jamal called Zeina to tell her they were on their way.

The bazaar had changed a lot since the last time he'd been there with his parents. In the winding streets there were few traditional businesses left. Many medieval buildings now housed foreign families. Fleeing the chaos that reigned in the cities of their own countries, they had found refuge in the ancient mansions that still survived in Tangier. Zeina was living with one of these families.

When Jamal and his uncle reached the big house, Zeina was already at the door, saying goodbye to her employers, clearly happy to be leaving them. "Little bro!" she cried, throwing an arm around Jamal and patting Brutus. She'd been thrilled at the chance to be reunited with the Homsi family.

Ramon greeted her and her employers and chatted with them for a while. Then he pulled up his shirtsleeve to reveal the outlines of a touchpad on the skin of his forearm. With a few taps, he summoned the Rent an Automatic Automobile car service—or RAA, as it was called. Jamal was always struck by the long sleeves worn by his uncle and other Moroccans, even when it was a hundred and five degrees in the shade. The car arrived and parked itself outside, and Jamal helped load Zeina's bags.

Looking again at the touchpad, Ramon asked a few questions, and the information popped up immediately, glowing through his skin.

"You have your return ticket for the one o'clock ferry, right? So we should go," he said, urging them into the RAA. It was an older model that still had a steering wheel, but it was clean and fully automatic. Ramon told the vehicle where to go, and it sped off as they both chatted with Zeina, whom Ramon had seen more recently than Jamal.

Jamal and his uncle both wished they had more time to spend together, but with *The Dreamer* scheduled to leave in two days, the teens needed to get back. They arrived at the ferry terminal fifteen minutes before departure.

"Want me to wait with you two?" Ramon asked.

"Nah, we'll just wait in the terminal," Jamal said. "You and Brutus should get to know each other," he laughed.

Ramon sighed and gave his nephew a big hug, knowing it would be years before they saw each other again.

"You'll be at least nineteen next time I see you, kid, and Brutus will be an old dog. Take care of your parents and this nice young woman, okay?"

"I will, Unc. And thanks for taking care of Brutus." Jamal

bent down and wrapped his arms around the dog's neck, giving him a big kiss on the head. Zeina laughed and wrinkled up her nose, but she'd spent so much time at the Homsis' home that she, too, had grown to love the dog.

Standing at the terminal doors, Jamal and Zeina watched Ramon load Brutus into the RAA before getting in himself. Ramon dictated his address to the GPS drive, and the car pulled away without making a sound, though Brutus could be heard whimpering for the boy.

Jamal felt terrible but was glad to have Zeina with him. He'd had to abandon his dog, but at least he'd regained his old friend.

They walked into the ferry terminal, left the luggage at the luggage drop and changed their one o'clock ferry tickets for the two o'clock, as he'd promised Zeina he would. Once on the ferry, he'd give his parents a call to tell them about the delay. Right now, the important thing was to go ahead with the plan he and Zeina had cooked up.

"We can walk there, Jamal. The mosque is just around the corner," Zeina said.

Along the streets of Tangier, solar panels glittered on the roofs of houses and businesses. Tiny surveillance cameras were on every corner and in front of each store, sometimes plainly visible, sometimes camouflaged in a billboard—where they might even lurk behind the luminous eyes of a child eating a banapple, in one of those ubiquitous advertisements that could be seen throughout North Africa.

Soon the two teens came to a portal. A man with a begging

bowl sat against a wall, directly under a large billboard announcing:

Do not go blindly through life!

Tangier Eye Clinic—Stem Cell Vision Treatment

As they approached him, the beggar reached out with his bowl.

"It's me, Uncle Nabil—Zeina. Remember, you promised me a story?"

"Oh yes, yes, my dear," the man said, shooing some flies from around his turban. "I was waiting for you."

"I'm here with my friend Jamal," Zeina said.

The beggar looked up with watery eyes. Only then did Jamal realize that he was blind.

"Come with us," Zeina said, taking the man's hand. "There's a café nearby."

They sat at a table on the sidewalk, shaded by an umbrella. A waiter brought meatballs and strong black coffee, and after a few quiet sips, the storyteller began the tale he had selected for the young travelers.

The Merchant and the Indian Parrot

This story, which the poet Rumi put into verse, relates that once upon a time, a certain merchant and his wife owned a parrot. This parrot lived a rich and tranquil life. He was fed a variety of sweets and other delicious foods. He enjoyed conversation and entertainment—because he knew how to talk like a human—and had every luxury in his golden cage. The only thing he didn't have was that which he most wanted—namely, his freedom.

One day, as the merchant was preparing for a business trip to India, he remembered that India was the parrot's homeland. He asked if the bird would like him to bring it back something from his trip.

"Bring me my freedom," the parrot said without hesitation.

The merchant smiled. "That's not within my power, because you belong to my wife. Ask for something else."

So the bird said, "If you can't bring me my freedom, at least tell my free relatives there that I'm imprisoned in a cage, and ask them what I need to do to find happiness."

"And how am I to find your relatives?"

"Just go to the jungle, and when you see a flock of parrots with the same plumage as mine, you'll know that they're my relatives. Give them my message."

This request surprised the merchant, but he promised the parrot that he would do as it asked.

On his arrival in India, the merchant was riding through the jungle when he saw a flock of parrots that looked just like his bird back home. They were resting in a tree, so he decided to give them his own parrot's message, as he had promised.

"Listen to me, birds," the man said. "I bring greetings from a relative of yours."

The parrots stopped their chattering and turned to listen attentively to the man.

"It asked me to tell you that it lives in a golden cage rather than a tree. And that it eats the most delicious meals, but can't obtain them for itself in the forest.

And it also said to tell you that it's well protected from aggressors but can't fly freely. It only wants to know how to find happiness."

As soon as the merchant finished this speech, one of the birds cocked its head to one side as if lost in thought. A moment later, it began to tremble and then fell senseless to the ground.

"Oh heavens, the news I've brought has been a tremendous shock to this poor parrot, who must surely be related to my own dear bird!" lamented the merchant. "The poor thing has been affected to such an extent that it's fallen dead at my feet!"

The man tried to revive the bird, but it remained as still as before. So he left it on the ground, covered it with leaves and, with great sadness, continued on his way.

As soon as he returned home, he went to greet his parrot. Noting the sad expression on the merchant's face, the bird asked, "Did you meet my relatives? Do you bring news of them?"

"You should never have sent that message!" said the man. "Do you know what happened? When one of your relatives heard it, it fell dead at my feet!"

Within seconds, the merchant's parrot uttered a cry of grief and fell to the floor of its cage.

"Oh, no! The news of its relative's death has killed it too! It's died of sorrow!" the merchant thought. "These

birds must have such sensitive hearts that they can't bear to hear any bad news."

Sorrowing over the death of his wife's dear parrot, the merchant opened the cage and, with great tenderness, picked up the motionless body and placed it on the windowsill. As he was leaving the room, however, he heard an unusual squawk—as though the parrot was laughing. Turning around, he saw that his bird had flown away!

Perched on a nearby tree branch, the parrot said, "Thank you for bringing the answer from my relatives in the forest!"

When the merchant had somewhat recovered from this surprise, he understood that what he had taken for a tragedy was actually a message to his imprisoned parrot—a way of demonstrating to the caged bird how to gain its freedom. Without understanding that message, the merchant had been the unwitting messenger. But the bird had immediately understood.

Looking upward through the open window, the merchant saw the parrot, free at last, flying high in the sky.

"Thank you, Nabil! I knew you were going to tell us a good one," Zeina said between bites.

The blind storyteller could have told them other stories, but it was time to return to the ferry terminal. As they walked the storyteller back to his spot by the mosque, Zeina slipped some money into his bowl and bid him goodbye.

The Mediterranean sky was dotted with color, as if loose flower petals were dancing in the breeze. Days like these, when the wind didn't blow too hard, were ideal for flying remote-controlled electronic balloons—a popular pastime for those who could afford them. From the railing of the ferry, Zeina watched in awe.

"Thanks for coming to get me, Jamal, and for coming with me to talk to Nabil," she said. "I just don't feel ready for this job. Of course I know lots of stories, but your mother asked me to tell them for the whole community, not just for kids. So I need to talk to real storytellers, like Nabil. I need the guidance of wise people like him!"

"I don't think so. I think your stories are great, Zeina," Jamal said. "But if you want to talk to other storytellers, I know all the ports we'll be stopping at, and we'll have time there to go find plenty of those old dudes. You can listen to their stories and store them in that elephant memory of yours, okay? Or do you want me to record them?"

"Nah, I'll remember them. But let's keep this between us, okay?"

Jamal was thrilled. This would give him the chance to visit all the exotic places he'd always wanted to see—and without his parents tagging along! Zeina was a good friend. A little bossy, he thought, but a good friend.

"Look, more balloons," Zeina said, pointing to the sky.

"It's the rich kids' favorite toy," Jamal explained. "You know, the kind of kids whose parents spend their holidays in space hotels."

"Politicians?" Zeina asked.

"Some. Others are cybersecurity consultants, executives or corporate lawyers."

"Oh, those. The elite few who can afford tuna fish."

"And order perfect babies from the geneticist. Intelligent, athletic, good-looking, not too shy, just the right height! That kind of thing."

"And the soul? I wonder if *that's* also custom-made," said Zeina, raising her eyebrows.

The balloons wafted over their heads, light as bubbles, and sailed away.

The ferry was still plying the water ponderously, as ferries had for hundreds of years.

The next morning, the day before departure, Omar had scheduled another meeting with the other travelers. Last-minute issues were discussed, and Zeina was introduced.

"Please meet Zeina, our new passenger and storyteller," Omar said. "The meeting is now over, but for those who want to stay a little longer, Zeina will tell us a story, as a way of introducing herself. It's about a traveler."

Nobody moved. They didn't know what to make of Omar,

his family or this Mauritanian girl, but were definitely curious.

"You've got the floor, Zeina," Omar said.

The girl cleared her throat and stood up in front of the group. Timidly at first, but with growing confidence, she began her telling of "The Merchant and the Indian Parrot." A natural storyteller and performer, she enhanced the tale with a repertoire of facial expressions, hand gestures and variations in vocal pitch and tone. By the time she'd finished, all eyes were fixed on her.

"An excellent story!" one person said, while others applauded.

"Now, *that's* what I call a wise tale," Igor added. "Full of meaning."

"And how do you remember so many details, Zeina?" someone asked.

"Zeina has always had that ability," Omar interjected. "She learned it from her mother, who was illiterate and taught her the importance of memory for those who can't read. Right, Zeina?"

"Yes. When I was a kid, my mother taught me the art of storytelling and the value of memorizing the tales," Zeina said modestly. She took care to hide her emotions whenever she spoke of her mother, but Jamal, who knew her well, didn't miss the glimmer of sadness in her eyes. The girl had lost her mother a year before, and still felt an enormous emptiness in her heart. She remembered with sorrow her mother's last words: "Poor girl! I'm not leaving you anything ... just stories!" Zeina had wanted to tell her that the stories were more than enough, but didn't get the chance.

"Well, folks, see you tomorrow at the port," said Omar, walking the last of his guests to the door.

3: Gibraltar

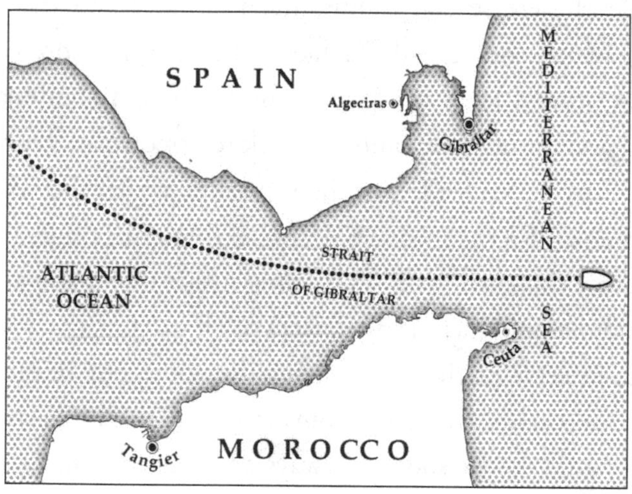

The clouds had opened up and blessed the earth around Cádiz with a sudden but short downpour before the storm moved on and left the coast hot and dry again.

The Dreamer's passengers gathered at the port at midday. Somewhat ceremoniously, Omar summoned everyone up the ramp, while a photojournalist from a science magazine took pictures and interviewed John, who was second-in-command. A flock of hungry gulls perched on the ship's railings, shrieking loudly, hoping for crumbs.

Some of the travelers asked themselves if perhaps they were making the greatest mistake of their lives, but it was too late to turn back now. So they gathered up their courage and climbed the ramp as Dr. Roble handed out motion-sickness patches.

The ship was an X-bow icebreaker—a dark-green, medium-sized vessel just over a hundred-and-sixty feet long. On the first level were several cabins, the infirmary and the main deck, which they called "Galileo." There were more cabins on the second level, along with the kitchen, a combination living and dining room and the deck referred to as "Darwin." Above that, a bridge led to the top deck, which they named "Einstein." There, on one side, were three huge globes that protected the satellite dishes twirling inside them, and a series of antennas and measuring devices of all sorts.

The interior of the ship was neither neat nor linear. The fourteen cabins, six bathrooms and other compartments were connected by short stairways and narrow hallways that appeared in the most unexpected places. Each section was tightly sealed off from the others.

Below the water's surface, in the hull, there were two levels. One housed the engine room and desalinization equipment, and the other was used to store food—not only for the ocean voyage, but also to ensure that the group wouldn't starve during its early days on the island.

Omar and John divided the group in half, and each man gave a tour of the ship, distributing the schedule and responsibilities, and showing the families to their cabins. After settling in and unpacking, the whole group gathered in the dining room.

"The layout seems chaotic," Omar explained, "because the ship's been modified in order to get the most out of the space, and also for safety's sake. Each compartment can be sealed off from the others by latching its door. That way, any kind of trouble in one section can be contained rather than spreading to the rest of the boat."

John explained that the ship was equipped with two kinds of engines: one that ran on solar energy, and the other that ran on liquid nitrogen gas—or LNG, as it was more commonly called. The former would be the ship's primary engine, with the latter, which had more power, used only in an emergency.

Some of the passengers felt a knot in their stomachs when they heard the word "emergency," and a few even looked at their HWatches to note the spike in their heart rates. But these were temporary reactions.

The children, who didn't understand how momentous the journey was, launched themselves on a tour of the ship with wild abandon, and were soon taking joyous advantage of the maze-like passages, which were perfect for hide-and-seek.

The deep sound of the horn announced the ship's departure.

Their hearts full of trepidation and excitement, the passengers didn't notice when John started up the solar-powered engine. It was almost inaudible, its sound just a whisper. Only when the boat began to move did they realize they'd finally left the shore to begin a new stage in their lives, perhaps the most important one they would ever experience. The voyage from Cádiz to the island in the Antarctic Circle had begun.

Zeina and Jamal were happy with their assigned jobs: Zeina as Mrs. Piscarelli's assistant in the kitchen, and Jamal as part-time deckhand. Even the younger children were given regular chores to do, but when they weren't busy they followed the teens around.

On the first leg of the trip from Spain to the north coast of Africa, Tapio, the twelve-year-old Finnish boy, tagged along behind Jamal like a lost puppy. Ming-Jung, who was a year younger, copied everything Tapio did. Ming-Jung was trailed by the ten-year-old Roble twins, who in turn led the two youngest: Kimiko Taniguchi, seven, and Liyang Wang, nine. So Jamal and Zeina had a court of followers, who ranked themselves by age.

As *The Dreamer* sailed through the Strait of Gibraltar on its way to the Mediterranean Sea, Mirta gave a short history lesson for the benefit of those who had come from far away. She explained that the name of the region's landmark, the famous Rock of Gibraltar, was derived from Arabic *Jib al Tariq*, or "Mountain of Tariq." It had been named after the Moorish commander who had crossed from Morocco to Spain in the year 711 with his army, beginning an occupation that lasted eight centuries.

"And that's why Moorish blood is mixed with Spanish. Just look at Mirta's lovely dark eyes," observed Mrs. Roble.

"Sometimes," Omar added, "this strait is very rough, because it's where the Atlantic Ocean and the Mediterranean Sea meet. Countless ships have sunk here, including quite a few that were bringing immigrants from North Africa to Europe—which wasn't too long ago, really."

Mirta glanced at Zeina and thought how lucky the girl's mother had been to have survived such a dangerous crossing.

Some of the children looked excited; others, worried. Omar immediately regretted his comment about shipwrecks and hastened to explain that *The Dreamer* was sturdy and seaworthy, and that the unfortunate vessels he'd referred to were small inflatable boats, as fragile as leaves drifting on the ocean.

"Modern boats don't sink anymore," Mirta chimed in. "A long time ago, when all boats were sailboats, they would sink. But not these ships. That reminds me of the story of a ship that sailed from Tunisia to the coast of Spain with a slave girl on board. What's that story called…?" She stared off in the distance, lost in thought.

"You mean 'Maiden Teodor'?" Zeina asked.

"Exactly! Do you know it? "

"Of course."

"Would you tell it tonight, Zeina? It's such a good tale!"

"I'd be glad to," Zeina smiled.

After dinner, everyone gathered around her, and she began.

The Story of Maiden Teodor

Once upon a time, there was a merchant from North Africa named Abulhasan, who was already quite rich, even though he was still a young man. As he was walking through the market one day, he saw a slave merchant. At that time, as you may know, slavery was common, and slaves were bought and sold as if they were animals. Among these slaves was a girl who attracted Abulhasan's attention, not only because she was beautiful, but also because of the intelligence shining in her eyes.

Her price, said the salesman, was high because this girl, who had been seized in war, was from a good, refined family. She knew how to play musical instruments and sing, as well as how to draw and paint, and she could recite poetry by heart.

The merchant became even more interested in the girl and, without thinking twice about the price, bought her and took her to his home to serve as maid to his mother. Teodor—that was the girl's name—would be perfect company for her.

Teodor quickly proved not only that she was intelligent, but that her knowledge of art, science and philosophy surpassed that of her master.

One day, as the merchant was preparing for a voyage that involved merchandise of very great value, he asked his mother if he could take Teodor with him. Someone had to keep the books, and the girl was faster with numbers than he was. The request was granted—and Teodor was thrilled. She was in love with Abulhasan, but of course she had to conceal her feelings. A slave didn't have the right to harbor such sentiments, much less to reveal them.

In those times, ships were made of wood and had sails, and were not as strong as our ships today. Well, it happened that Abulhasan's ship sailed into a huge storm and was lost at sea.

Abulhasan and his young slave found themselves

cast upon a desolate beach. They had survived the shipwreck, but the entire cargo was lost beneath the waves, and with it, Abulhasan's entire fortune. The two walked along the coast until they arrived at an important city. Their clothes were in tatters, and they themselves were in total misery.

Seeing the merchant's great distress, Teodor said, "Don't be sad, sir. I have an idea that may save us. Take this ring to the jewelers, and buy a good dress for me and an outfit for yourself. Then request an audience with King Miramolín Almonzor. When he receives us, tell him that you want to sell me, and when he asks my price, say it's ten thousand gold doubloons."

At first, Abulhasan thought the idea was ridiculous. He had never heard of anyone paying such a fortune for a slave—much less Miramolín, the emperor of North Africa, who probably possessed thousands of beautiful and talented slave girls! In the end, however, Abulhasan agreed to Teodor's plan.

When the day of the audience arrived, the two were ushered into the royal chambers. Teodor was beautifully dressed and adorned, and Abulhasan, too, had done as much as possible to present himself well. Both of them bowed deeply and kissed the ground in front of King Miramolín. Then they rose and kissed his hand.

The merchant asked Teodor to lift the veil that covered her face, and then he turned to the king and said, "I bring before Your Majesty this beautiful maiden. Perchance you may be interested in buying her."

But when the king heard Teodor's price, he laughed. "What makes you think I would pay such a fortune for a slave, no matter how pretty she might be? Certainly she's beautiful, but I have many lovely slaves, and I've never paid for any of them even a hundredth of what you're asking for her."

"Your Majesty, if I may ... There's no doubt that the slaves in your harem are beautiful, but they aren't worth a hundredth of what Teodor is worth in terms of knowledge. I'm not asking this price because I've lost my senses, but because I know her value. She knows all the sciences as well as the seven liberal arts, and she can converse with philosophers and men of letters with equal knowledge. Not only did she learn from me but also from the best masters of Andalucía. Would you care to test her?"

When the king heard this, he thought it not a bad idea. No harm could come of it, and such a test would provide some entertainment. So he asked his vizier to round up all the wise men in the kingdom, so that seven who were the most knowledgeable could be chosen.

Once the selection had been made, King Miramolín let it be known there would be an extraordinary session that night: The wisest men in the land would debate with a slave!

The merchant was also present at the debate, as were the vizier, a secretary to take notes and, off to one side, Maiden Teodor. When the king entered the room, everyone rose and bowed reverently, and then remained standing until the king bade them be seated.

"To see if this slave girl is as enlightened as her owner claims," said the king, "I've summoned these gentlemen to offer their verdict. Know, however, that I'll only buy her if she can outwit all seven wise men, which I seriously doubt. For not only are they the wisest men in the kingdom, they also have the advantage of age and experience. But let us proceed."

The king ceded the floor to the first wise man, who questioned Teodor about the planets and astrology as well as other things I won't describe because they correspond to the science of those times, which we now know to have been wrong.

"Why wrong?" asked Ada, one of the twins.

"'Cuz they believed that the sun and the planets went around the Earth. Duh!" Ming-Jung put in.

"And they thought there were seven skies!" Tapio added.

"That's true," Zeina responded before continuing with the story.

Teodor answered all of the first wise man's questions with clarity, and he was satisfied.

The second wise man tested her on music theory and

the scales. Teodor answered without hesitation, and even gave a demonstration of the major and minor scales, using her own voice. This second wise man also acknowledged Teodor's knowledge and talent.

The third sage inquired as to the conquests of Alexander the Great, which Teodor described in rich detail. This impressed even the king, who knew quite a bit about history.

The fourth sage questioned Teodor about some mathematical theorems, and the maiden explained them and their proofs, drawing geometrical figures as well as formulas in a beautiful hand. So the fourth sage also had to admit defeat.

The fifth sage asked Teodor to name the plants that cured certain illnesses; the sixth asked about creatures of the oceans, valleys and mountains; and the seventh asked her questions regarding jurisprudence.

"What's that?" interrupted Ming-Jung.

"It just means the legal system, the law," explained Zeina. Then she continued.

Again and again, Teodor answered eloquently and with a richness of detail that exceeded the knowledge of the wise men.

However, when the king signalled that he was satisfied, one of the erudite gentlemen said, "Very well, everything this girl has stated is true, and it demonstrates a wide and encyclopedic knowledge. This, however, is not wisdom. Given enough time, anyone of intelligence can memorize texts and recite them at will. Wisdom is more than information. In order to see how deep her knowledge is, I propose she tackle certain issues not found in scientific books—issues that require insight, judgment and wisdom, not just facts."

The king voiced no objection and asked Teodor if she would like to continue with the test, which was about to become more difficult.

"Yes, Your Majesty," she responded, "but since this second round was not part of the agreement made with my master, I would like to impose one condition.

"And what is that, Teodor?"

"Each sage may ask three questions. With each question I answer correctly, the gentleman who asked it will remove one article of clothing."

The wise men murmured in dismay. "One article of clothing? What are you saying?"

"One article of clothing: jacket, shirt, pants and so on," was Teodor's reply.

The sages exchanged horrified looks. The king, however, smiled complacently and said, "Granted! Each one of you gentlemen must write the question and answer in advance, and pass it to my secretary, just in case you change your minds afterward."

With these arrangements clarified, the first wise man

said, "This is my question: Yesterday I was walking along a path, when I realized that a horse that was blind in one eye had gone that way a short time before. How did I know this?"

"Because you saw that the grass was eaten on only one side of the road and not on the other," Teodor answered without hesitation.

The secretary checked his notes and nodded. Everyone watched as the poor sage reluctantly removed his jacket.

"But I also knew that the horse carried vinegar on one side and honey on the other," the scholar added.

"That would be easy to deduce by looking at the ground," said Teodor. "On the vinegar side, the earth would be barren, and on the honey side there would be bees, ants or other insects."

Again the scribe nodded. The sage angrily took off his shirt.

"And I also knew that the horse was missing a tooth!" roared the wise man, furious. "How did I know that?"

"Clearly, instead of having been cleanly bitten off, the foliage would have been shredded, which would indicate the lack of a tooth," said Teodor.

The embarrassed expression on the secretary's face told everyone that this was indeed the correct answer, though he was reluctant to say so out loud.

There was a moment of uncomfortable silence in the

room. Then King Miramolín, who could barely suppress his laughter, said, "Your pants, please."

The sage, who was beside himself with rage and shame, had no recourse but to remove his pants.

"Perhaps the good sage would like to ask me how one would know that the horse was lame in one leg?" asked Teodor.

"No, no!" the man shouted angrily. "You've won, young lady! Let my colleagues proceed!"

The king said, "Give us your answer, Teodor, if only to satisfy our curiosity."

"Of course, Your Majesty. It would be enough to observe the hoofprints. One of them would be shallower than the other three. That would be an unmistakable sign of lameness."

"Very well, Teodor, you have responded intelligently," said the king. "The second examiner is up now."

The second examiner cleared his throat and said, "Since you are much younger than we are, I want to ask you about age. Which is better: to be young or to be old?"

"They are equal, sir," said Teodor, "because to be young is to have more mistakes in front and fewer behind, while to be old is to have more mistakes behind and fewer in front."

Very sorrowfully, the man took off his fancy new shirt. In order to show it off, he'd gone out that day without a jacket. What bad luck, he thought. If the girl answered correctly three times, he was going to have to stand there naked!

"This is my second question," he said. "What is humankind's most important duty?"

"The search for knowledge."

The poor man bent, ready to remove his pants.

"Your Majesty," he blurted out to the king, "I hope you'll agree that shoes come under the category of clothing. Right?"

"No," said the king. "Your last question, professor?"

Being Christian, the man crossed himself. Then he stammered, "Ah, er ... Teodor, what is the best way to answer a fool?"

"With silence."

Oh, how he'd let that young woman overcome him so easily, he lamented to himself. Then, suddenly, the professor remembered he had a hat on his head. He quickly and merrily took it off, threw it into the air and heaved a long sigh of relief.

At this point, two very shamefaced sages were walking around in their underwear, doing their best to conceal the holes in those garments. The king found it all great fun.

Finally, the third sage approached Teodor and, with tears in his eyes, whispered to her, "Please, please, my most esteemed maiden, it's obvious that you're a well-

raised girl, so have mercy on me! I plead with you." Kneeling before her, he implored, "I beg you, don't make me humiliate myself. I prefer pulling the hair from my head to—"

"Enough!" shouted the king, taking pity on the professor. "I think that this slave has answered all the questions she needs to answer and has solved all the riddles. Isn't that right?"

"Yes, yes, Your Majesty. We're convinced! Of course, of course, we have no doubts!" the wise men shouted.

The third wise man collapsed into a chair, wiping perspiration from his face.

The king asked Teodor and Abulhasan to leave the room, and instructed the first two professors to gather their belongings and get dressed. After a few minutes, the slave and her master were called back in to hear the verdict.

"The wise men gathered here," said the vizier, "have certified that this maiden's knowledge is equal to theirs, and the king has decided that the price asked for her is acceptable."

The merchant looked at Teodor with a sad expression. He hated to let her go, because he was deeply in love with her.

"Teodor, you've impressed me greatly with your knowledge, gentility and intelligence, to say nothing of your beauty," said the king. "I give you the right to ask

me anything you desire. Anything you wish for, tell me and I'll grant it."

"Anything, Your Majesty?" said Teodor, with her head bowed but her eyes still fixed on those of the king.

"Anything within my power. You may not ask for the moon and the stars, of course. But anything that's possible. I give you my word."

"Then my desire is that Your Majesty give me as a present to Abulhasan."

A deathly silence filled the room. The king grew pale, then red. He sat down, took a sip of water and wiped the sweat that had begun to trickle from his brow. He had not foreseen this request. What an astute girl! Honor forced him to comply with what she asked, because he had given his word. Composing himself, he took Teodor by the hand and led her to the merchant."

Zeina looked at the rapt little faces of her audience.
"But she's going to become a slave again!" yelled Ada.
"No, just listen; I haven't finished," said Zeina.

The merchant took Teodor back to his mother, who was very concerned about the whereabouts of her son. Moved by the story they told her, she gave Teodor her well-deserved freedom. Only then was Abulhasan able to confess his love to her, which he could not have done while she was still a slave. And Teodor loved him just as much. In due time, they married and had many children, who were blessed with growing up in a family where knowledge was the most precious treasure.

"Thank you," Zeina said upon hearing her audience break into spontaneous applause.

Just then, Omar received a message that all flights to Tripoli had been canceled. There were riots in the streets there—political protests—and the Chissano family from Mozambique had to change plans for where to meet the ship. Instead of Tripoli, the Chissanos would wait at the port of Oran in Algeria. John Wood took over the helm and modified the boat's course.

Sleep didn't come easily to the passengers that night. The excitement of the first day of travel, and the mental images parading one after another—the vastness of the ocean, even the shipwreck in the story—kept them awake. But sleep finally came and, like mist from the sea, silently wrapped them in its soft embrace.

While the rest of the ship's passengers slept, Jamal and Zeina huddled on the main deck, planning in whispers their excursion at the port of Oran.

4: **Oran, Algeria**

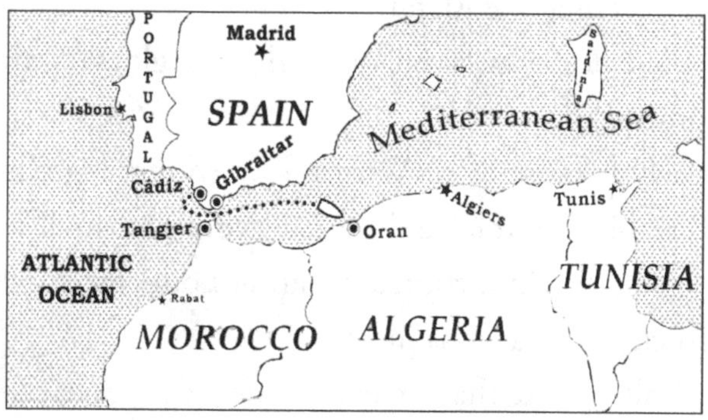

Omar radioed in *The Dreamer's* information and was allowed to enter the port of Oran. The ship would be there in about thirty minutes.

The morning was warm. Passengers leaned over the railings, watching the flying fish leap out of the sea and fall back with a splash. Others waited their turn to go to the bridge, where John had invited them for a brief navigation-training session. It had been decided that in case of emergency, everyone should be familiar with the various instruments that helped guide the ship.

The bridge had a one-hundred-eighty-degree window display screen, and different monitors showed the ship's route, the position of nearby vessels and other navigation information. Jamal, who had been trained by his father, explained how to read the charts.

"The superimposed images from the new thermal camera,"

John said, "allow us to detect and monitor any obstacle in the dark. This will be useful for seeing icebergs at night when we're approaching the island."

"Are there icebergs, even with all this global warming?" somebody asked.

"Precisely because of it. With the warming, big chunks of ice are breaking off the ice shelf. But we're prepared!"

The lesson was interrupted by an announcement that the Algerian city of Oran was in sight.

They'd all agreed that at every port, the travelers would disembark in two groups rather than all at once, and that two men would remain on board to keep guard, since theft was not uncommon. Entire ships had been known to disappear completely while crew and passengers were ashore.

A number of the families had never visited North Africa before and were excited.

"All back to the ship before dark," announced Igor, who was in charge of keeping track of the passengers and organizing outings.

Like all coastal cities at sea level, Oran had suffered in recent times. The Mediterranean Sea had risen nearly two feet and had flooded entire towns. But at Oran's port, the travelers were informed that *le Marché Medina Jedida,* the old market, was still standing and was the most active place in the region.

Omar, Mirta and Urho Ullakko went to meet the Mozambican family, *The Dreamer's* newest passengers: Joaquim Chissano, a biochemist; his wife, Vera, a zoologist and painter; and their eleven-year-old son, Joãozinho.

The other passengers went to the bazaar to barter with items they'd been advised to bring along with them. They swapped medicine for nuts, eyeglasses for vegetables, and a holophone—a big hit with all the merchants—for pistachios and *burek,* a type of meatball. This would provide dinner for the whole crew. Jamal and Zeina bought some *burek* for themselves and then scurried down the alleys, unnoticed. They were on a mission of their own.

The two teens walked for a long time through the narrow streets of the *medina,* aware of the ever-present surveillance cameras at the entrance to each store. They also noticed the suspicious stares from some of the Algerians, perhaps because of the unfamiliar sight of a dark-skinned girl walking with a much lighter-skinned boy.

Finally, in a beautiful carpet shop tucked into an ancient alley, they found an old man who was willing to talk. The carpet seller chatted about the *medina* and its history, the changes that had taken place in Oran since the rising of the waters, the things he'd seen during his long life. Zeina and Jamal let him talk as they sat, sipping tea, on top of a huge stack of colorful handmade carpets.

"Do you know of any traditional storytellers?" Zeina asked.

"Ah, young people still interested in the old stories!" the old man exclaimed with surprise. "Yes, I know of one." He sent them to the Pacha Mosque, in the portal of which, he assured them, they'd find old Ahmed, dressed in a white tunic and a blue turban. "Tell him I sent you, and I'm sure he'll spin you a wonderful tale."

As Zeina and Jamal headed to the mosque, they saw two armored vehicles stationed at the entrance to the bazaar, but there was no sign of the soldiers, who must have taken cover. It was midafternoon, and a stinging wind had begun to blow through the streets, raising a cloud of thick, choking dust.

These storms had become increasingly common. Although Dr. Roble had distributed protective facemasks to all the passengers, Jamal and Zeina hadn't brought theirs with them on their walk. Instead, they wore their B-goggles, which were equipped with microcomputers and GPS, and which showed them the way to the mosque and protected their eyes, but not their mouths. The sun was momentarily obscured by a thick dust cloud, which turned everything a hazy orange-brown. The two teens shuffled down the narrow alleys, covering their mouths with their shirtsleeves as best they could, trying in vain not to inhale the dust.

They arrived coughing at the mosque to find Ahmed in a protected stone cove, with dust swirling at its entrance. As a sign of respect, they took their goggles off while recovering their breath and greeting him.

"Peace be upon you, good Ahmed," said Zeina in her Mauritanian-accented Arabic. "We're students, looking for a storyteller. We were told by the carpet seller to come and speak with you." She pointed in the direction of the carpet seller's shop.

"You've found the right place," answered Ahmed, "but people are too busy these days and don't come to me anymore. Now I only count and recount the stars, and they never end."

"Do you know many stories?"

"Too many to count! Like the stars in the sky!"

"Do you have any good ones for us?" Jamal asked in his halting Arabic. "Here's something to eat if you'd like," he said, extending two *bureks* that still smelled delicious.

Ahmed accepted the *bureks,* ate one and put the other in a hidden pocket in his robe.

"Since you're young students, I'll tell you a special story, about someone who wanted to be a student."

Zeina and Jamal sat on the floor beside the old man as he began.

The Wise Man, the Merchant and the Fish

In a village near Oran, there was a wise man who had various students. One day, a merchant with a desire to learn the Science of Man decided to visit this wise man to ask for acceptance as his disciple.

The master received the merchant with much courtesy. The merchant told the master of his desire and gave assurance that he would do everything necessary to become an ideal student.

"Very well," the master said, "we can proceed immediately. But first I'm going to order some food for the two of us."

So he called the cook and asked her to prepare a fish with tamarind sauce for dinner, but not to begin broiling it until he told her to. Then he invited the merchant to his study and showed him some books full of magic symbols. The instruction was to begin with these.

A short while later, the merchant's servant called at the wise man's door with a letter. In it was news that the merchant's wealthy uncle had died, and that the merchant was the sole heir. The wise man offered his condolences to the merchant and suggested that, since he was now a rich man, he could perhaps leave a donation for the town orphanage, where some of his fellow students were working as volunteers. The merchant replied that he would first have to reconcile his accounts and see what was left over after paying any creditors, and that the wise man should send a disciple to him for a donation the following day.

When the disciple presented himself at the merchant's house the next day, he was told he should come back later, because the merchant had paid off his creditors and was at the moment short of cash.

The day after that, the merchant again studied magical formulas and invocations with the master, until another messenger appeared, again kissing the merchant's hand and delivering a letter to him. This letter announced that the merchant had been elected town mayor. Upon hearing this news, the master congratulated his student for having obtained such a high and dignified office, and he begged that a certain plot of land be ceded to him in order to construct a place for meditation and exercises. The new mayor replied that he first had to see what else needed to be done, but that he would think about the case, and that the master should send someone to his new office in a few days.

But when that period had passed, the merchant's answer was that unfortunately he couldn't comply with the request, because the plot of land was needed for other uses.

The following week, while the merchant was again in the master's studio memorizing certain spiritual exercises, another letter arrived, announcing that the mayoralty had been given to someone else. The merchant, because of his experience and administrative talents, was needed to fill the office of governor of the province, if he accepted that honor. The merchant's joy was indescribable, and the master celebrated the good news with him.

"I congratulate you on this nomination and wish you every kind of success in your new career," said the master. He also reminded the merchant to donate money to the orphanage and land for construction of the place of meditation. The merchant replied that he would take note of these requests but couldn't promise anything, because he had many matters demanding his attention. The master, he said, should send a student for an answer in about a week, after the merchant had

assumed his glorious public role.

On the appointed day, the merchant saw the wise man himself coming through the door of the governor's palace. The wise man reminded the merchant about the donations—but the newly appointed governor became irritated with the master for not having scheduled an audience, and told him so. If the master continued to insist, the merchant-governor would have him jailed as a heretic and magician, because he knew very well that the master had been practicing magic his entire life.

The master replied that he was going to leave but was in need of a bite to eat first. He hadn't eaten anything on the way there, and would now call for the fish he had asked to be prepared when he arrived.

So saying, he clapped his hands.

The palace disappeared, and the merchant found that he was sitting in the wise man's study.

The wise man called the cook and asked that the fish finally be broiled. Turning to the merchant, he said, "Now you may leave my house, because we have proven, you and I, that one can't hope for anything from you. If you, in your greed, could not distinguish reality from fantasy, how could you aspire to learn something real from me? I have nothing to teach you, and to try would be bad use of my teaching skills. So, if you'll excuse me, I'm going to eat the fish with tamarind sauce."

"I'll never forget that story," said Jamal.

"Good. Don't forget it," said Ahmed. "Pass it on to your children."

Jamal quietly left the kind old man some money in gratitude, and the three said goodbye. It was time for the teens to return to the ship.

On the way to the port, Jamal and Zeina passed in front of a French colonial building. Two imposing bronze lions guarded the entrance. Jamal stopped and placed his hand over one of them. Zeina noted that Oran, or *Wahran* in Berber, meant "lion."

The dust storm had subsided, and the two teens picked up their pace as the last rays of sun reflected off the windows of the tall buildings near the port. Looking for a shortcut, they entered a narrow alley they'd noticed on their way into town. On one corner of the street was a café, and Jamal, who needed to use a bathroom, peered through the window.

"You'd better stay here, Zeina," he said. "I don't see any girls inside. I'll be right back."

"That's fine, but don't be long. I'm going to that store over there to buy water," she said, pointing across the street.

When Zeina left the store a few minutes later, dusk had settled over the city. As she crossed the street, she found her path blocked by a group of young men in their late teens.

Two of them approached her from either side, grabbing her arms. Her heart started to pound as she looked wildly around for Jamal, who should have been on the corner by then. "Let me go!" she shouted.

"Calm down, sweetheart," one of the boys cooed. "We just want to talk to you."

"What's a girl like you doing out here all alone, anyway?" another boy asked.

Zeina recognized their accent. "And what are illegal immigrants doing here, bothering a Mauritanian sister in a foreign country?" she snapped. "Or did you lose all sense of shame when you left your people? Do you want me to report you to the authorities?"

As Jamal opened the café doors and stepped into the twilight, he saw Zeina with the young men.

"What's going on?" he said.

"Nothing. These guys and I were just chatting," Zeina replied without taking her eyes off them. "Nice talking to you, boys," she said calmly. Then she added, more sharply, "My father is inside the café, and my cousin is waiting for me," and she yanked her arms free and pushed past the troublemakers. Holding her head high, she strode over to Jamal, taking his arm and leading him back inside the café.

They watched as the gang left, and then the two sprinted back to the port in the dark. Zeina ran like a gazelle on the African savannah, with Jamal following close behind. They arrived breathless and sweaty.

"How did you know they were undocumented?" Jamal asked after hearing the story.

"They all are, because Algeria doesn't give visas to young Mauritanians. It was obvious those guys crossed the border illegally," Zeina said as they made their way up the gangplank and onto the deck of the ship.

Fortunately, the bulk of *The Dreamer's* passengers had arrived back at the ship at the same time as the teens, so Jamal's parents—who had separated from the group to go meet the Chissano family—didn't suspect that he and Zeina had gone off by themselves.

Dinner was served while Omar introduced the Chissanos to the rest of the passengers. Jamal unenthusiastically pushed the cultured meat and vegetables around his plate, wishing for more *burek* instead. At Mrs. Piscarelli's request, Joaquim Chissano, who as a biochemist knew the properties of the synthetic food, gave a brief explanation.

"With cultured meat, the meat substance is the result of a chemical reaction," he said, "involving carbohydrates and amino acids in a warm and slightly damp environment. It's a clean and simple process that can result in something nutritious that tastes just like red meat. Thanks to this, my friends, the world's children can now have all the protein they need."

Jamal made a face at Zeina, who covered a smile with her hand. Most people still preferred the real thing, but the younger children, who had grown up with laboratory sausage, didn't notice the difference.

After dinner, Mirta asked Zeina if she had any stories to share. Some of the passengers considered storytelling to be nothing more than a childish pastime, but they remained in their seats so as not to be rude. Others, recalling "The Merchant and the Indian Parrot," were genuinely interested. Perhaps there was something in these tales, they thought, something worth thinking about.

The night sky sparkled with stars. Omar suggested they arrange chairs on the Darwin deck, which was the largest, and placed a stool in the front for the storyteller. It was a splendid night, and Jamal turned off the lights. In the dry, clear air, the Milky Way shone across the sky from end to end, a river of stars. Silently thanking the universe for the glorious light and the happy ending to the day's adventures, Zeina began telling "The Wise Man, the Merchant and the Fish." She remembered it in minute detail and recited it as if she'd known it her whole life. The group was delighted—and even Jamal was impressed.

Omar had received an offer for olives at a good price by the barrel from a vendor in the port of Tunis, so he decided to go there the next day for a few hours. A severe blight had wiped out the olive harvest in Spain, so this would be an ideal opportunity to stock up. The news was music to the ears of Jamal and Zeina, who were in no hurry to get to the "island wasteland," as they now called their icy destination, and wanted to see as much as they could of the lands between Spain and the Antarctic Circle. Jamal would have another chance to explore a new city, and Zeina could continue her quest to find stories before they faded from human memory. She had begun to feel that this was her mission in life.

5: Tunis, Tunisia

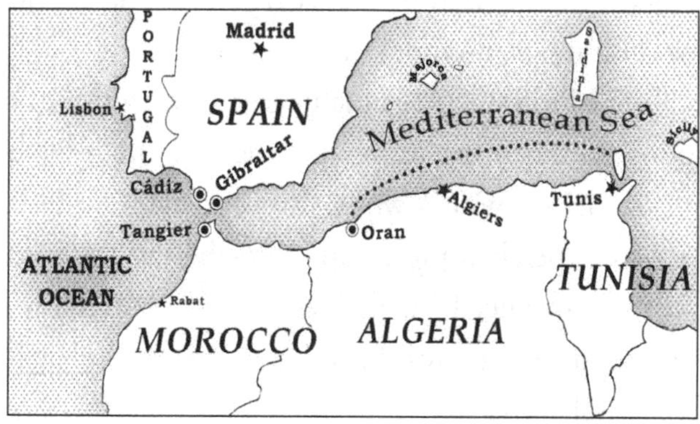

A commotion woke the travelers on *The Dreamer*. They jumped out of their beds and went to the main deck, where they were greeted by a flock of seagulls.

"Tunis ahoy!" John's Australian-accented voice boomed from the bridge.

The port of Tunis was located on a bay that was ringed by white buildings with identical carved-out windows. From a distance these structures looked like great dovecotes, their backs to the mountains.

It was midmorning and already one hundred and four degrees Fahrenheit when the passengers started up the stairs to the top of the hill where the market was located. Omar, Mirta and the Kims went directly to a warehouse to pick up the olives, while the rest of the group walked to the *medina*. Jamal and Zeina walked there with them but took off on their own as soon as they arrived. The night before, Zeina had researched the city on the UNet and learned that at the University of Al-Zaytuna, one of the oldest in the Islamic world, there was a professor who specialized in collecting traditional stories. His name was Rahman Al-Andalus.

They found Professor Al-Andalus in a small office in one of the older sections of the university. Despite the heat, he was wearing a blue suit with a white shirt and tie. Old-fashioned reading glasses perched precariously on the tip of his nose.

The teens introduced themselves, and then Zeina told the professor about her interest in storytellers. He explained that he was a scholar and not a storyteller, and that his expertise was in collecting and translating folklore narratives.

"At the moment, I'm working on King Solomon's stories, together with a colleague in Beirut. However, a few years ago, while doing research on the kind of narrative that the Andalusian Moors brought back from Spain to the lands of the Maghreb, I found a very unusual one. If you want, I can make you a copy."

"We'd really appreciate it, Professor," said Zeina.

He replied, "It's called 'The Knight Zifar.' Like you, this knight had to abandon his home country and travel to a faraway and unfamiliar place. It's obvious that the origins of this story are Middle Eastern, because Zifar is the same as *sifr*, which in Arabic means..."

"'Numbers?'" said Jamal.

"Right. Now, in medieval Europe, this word, *sifr*, was understood to mean 'secret code.' You can see the connection with the English words 'cipher' and 'decipher.' Well, stories like these are said to have multiple meanings that can be 'deciphered.' … But I don't think that's exactly right …" The professor stared out the window at the courtyard below.

"What do you mean, sir?" Zeina asked.

"Well, I mean we don't need to 'decipher' the stories, just know them well enough to keep them in our hearts. Then, as we travel through life, we come to understand more and more of what they have to offer."

"It's interesting to meet a man named Al-Andalus, Professor," said Jamal, "because my family came from Andalucía, in Spain."

"My ancestors also emigrated from Andalucía, and the most famous of them was Abd al-Rahman bin Khaldun—or Ibn Khaldun, as you call him. He was an Arab and the forerunner of today's historians. That's why I've taken his name as well as the name of his birthplace. He was at this very university all those centuries ago."

It occurred to Jamal that he could change his own name, perhaps to "Jamal-Al-Sirius" to honor his Syrian ancestry. It sounded cool, he thought, because "Sirius" was the brightest star in the sky and was actually composed of several stars.

"Did you say you have a friend in Beirut, Professor?" Zeina asked.

"Yes. His name's Ali. Are you going there?"

"Yeah, we're picking up another passenger in Beirut," Jamal replied.

"Well then, if you'd like to visit him, I'll give you a letter of introduction."

"That's very kind of you. I wish there was something we could do for you," Zeina said.

"I'll be happy just knowing that you're keeping the story alive," said the professor, wishing them a safe trip and handing them the letter together with a copy of the story.

They arrived back at the *medina* just as the last group was getting ready to return to the boat. After dinner—as, one by one, the stars began to rise and take their places in the night sky—the passengers once again spread themselves out on the boat's deck, young and old settling down to hear the story of Zifar.

The Knight Zifar

It's said that in a far corner of the Earth, there lived a knight named Zifar. He was from a royal family, and

his grandfather had been king. However, due to a series of palace intrigues, the family had fallen into disgrace, and the throne had passed into other hands.

This didn't bother Zifar, who was happy just to have a wife who was honest and wise, and two children who were the light of his eyes. He harbored no bitterness toward his ancestors for having lost the throne. Zifar accepted his lot, telling himself that it was the will of God. What's more, he bore no ill will toward the king who reigned at the time. Zifar was his subject and fulfilled his knightly duty with honor. The king was grateful for Zifar's services and praised him far more often than he praised anyone else.

But this aroused a great deal of jealousy in some of the king's ministers and counselors, and they decided to do away with Zifar. So with the help of false stories they had concocted, they managed to convince the king that Zifar was a threat to the crown, that behind his amiable expression lurked hatred, and that it would be better to banish him from the kingdom. Eventually the king, pressured by these evil men, agreed to do as they suggested.

So it was that one night, under cover of darkness, the king's troops surrounded the knight's house, set it on fire and then galloped away. Zifar had just enough time to gather his children and his wife, Grima, and snatch up the money and jewels he had hidden under his mattress. With flames already licking at the stable walls, Zifar quickly saddled two horses, and then he and Grima fled, each carrying one of their children. As they rode off, their home collapsed in smoke and flames behind them.

They galloped throughout the entire night, getting as far away as possible from the kingdom that had turned against them. At dawn they dismounted to eat and rest under a tree. They had hardly finished their meal when a band of passing highwaymen saw this seemingly wealthy family and lost no time in robbing them of their money, jewels, horses and weapons, leaving them with only the clothes on their backs.

The children, Roboán and Garfín, held each other, weeping on their mother's lap. A pale and trembling Grima gave thanks to God that at least they had escaped with their lives. Zifar, not wanting to let the children see his dismay, told them that this was just another of Destiny's tests and assured them that they would overcome this and every other difficulty.

So it was that, after comforting one another, they set off walking toward the coast.

They walked until they reached the edge of a long and narrow inlet. From there, they could see the opposite shore, just beyond the king's reach. Zifar, who was the only one in the family who knew how to swim, set out for the opposite shore, carrying Roboán on his back.

When he reached it he left the child to wait on the beach and returned to do the same for Garfín. Once Zifar had made sure both children were safe, he returned for his wife. But when the parents reached the opposite shore, their boys were nowhere to be found.

"Garfín! Roboán!" Their parents shouted to the four winds until their throats ached. The more they searched, the more desperate they became. The children had disappeared into thin air.

Sobbing, Zifar and Grima plunged into the thick forest. They hurried over trails and pathways, and even climbed trees in hopes of spotting their children from above. But all they saw was the green forest canopy. Never were parents as downcast as they were. Sometimes they ran, sometimes they knelt, beating their chests, tearing their clothes, making promises and pleading for God to return their boys. Eventually their strength ran out, and it was all they could do to drag each other along.

At nightfall, exhausted and hungry, they lay down and tried to sleep. The worst thoughts went through their heads: Had their children been attacked by a tiger and carried off to its lair? Had they been kidnapped by pirates to be sold as slaves? Or had some evil magician cast a spell on them—or a witch carried them off for some unholy ritual?

Zifar and Grima ate some fruit they picked from

a tree, and this eased their hunger and thirst but not their distress. Finally they closed their eyes and slipped into a terror-filled realm of endless nightmares.

Just before dawn, they woke up and walked toward the interior of the territory, which they soon discovered was an island. They had gone only a little way when they met an old man and his wife, who were building a little straw hut not far from the sea. Asked if they'd seen the boys, the elderly couple said no but shared some of their food and allowed Zifar and Grima to rest there.

As it happened, Garfín and Roboán had gone into the forest the day before in order to answer the call of nature, and there they'd seen a strangely dressed man on a horse. The boys had been irresistibly drawn to follow him, but at a turn in the path, the horseman had suddenly spurred his mount and disappeared among the trees. When the boys tried to return to their parents, they got themselves turned around and were soon completely lost.

The island contained a network of pathways, some leading nowhere and others crossing and recrossing, as if part of a labyrinth designed to make people lose their bearings. Zifar and Grima spent several days walking back and forth, looking for their children. Each night, they went back to the hut near the bay.

One morning, Grima saw a ship approaching. Full of hope, she asked her hostess if it would not be a good idea to speak with the crew. Perhaps someone on the ship had seen the boys walking on the beach. What Grima didn't know was that this was not an ordinary merchant ship, but one captained by an evil magician who had sailed to the island to replenish his supply of fresh water. The old couple, who were the only inhabitants on that part of the island, knew this and were alarmed at the sight of the infamous ship. Partly out of fear, partly out of a desire to get into the magician's good graces and partly out of greed—in hope of receiving a reward—they told Grima that she should let them speak with the ship's commander.

"A beautiful woman is going to appear soon," they told him. "She's a foreigner. Act quickly, before her husband returns!"

Hearing this, the magician hatched a plan and then made straight for Grima.

"Madam, how fortunate we are to have found you!" he said to her. "A woman is about to give birth on our ship, and we urgently need maternal hands to tend to her. Do you have any experience with childbirth? Might you be so kind as to come aboard and help us in this most difficult circumstance? I beg you, by the life of my sons."

Grima, who was both soft-hearted and extremely generous, agreed to his request without a thought and hastened aboard. But the instant she stepped onto the deck, the magician gave the order to hoist sail and pull up anchor—to the horror of poor Zifar, who was running down the beach toward the ship.

When Grima realized she'd been the victim of foul play, she screamed and cried and threatened to throw herself into the sea. The magician ordered her to be tied to a post and, taking advantage of favorable winds, swiftly sailed away from the coast.

Zifar shouted and made threats from the shore, but to no avail. The magician's ship, with Grima on board, sailed farther and farther into the distance, and there was nothing Zifar could do about it.

As for Grima, the magician determined that she would remain tied to the post until she willingly agreed to be his new wife.

The unfortunate Zifar threw himself onto the sand, crying and cursing Destiny for having robbed him first of his possessions, then of his children and now of his beloved wife. What more was left for him to lose except his own life? A pain shot through his heart. Finally he lost consciousness and lay there motionless on that dry and desolate coast.

Zifar spent a tormented night on the sand in a state of semi-consciousness. At first light, he got up and, without knowing what to do or which direction to take, began to walk along the shore.

An entire day passed without him seeing another

living soul. When he grew so thirsty he thought he would die, he prayed, put his trust in God and set off into the island's interior, where he found wild herbs and fruit to eat and drinkable water in the hollow of a tree.

The next day, Zifar reached the top of a mountain, on the other side of which he found a road. "If there's a road, there might be villages," he thought, picking up his pace.

On the third day, he passed some farmland and, farther on, saw a city right by the sea. By afternoon, he found himself at the gates of the city walls. The guard, however, would not allow him to pass, so Zifar just sat there on the ground. He spent another night tormented by anxiety, hunger and cold, praying that dawn would bring an end to his misery.

Now, it happened that the king of the city had recently passed away without leaving an heir. The citizens were anxious to find out who would reign in his stead, and above all were afraid a civil war would break out. After much deliberation, they came to an agreement: They would leave the selection of their next king to the deceased monarch's wise old elephant, which lived in a corral some distance from the city. The person to whom the animal bowed down would be the city's next sovereign.

The citizens placed the throne on the elephant's back and gave it the crown to carry with its trunk. Adorned with ribbons and banners, and bearing the royal crest, the elephant began carrying out its task. It sniffed many of the people who entered and left the city, always indifferently and in a haughty manner, until it came to Zifar, who lay curled up on the ground beside the gate. The great beast lay itself down in front of him, placed the royal crown on his head, took him up by the waist with its trunk, raised him high and delicately placed Zifar on the throne that was secured to its back.

Zifar offered no resistance, convinced that his troubled mind was playing tricks on him. Then the drums began to roll as the animal marched back through the city's gate, and the excited citizens bowed before Zifar. It was only then that he realized he wasn't delirious.

The elephant, for its part, didn't stop until it arrived at the royal audience chamber. There it sat down with the astonished Zifar, while the courtiers entered to congratulate their new monarch.

Thus the knight Zifar became king of the island of Mentón.

Since he was well-versed in royal matters because of his lineage and his experience as a servant of the king of his native country, Zifar had no difficulty in ruling Mentón with wisdom and justice.

But in spite of this unexpected turn in his life, and in spite of the honors and privileges that had been given to him, in his heart Zifar harbored only one desire:

to be reunited with his family. He fasted, prayed and ruled his subjects well and wisely, always asking God to return his loved ones to him.

Three years passed. Then, one fine day, a merchant ship laden with rich cargo tied up in the harbor. In accordance with custom, the king sent a delegate to inspect the goods that were unloaded there and collect the required taxes and duties. As it happened, this delegate asked for help from two boys who were working in the port.

After unloading the ship's cargo onto the dock, the two exhausted pages sat down to rest beside a trunk.

"Brother, how I would like to hide myself in this trunk, so as to board this ship and travel the world to see if we might find our mother and father. Do you remember how we lost them, Garfín?"

"Of course I do, Roboán. How could I ever forget how our father carried us on his back across the water, and how you and I went into the forest and got lost. Our parents could be anywhere now."

"The lost boys!" exclaimed Leia.
"Hush," her sister said.
Zeina continued:

Just as the second page finished speaking, they heard a pounding on the trunk lid.

"Open the trunk, Garfín and Roboán!" cried a voice

from within it. "I'm Grima, your mother, the wife of your poor father, Zafir. Open this trunk, for the love of God!"

The brothers went white from the shock of hearing their mother's voice. Then Roboán shouted out to anyone who could hear, "Bring us a crowbar!"

"Quickly!" added Garfín.

When the trunk was pried open, there was poor Grima, who had been kept inside of it to punish her for not giving in to the magician's demands. Together, the brothers lifted her up and embraced her tenderly. Tears streamed down their cheeks.

Garfín and Roboán had grown up a lot in the three years since they'd been gone, but they were still the boys their mother remembered, and the intense emotion from seeing them caused her to faint. They held her in their arms, while the crowd that had gathered marveled at the poignant scene that was playing out.

Attracted by the commotion, the magician-captain appeared, brandishing a sword. He became furious when he noticed the open trunk, which had been unloaded by mistake.

"Who ordered you to unload that trunk, and to break its seal?" he shouted at the two boys. "Would you rob the jewels I've kept there? And what are you doing with my slave? I'll denounce you immediately to the king of this city and claim compensation!"

"This woman is not your slave; she's our mother!" shouted Roboán.

"Whom you've kidnapped!" Garfín added.

Several soldiers ran up to restore order to what seemed to be a dispute among merchants. But onlookers who had witnessed the entire encounter between the boys and their mother gave testimony, and it was finally decided to take the case to the king for resolution.

Followed by the crowd, the two brothers arrived before King Zifar, whose mouth fell open as soon as he saw his sons and their mother. Although Grima's appearance had been changed somewhat by her years of suffering at the hands of the magician, Zifar could still see that she was his beloved wife. And the boys had grown quite a bit but were still recognizable as Garfín and Roboán. Realizing that the glorious day he had longed for had finally arrived, Zifar dismissed everyone except for his loved ones and ordered that the magician be arrested.

Once alone, the family gave free rein to their emotions. They each recounted their own story, and Grima—who, under the magician's tyranny, had suffered the most—threw herself into the loving arms of the former knight and now King Zifar.

The king seated himself on his throne, with Grima beside him and his sons flanking their parents. Thus reunited, they thanked God for their good fortune.

From then on, the four lived together, enjoying each other's company, until old age delivered Grima and Zifar to the Celestial Kingdom.

6: Alexandria, Egypt

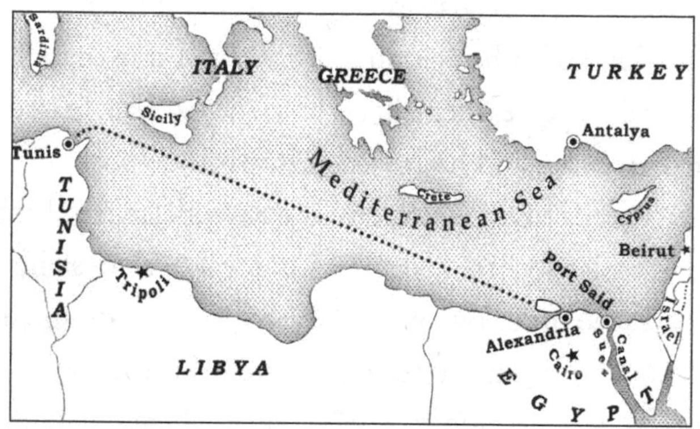

Omar called everyone to the dining room. He had an announcement to make.

"We've been advised not to stock up on LNG in Tripoli," he said. "Thousands of climate refugees from the Sahel and East Africa have overwhelmed the city, and anti-refugee protesters have blocked the roads. Our best chance is Port Said. In any case, Egypt has the best fuel prices right now."

The agreement was unanimous, and John set a new course.

Hours later and hundreds of miles to the east, Captain Cabra of *The Concordia* was put out by *The Dreamer's* delay. After a very long wait, he was finally informed by a reliable source that the Spanish vessel had stopped in Oran and Tunis as planned but had skipped Tripoli, where *The Concordia* was waiting, and had instead sailed for Port Said.

In Luxembourg, accusations flew back and forth.

"What kind of imbeciles do you have working there?" Palvo shouted when he learned that *The Dreamer* had passed right under their noses and hadn't been stopped.

"Alert! Alert!" his HWatch chimed to indicate that his blood pressure had risen to a dangerous level. Palvo sighed and scowled at the other two men. "You're going to do me in!" he hissed, shoving a nitroglycerin pill under his tongue.

"Sir, the Mediterranean isn't a pond," Dement said. "*The Dreamer* took a northern route past Malta. But our guys can easily intercept it in Port Said."

Palvo looked at him skeptically, but Dement continued. "*The Concordia* is a smaller ship, with plenty of fuel on board. *The Dreamer* is bigger and much slower, plus it's low on fuel, so it can't go at full throttle."

"What if they change their itinerary again? Because that seems to be what this Spaniard—or Syrian, or whatever he is—likes to do," Palvo added.

"It's just a matter of asking the authorities at each port to check whether any boat from Cádiz asked permission to dock," replied Beremolto. "And greasing a few palms when needed."

"Until we find a better way to trace them," mused his boss.

Dement swallowed his second Neurocrop, hoping it would bring some fresh ideas.

On *The Dreamer*, Mrs. Ullakko was monitoring the children's schoolwork at the computers. They studied for three hours a day, and while that wasn't a lot of time, the intensity of the sessions made them much more productive than they would have been in a typical classroom. Zeina helped Jamal with his Arabic lessons, while the other students worked independently.

Suddenly the sky turned an eerie ashen color, and the boat, which had been steady up to that point, began to rock back and forth as the waves grew higher. The swaying of the ship could make passengers feel ill, so Dr. Roble carefully made his way down the narrow passages and stairways, distributing more motion-sickness patches. Mrs. Ullakko noticed the students' attention flagging and ended the lesson. No one was in the mood to stare at a screen.

The barometer on the ship's bridge showed very low atmospheric pressure, and a message soon came in announcing an eighty-percent chance of a cyclone. Formerly rare in the Mediterranean, cyclones had become common there. Omar told John to head for Alexandria's harbor, which was the nearest port.

The Dreamer arrived at dusk and tied up as the storm blew around them. Even in the relative safety of the harbor, the ship rocked so violently that Omar arranged for the group to stay in a hostel not far from port rather than spend a stormy night on board. Luckily, Dr. Roble and John Wood seemed to be handling the choppiness well, so they volunteered to stay behind to guard the ship. No one wanted to take any chances, even in such dreadful weather.

Rising water had threatened the legendary metropolis of Alexandria before. Only sixteen feet above sea level, it was the most vulnerable of all Mediterranean cities. But the enormous dikes and seawalls that had been built with United Nations financing had enabled the city to resist the pounding waves so far.

The Dreamer's passengers walked to the hostel in the torrential rain. As they went inside, the storm turned into a full-blown cyclone. The roar was tremendous.

"No reason to panic. It's noise, nothing more. We have a zinc roof, so the storm sounds worse than it is," said Emir, the hostel's owner. But his words didn't match the expression on his face. The noise was unusual. Suddenly something solid hit the window, and they realized that in addition to the rain, it was also hailing. In the strong wind, the large hailstones slammed the sides of the building almost horizontally.

Emir closed the wooden shutters and secured them. Then he disappeared into the kitchen, clutching a rosary in one hand and muttering something about biblical plagues.

Soon he emerged to bring his guests dinner: meatless *fatta*. Desertification of the former agricultural lands had changed the population's eating habits. Since plants required less water than cattle did, large numbers of people had become vegetarians. But now even vegetables were scarce.

"That's it, gentlemen, you can't rely on the seasons anymore," Emir lamented. "After this rain, the cisterns will be full, but there's a good chance the wind and hail will have ripped the vegetables up by their roots. Lettuce, carrots—all gone. Tomorrow the garden will be a cemetery!"

"Can't you put the roots back into the holes?" Kimiko asked.

"Maybe, girl, maybe," answered Emir with a sad smile.

It rained and howled well into the night, but daybreak brought blue skies and a calm sea. Emir served breakfast as he and the guests talked about the lives and property that had been lost the night before.

"All that water brought down an entire hill, with all the buildings and their occupants," Emir told them. "Who knows how many dead. Volunteers are in the streets now digging through the mud and rubble, looking for survivors." Dr. Roble volunteered to tend to the victims, and others offered to accompany him to help. Rescue efforts were being coordinated from a place near the museum.

Zeina and Jamal wanted to join the group of volunteers, but by police order minors were not allowed. So the teens headed to the Grand Bazaar instead.

Omar was told that to attract money into the city after the disaster, the price of liquid nitrogen gas was being cut, and they could get their supply right there, without having to go into Port Said. So he made a phone call to cancel the ship's visit there. After he'd hung up, the officer he'd spoken with in Port

Said wasted no time, immediately passing the information on to *The Concordia*. The man felt a twinge of guilt, but his job paid poorly, and he needed the extra cash he'd been promised.

"Change of plans, sir," Dement said to his boss, bracing himself for the expected outburst. "*The Dreamer* is in Alexandria. Their stop in Port Said was cancelled."

Palvo swore several times. "You have other plans in the works, I hope," he said flatly. "Or is that melon stuck on your neck just ornamental? Or maybe you forgot to take your Neuro-*Crap,* Dement?"

Dement felt the heat rise in his face but kept his cool. "We still don't know what their next destination will be, but we have other information. Two teenagers from the ship appear to be in the habit of going on foot to the bazaar at each port, looking for people who tell stories."

"What? Stories? And what do I give a crap about kids who want to be told stories?" Palvo bellowed.

"One of them is Omar Homsi's kid. He's accompanied by a girl who's slightly older than him."

"And what do you plan to do with that invaluable information?" Palvo said with his usual sarcasm.

"We're taking the kids."

There was a moment of silence in the room as the implications of this idea became clear. Omar wouldn't continue on the voyage without his son, and without Omar, the group would be leaderless.

"Your job's at stake, Dement," Palvo said quietly.

Alexandria, like other cities, offered an RAA service, but because the cars were not completely automatic, neither Zeina nor Jamal was old enough to hire one. Even if they could have, rivers of muddy water were pouring down the old cobbled streets, tangling everything in palm branches and other storm debris. Men walked with their pants legs rolled up, and women hiked up their skirts and *abayas* discretely. The streets were in chaos, and the automatic cars didn't respond well in the midst of old-fashioned, more-aggressive vehicles. There was no point looking for an RAB bicycle-rental stand, because it would have been impossible to ride a bike in these conditions. Jamal asked his Hwatch where to catch a bus to the bazaar.

It turned out the bazaar was only a few steps away. Because of the storm, less than half the usual number of vendors had set up shop there. Jamal and Zeina walked from stall to stall asking if there was a storyteller around, but the Alexandrians were distracted and didn't seem inclined to talk about anything except the storm. Those who did answer the teens' questions tried to convince them that storytelling was a thing of the past.

Eventually they found an open café and sat down. A middle-aged gentleman began speaking to them, asking where they were from. He described the damage that had been inflicted by windblown objects flying over the city like missiles, and spoke of the drowned animals at the zoo and other disasters in his own neighborhood.

"Climate change, so-called global warming!" said the man. "They say it's because we used coal as fuel. Or they blame oil. Or deforestation. Or El Niño, which has gone mad. Or God knows what else. Divine punishment. But we all know deep down that the real reason, my friends, is the desire for profit. That's all! Human greed and nothing else!"

The teens nodded in agreement, but it was obvious that the man, whose name was Iskandar, wanted to continue his rant.

"No one wanted to give up anything, that's for sure," he said. "Or as they say, nobody wanted to open their hands, you know? They were as tight-fisted as the monkey with the gourd."

"What monkey?" asked Jamal, not understanding the reference.

"It's a story people tell around here, and it's a true one, from the sub-Saharan countries, where there used to be many monkeys. Hunters devised a method of catching them, based on what they knew about monkey psychology. We humans are like those monkeys, you know"

"Would you tell us the story?" asked Zeina.

"With pleasure," he said.

The Monkey and the Gourd

Once upon a time, there was a monkey jumping from branch to branch in the trees, in search of amusement. Suddenly he smelled a banana. He sprang to the ground, landing next to an enormous gourd.

"Aha!" he said to himself, "this is where the smell is coming from!"

In fact, the banana had been slipped into the gourd through a small hole, and the monkey thought it would be clever to squeeze his hand into that hole and take the fruit. So he inserted his hand, and when he felt the banana, he closed his fist around it and tried to pull it out. But right away he discovered that it was impossible to withdraw his fist from the gourd while still holding on to the banana. The hole was just too small. Or, you might say, the fist with the banana was too big.

The monkey became very angry when he realized he couldn't get the banana out, so he screeched and screeched.

As you might already have guessed, the gourd with the banana was a trap set by a monkey hunter, who approached as soon as he heard the screeches.

The monkey, who was very frightened because he knew what the man meant to do, wanted to run away, but his hand was trapped inside the gourd. He was so greedy for the banana that he wouldn't let it go, so he couldn't run away, because the gourd was very heavy.

"Woe is me! I can't get my hand out!" the monkey lamented. "But at least I have the banana!"

The man picked the monkey up by the neck and gave him a sharp tap on the elbow, which made the monkey's hand open. The gourd fell to the ground with the banana still inside, and the hunter carried off the monkey, along with the gourd and the banana, with which he meant to trap his next foolish monkey.

The man congratulated himself for knowing monkey psychology so well.

And the monkey could only screech, "Not fair! Not fair!"

"Great story," said Jamal. "Do you know many others?"

"Not really. I remember that one because I read it in a book at school, back in my youth."

Jamal called the waiter over and paid the bill with a hundred-dinar note. The waiter grumbled. With limited currency circulating in the country, it was difficult to come up with change. But he managed to find a bundle of worn, crumpled banknotes.

Sitting at a table by the window, two girls Jamal's age were lost in an alternate universe behind virtual-reality goggles, laughing and giggling. Jamal watched them closely as he walked toward the door, trying to determine how pretty they were behind their goggles. He was so distracted that he ran right into someone. For a second they were face to face. Jamal apologized, but the man didn't look friendly.

"That's what you get for checking the girls out," Zeina smirked.

"Whatever, Auntie," he teased. That was what he called her when she was being bossy.

Jamal and Zeina left the café and continued on through the half-empty bazaar.

"At least you got a new story," Jamal said.

Zeina didn't respond. She had an uneasy feeling and kept looking over her shoulder. "Let's turn here, Jamal. I think somebody's following us."

Skirting storm rubble, they took a side street. As there weren't many passersby, they picked up their pace, jumping over puddles of murky water. Jamal shot a glance behind them and saw a man turn the corner they had just come around. He seemed to be talking on his phone, but his eyes were glued to them.

"Don't turn around," whispered Zeina as she picked up the pace.

Seconds later, another man came from the opposite direction, walking toward them intently. Jamal risked a glance over his shoulder again and saw a black van with tinted windows turn the corner. The man behind them signaled to the van, then pointed at the two teenagers.

"In here!" said Jamal, now in no doubt about the danger they were in. He pulled Zeina into an open doorway and then up a flight of stairs. The van's electric engine was silent as it raced down the street, but Jamal heard the squeal of the brakes and the opening and slamming of doors moments later. He didn't know if the pounding in his ears was the sound of the pursuers' footsteps or his own heart thudding against his chest. The two teenagers tried multiple doors as they reached the landing, finally bursting through one that led to a rooftop terrace. Slamming the door shut, they ran to the terrace's edge. The distance that separated them from the rooftop next door was about five feet. There was no railing, just a narrow ledge.

"Can we jump it?" asked Zeina quickly.

"Sure!" said Jamal."

They backed up a dozen steps to get some momentum, and then ran forward as fast as they could. As their toes reached the end of the roof, they jumped, eyes fixed on the neighboring roof. Zeina landed first and then grabbed Jamal under the arm as he stumbled to his knees. Then they got up and repeated the whole process again, until they had reached the last house on the block. Nowhere to jump now.

Looking back, they saw the silhouettes of two men at the edge of the first building's roof, who were clearly hesitant as they stared down at the alley far below.

"There!" panted Jamal, pointing to a stairway.

He and Zeina stumbled down the stairs with no other plan in mind but to elude their pursuers. On the bottom floor was a long, narrow hallway. On the right, a door opened onto the same street they had just been on. Not a good choice. The left side of the hallway was dark. They rested with their backs against the wall for a few seconds, to catch their breath.

"Press the panic button, Jamal!" Zeina whispered, grabbing Jamal's HWatch.

"No, wait, I don't want to scare my parents," he whispered back.

"Then send them a message!" said Zeina.

The Auto Message feature on the HWatch had the preset phrase "Hi, we're all right," which was coupled with the GPS coordinates from where the message was being sent. Of course, they *weren't* all right, but there was no time—or desire—to send details.

They went down the dark hallway toward a dull light shining at the very end.

"That was the guy from the café, Jamal, the one you smacked into. Remember his face?" Zeina whispered.

"Think he saw how much money we had on us?" Jamal whispered.

"Yes! You shouldn't use big notes, bro! It attracts too much attention!"

"Too late. Hard to believe these countries still use actual money!"

"Let's knock," suggested Zeina when they reached the source of the light, which was trained on the area directly in front of a door.

The eye of a camera warned them that they were already being watched from inside. A small window opened, and they saw, behind thick glasses, a pair of human eyes that looked from Zeina to Jamal and then back again. Then the door opened, and a man greeted them with a smile.

"You must be Miss Katirayi! I was expecting you later in the afternoon. But no problem, I'm not busy. Come in, come in, please. Make yourselves comfortable," he said as he closed the door and locked it, to their relief. "I didn't think you were so young! And this is ...?"

"This is my cousin Jamal, from Spain," said Zeina quickly, glancing at Jamal.

"Ah, good, good. Ladies shouldn't walk around here alone. You have a lovely accent. Where is it from, if I may ask?"

"Time spent at college in Mauritania, sir."

"Oh, how nice. But sit, sit," he said and started bustling around the room, looking for something, while the teens seated themselves on the couch. Finally he brought a small box to Zeina and said, "Here's the ivory amulet you ordered."

Jamal's eyes widened as the man opened the lid and handed the box to her.

"And how much did you say it was?" asked Zeina, pretending to be interested.

"No worries, Miss Katirayi. I've already negotiated payment with your mother."

"Oh, good. But I won't take it now, because, you know, there are too many thieves around here in the bazaar, and I don't want to risk it. I'll come with my mother tomorrow. I only came today out of curiosity."

"But it's real ivory?" asked Jamal, with surprise.

"No, young man! How can it be real, if there are no more elephants left in the world? Real ivory costs a fortune. This is imitation ivory of the highest quality. But what's important is what it contains."

"No more elephants …" Jamal repeated to himself.

"But not all is lost, my boy," said the man, interrupting Jamal's thoughts. "At least we still have some rhinos and tigers. And in case you didn't know, the ground-up horns and bones of those animals are very good for human health."

"This dude is either really stupid or very, very smart," Jamal thought.

The man continued. "But an amulet is different. It's not the material per se, but what it contains—you know? In this case, they're ... secret things, serving different purposes. Sometimes it's to attract a person—a woman, or a man … a lover. Other times it's to … keep someone away, so to speak. Understand?"

"But those are just superstitions!" Jamal exclaimed. Then, feeling Zeina's sharp gaze, he corrected himself. "I mean, they're what people believe."

"Yes, yes, they're beliefs," said the man. "But sometimes things don't work the way we think they do, and we suppose there's magic where there isn't any. Because things can work in different ways, some of them quite unexpected."

"I'm not sure I understand, Mr…" Jamal stammered.

"My name's Muhadin," the man said, before continuing. "For example, do you think you can kill someone with a book?"

"It'd be hard, but I guess if you gave the person a good whack with one!" Jamal said with a smile.

"Well, it's possible to kill someone with a book, without a whack!" Muhadin said. "Do you know the story of King Yunan and the wise doctor?"

"No, but we'd love to hear it," Zeina said immediately.

"Gladly, Mademoiselle, since there are no customers now. Imen!" he called to someone lurking in a back room. "Bring us tea, please! ... Well, here goes!"

The Story of King Yunan and Sage Duban

There was once a king named Yunan, who reigned over a city in Persia. King Yunan was rich and powerful. He had armies, guards and allies. But he suffered from a horrible skin disease that doctors had been unable to heal.

One day, a sage named Duban came to the king's city. Duban was a man of considerable knowledge in many disciplines. He could read Greek, Persian, Turkish, Arabic and Syriac. He was versed in the natural sciences, astronomy and philosophy. But above all, he was a skillful doctor. He knew the properties—both beneficial and harmful—of different plants and all their parts. He was soon invited to court to see the king.

That night, Duban studied the king's case. When morning arrived, the sage appeared before the court, dressed in his best clothes. After prostrating himself and kissing the ground before the king, he was well received.

Duban said, "Oh glorious monarch! I've heard about the leprosy that ravages your body, and the many who've tried and failed to heal it. I've come to tell you that I have the cure for you. Not only that, but you'll get rid of your disease without having to drink any potions or apply ointments of any kind. You need only follow my simple instructions."

"If you can really cure me as you say, I'll make you rich, and your children too, and I'll grant you everything you desire and make you my friend and companion. Tell me what I should do!" said the king

The sage promised to start the treatment the next day. He immediately left the palace and rented a house. There, he took all his books, plants, aromatic roots and other medicines that he carried in his luggage, and then he went to work.

First, he selected the appropriate ingredients for curing leprosy. Then he made a mallet, of the kind that are used to play polo. But he made the handle hollow and porous, and he poured into it the curative mixture he'd prepared.

The next day, Duban headed back to the court and kissed the ground before the king, saying, "Get your horses ready, and gather your courtiers for a game of polo. You shall use this mallet and hit the ball with all your strength, until the palm of your hand and the rest of your body are drenched in sweat. Then return to the palace and wash yourself."

Without wasting a minute, the king called the emirs, the viziers, the chamberlain and other members of his court to start a polo match.

A short while later, he was mounted and playing. He rode his horse and hit the ball with all his might again and again with the stick that Duban had given him, until he was drenched in sweat.

When the game was over and he went to wash and dress, he found no trace of his illness. His skin was smooth and clear.

The king was beside himself with joy and was even more impressed by the fact that he had been healed without medicine or ointments of any kind. What he didn't know was that his perspiration had helped him absorb the remedies that were hidden in the handle of the mallet. That's how they had entered his bloodstream and produced their healing effects.

From that day on, Duban was honored in court and became a favorite of the king.

The amulet merchant took a sip of his tea and then he continued with his story.

Now, among the king's viziers was a greedy and malicious man. When he saw the king granting Duban favor after favor, this vizier was consumed by envy and jealousy, and he conceived a plan to do away with the sage.

One day, in the late afternoon, the vizier approached the king, kissed the ground before him and said, "Oh king of this age and all time, whose generosity knows no limits! I'm forced to speak, because I would never forgive myself if I didn't. Duty compels me to give you an important message to protect you from an evil that threatens your life—an evil I see clearly."

"And what's the message?" the king asked, alarmed by the minister's words.

"Glorious monarch! The ancient sages have said: 'Whoever doesn't measure the consequences of their actions, Fortune will not help.' And indeed, I've seen that lately Your Majesty has strayed from the right path and acts impulsively, lavishing wealth and favors on an enemy whose aim is none other than the fall of your kingdom. I fear for your life!"

The king's countenance changed suddenly, and he

said, "Who do you mean? Who should I be wary of?"

"Oh my king, if you've been asleep, let me wake you! It's Duban, of course."

"But Duban is my close companion and the best man at court! There isn't another like him in the world. His knowledge is second to none. Are you not saying this, my dear vizier, purely out of envy?"

"Your Majesty, it's Duban's very powers that I fear. If he was able to cure you without anyone seeing how, would he not be able to kill you in a similar way? Duban is an impostor! A spy!"

At first the king refused to think ill of Duban. But then, because he was one of those people who are easily manipulated, he began to feel confused. He thought it over and reasoned that if Duban really was a spy, he would poison the king at the first opportunity, using the same extraordinary measures he had used to cure him. The king decided to act.

"My dear minister, we must remove Duban before he removes us. Bring him here this instant!"

The sage came to the court, happy to oblige his king.

"Do you know why I've called you?" the king asked by way of greeting.

"Only Allah knows the secret thoughts of men," answered Duban.

"I've called you here to destroy you! I have proof that you're a spy and that you've taken advantage of my

innocence!" The king then asked the vizier to make the case.

Realizing instantly that it was all a plot devised by the vizier, Duban tried to defend himself, explaining that the accusation was false. But the vizier was well-prepared with all sorts of trumped-up charges, and the king, blinded by suspicion, couldn't see the truth behind the lies.

"If you kill me," said Duban, "Allah will kill you."

"Take him away!" roared the king. "Have the executioner cut off the head of this traitor and deliver us all from his evil spells!"

When the doctor realized that he was about to die, he accepted his fate and said, "Please at least give me a little time to go home, settle my affairs and give away my books of wisdom and medicine. Among those books is one, the rarest of rarities, that explains all of life's mysteries and reveals the greatest secrets. I wish you to have it. May it enlighten you!"

The next day, the doctor was escorted back to court by guards. He was carrying an old, worn volume, which he gave to the king before being taken away to be executed.

The king, who was anxious to know the secrets the book contained, sat down to read it. But he found that, as often happens with old books, the pages were stuck together. To separate them, he licked his index finger before using it to turn each page. He was surprised to find the first pages blank, and continued putting his finger to his tongue before turning each succeeding page. What he didn't know was that the book's pages—all of which were blank—were coated with poison, and that every time his finger touched his mouth, he received a small but powerful dose, which was the beheaded sage's revenge.

Within minutes, the king was dying. In his final moments, he realized his mistake, and then his limp head dropped onto the pages of the book, which still seemed so innocent—and so empty.

"What a story!" Jamal exclaimed.

"Yes, thank you, Mr. Muhadin," said Zeina, who had been listening to the story but also to the sounds outside the room. The thieves would be gone, and she worried about the possible visit of the real Ms. Katirayi. "Unfortunately we must leave now, but tomorrow I'll be back for the amulet with my mother."

"Of course, Mademoiselle."

"Mr. Muhadin, we came down this hallway, but do you have another way to leave? A gang was in the street when we came in," said Jamal.

"Of course. Nowadays you have to be careful. Don't walk those back streets by yourselves. There are so many thieves and smugglers, and all kinds of other people who are up to no good! I'll have Imen lead you the other way out, to the main street of the bazaar. Always stay in the crowd," said the merchant. Calling Imen to escort them out, he added, "See you tomorrow, then. And give my greetings to your dear mother."

"I will," Zeina said, smiling to herself.

The exit to the bazaar was through a small arcade without any signs. They looked up and down both sides of the street, saw only buyers and sellers and thanked Imen. Their pursuers were gone.

"Zeina, I can't believe you pretended to be his client," said Jamal.

"Well, I did study drama. But you did well, too, bro. And look where we ended up! The guy runs a totally shady business. Rhino horns and tiger bones! I can't believe it! No wonder he's down a dark hallway."

"We could have taken that magic amulet with us, since 'your mother' already paid for it," said Jamal. "And it was pretty cool-looking."

"Let's leave my mother out of it," Zeina answered.

Jamal's HWatch began to flash and vibrate. His father appeared on the display, asking where they were and ordering them to return to the ship immediately.

"And where did you find such a bunch of idiots?" snarled Palvo when his aides informed him that the kidnappers had failed to get the kids.

"You said no violence, sir. And apparently those teens were fast."

"You'll run faster when I kick your ass, Dement!" roared the boss. His HWatch gave a sharp "beep-beep-beep" to indicate another blood-pressure alert. Three beeps were a serious warning signal.

"No need to worry," Beremolto cut in. "Our crew learned that *The Dreamer* is going to Beirut, and this time they can't skip it, because a new passenger is waiting for them there. They should be arriving in about six hours. *The Concordia* will intercept *The Dreamer*, and the crew will board it before it reaches the port."

"It'd better. I'm getting fed up with this," Palvo said. The HWatch beeped again as he left, slamming the door behind him.

Dement downed three Neurocrop pills to sharpen his mind. He had to increase the dose, because the drug no longer made him feel as sharp as before, but he knew he shouldn't abuse it. Sometimes it was hard to slow his brain down, and he'd feel stunned by the unstoppable flood of images and the unbroken chain of trivial memories and random thoughts that scrambled together into one big, incomprehensible mess inside his head.

That night after dinner, the people in *The Dreamer's* cafeteria asked Zeina if she would share another story. The tales had become an evening tradition and a favorite part of the day. The passengers recognized that something in these stories spoke to everyone.

Zeina wondered whether, instead of a traditional tale, she should recount what had happened to her and Jamal that afternoon. She sent a quick message to his holophone, and his answer came fast: *Pts find out, we dead meat!*

"Yes, I do have a couple of tales you might like," Zeina said, putting away her phone. And she told them the two stories she and Jamal had heard that day.

7: **Beirut, Lebanon**

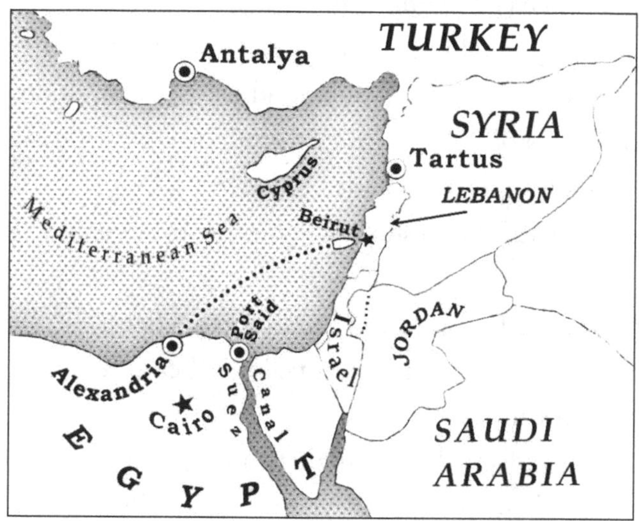

Having obtained a good supply of fuel, *The Dreamer* sailed north at fifteen knots per hour under a clear blue sky. There was no need to hurry. Antonio Mercado, the Chilean scientist, had already been informed of the ship's arrival time in Beirut, where he was attending a conference on the melting polar ice caps.

The sun was high in the sky. It was an autumn sun, although the word "autumn" was a bit of a stretch in those latitudes. It just meant that the sun didn't scorch the earth like it did in summer.

On the Galileo deck, a few people were reading. Urho Ullako was peering through binoculars at the city of Haifa on Israel's coast.

"Haifa is famous for its Bahá'í temple," he informed the passengers sitting nearby.

"What's Bahá'í ?" Ming-Jung asked.

"A minority religion from Iran. Take a look," said Urho.

He passed the binoculars around. A building of massive proportions stood on a hill, surrounded by gardens and stairways leading down toward the town.

"What's that?" Tapio shouted, pointing to something in the distance.

Mrs. Taniguchi raised the binoculars to her eyes. The sky suddenly darkened, as in a solar eclipse. "I can't see anything!" she said. "It's all dark!"

Enormous black clouds rippled through the sky, breaking apart and then coming together again, allowing rays of sunlight to shine onto the sea up ahead one moment, but blocking them out the next. Some of the passengers cried out when the form hovered over them like a spacecraft, casting its shadow over the entire ship.

"Locusts!" exclaimed the Chissanos.

Hearing the commotion on deck, other passengers made their way outside. They watched as the cloud changed form and shape again and slid through the air with a deafening sound.

In the control room, John ran to the monitors and saw the news. An invasion of locusts had attacked the winter flax and barley crops in Egypt, and in a feeding frenzy had stripped the fields bare. Standing next to him, Mrs. Kim, an entomologist, speculated aloud that the drought had probably caused the resurgence of the voracious insects.

"They don't know what borders are," she said, "only that there are fields to devour." She went to the main computer and entered the swarm's trajectory and estimated velocity, and soon the results came in. The insects would arrive at the Israeli-Palestinian coast in two hours.

The mass moved on, disappearing over the horizon, flying like a single organism with one mind and one purpose.

The Concordia also saw the locusts pass by, shimmering as the sun lit up their wings in a play of light and shadow. But the crew didn't think of the cloud of insects as a climate problem so much as a bad omen.

"One of the seven plagues of Egypt!" exclaimed the Sudanese helmsman, who refused to continue steering. Captain Cabra threatened to throw him overboard for disobeying orders. Several crew members intervened, and tensions mounted. Weapons gleamed as hands twitched. To ease the tension, the captain had the boat sail to a nearby port, where the mutinous helmsman was literally kicked off the vessel and was replaced by a less superstitious man. Then, having lost precious time, the captain ordered full speed ahead.

As *The Concordia* drew near the port of Beirut, Cabra was informed that *The Dreamer* was already there.

When this news was relayed to Palvo, he became furious. Gesticulating wildly from a three-dimensional hologram, he screamed that he was demoting Captain Cabra for letting *The Dreamer* beat his ship to port. Captain Wulandar was to assume command immediately.

The new captain announced that any further insubordination would be instantly dealt with, pointing to two sinister-looking dorsal fins that were glistening in the waters off the ship's starboard side, indicating the presence of sharks.

The day was grey and bleak. The locusts had destroyed what little vegetation had been left in the fields surrounding Beirut, and the farmers were already burning piles of the short-lived insects. A wind filled with ashes and charred wings enveloped the city. The sky became duller than ever.

The Dreamer's passengers didn't feel like venturing into the city. At the port, the air quality was a bit better. Putting on surgical masks to act as filters, Omar and Mirta took an RAA to the hotel where they'd arranged to pick up Antonio. Jamal had told his parents he wouldn't stray far from port. He seemed interested in observing the white-chested birds with black plumage that made their nests on the piers. Mrs. Kim told him they were called cormorants.

"Zen, do you have the letter from Rahman?" Jamal asked when his parents were gone.

"Yeah. Did you talk to your parents?"

"I left a message."

In fact, the message merely said "We're going for a walk to see the cormorants."

"We probably don't have much time," Zeina said, looking at her HWatch.

A man sitting at a sidewalk café that looked out on the port saw the two teens walking along the pier and gave a signal via his own HWatch.

Following Rahman's instructions, Zeina and Jamal asked some locals for directions to the old Jewish quarter. They were told to take a bus downtown and, from there, to catch the Number Four bus.

Tall, modern buildings stood side-by-side with oriental arcades and French facades, a common mix in many Middle Eastern cities. Life in Beirut seemed pretty normal, despite the dirty air after the locust infestation. Streets and coffee shops were packed with people. However, the atmosphere was tense. Zeina and Jamal first noticed this when they boarded the bus, whose door bore a sign barring passengers if they wore bulky clothing—which could easily hide explosives.

The ride downtown took only a few minutes. Near a plaza with a clock tower, Zeina and Jamal sat on a bench waiting for the Number Four bus. Some people crossed the plaza with surgical masks on. A smartly dressed man approached the two teens.

"Aren't you Omar Homsi's son?" he asked in perfect English.

"Yes, I am," Jamal replied, surprised.

"And you're Miss…"

"Zeina Moura," said Jamal.

Zeina greeted the man with a nod.

"I'm a friend of your father's. You remember me?" the man asked Jamal with a smile.

Jamal didn't want to be rude, but he shook his head hesitantly.

"No," continued the man, "I guess you were too busy on your computer last time I visited your parents in Cádiz! But what on Earth are you doing here?"

"Well, we're traveling with a group of friends," Zeina said, interrupting Jamal before he could answer.

"I see. And doing some shopping downtown."

"Actually, we're going to the old Jewish quarter to see an acquaintance," Jamal responded. Zeina scowled at him, but he didn't understand why.

"What a coincidence!" the man said. "I'm heading there right now. I'll take you in my car. Come on, it'll just take a few minutes."

"Oh no, sir, we're happy to take the bus, but thank you anyway," said Zeina.

"It's not a problem. Come on. My car is just over there, see?" He pointed to a blue van parked half a block down the street.

The offer was attractive. The three of them crossed the plaza. When they were close to the van, Zeina noticed that the license plate was covered with mud, and the numbers couldn't be read. She had a bad feeling and wasn't about to get in.

"Oh, I left my purse on the bench!" she cried. "Come on, Jamal, before someone takes it!"

"What purse, Zeina?" said Jamal, as Zeina wheeled him around and pinched his arm hard. "Oh yeah, your purse! We'll be right back," he called over his shoulder.

The two ran toward the bench, just as the bus pulled up.

"It's a trap!" Zeina said angrily, pushing him into the crowd of people getting aboard. "That guy isn't your father's friend, dummy!"

The bus was packed. As it pulled away from the plaza, they saw the van pull around and follow, a few vehicles back. Two men were in the front seat.

"What the hell, Zeina? How do you know that?" Jamal said irritably.

"You think some random guy you've probably never laid eyes on would recognize you in a crowded plaza in Beirut, of all places? What kind of a coincidence is that? Jeez, Jamal, what's wrong with you? Use your brain!"

"Jeez, you're right!" Jamal said. "That means we can't get off in Ali's district. They'll be waiting for us."

"But we can't go to the end of the line either. It's probably a ways off and isolated, which is even worse."

"Let's talk to the driver. He could call the police."

That was a bad idea. The driver got scared and immediately ordered the teens off the bus. He didn't want to risk there being a kidnapping or police shootout, both of which had been known to happen on public transportation.

Jamal and Zeina were forced to jump off the bus as it rolled slowly on, because the frightened driver refused to come to a complete stop. They ran down a busy alley, quickly glancing over their shoulders. The van was definitely following them. Suddenly an RAA came down the alley from the opposite direction. The street was too narrow for both vehicles at once, so the van had to wait for the other car to exit before turning in. Just as the van finally made it into the alley, a mother and child crossed the street right in front of it. Even though they had already slipped around a corner, Jamal and Zeina could hear the van's brakes screech to a stop.

"Let's get in here!" said Jamal, climbing onto the bed of a half-unloaded truck. In seconds, the two teens had hidden themselves under a tarp that covered boxes of merchandise. Just then, the van came barreling down the alley and passed the truck without stopping. Jamal and Zeina remained hidden, their hearts in their mouths, not knowing if their pursuers were nearby or far away.

They heard the truck door open and slam shut, and then the old diesel engine roared to life as the driver started it up. They felt the truck lurch forward. Jamal touched his HWatch and sent a text to his mother, telling her they were downtown.

"Next time he stops, we'll jump for it, okay?" Jamal said to Zeina, hoping his voice didn't let on how scared he was.

At the next red light, they peered over the side before

crawling out. A few passersby looked at them curiously but minded their own business.

"Taxi!" Jamal called when he saw a human-driven cab.

"To the port, please," said Zeina, climbing into the tattered back seat.

"No, to the old Jewish district," Jamal corrected.

After a ten-minute ride, the taxi stopped in front of a large, old building.

"Can you come back in forty minutes?" Jamal asked, after paying the driver.

"I'll be here," the man assured them.

Before going in, Jamal sent another message to his mother, promising to be back soon.

The two teens found Ali in a set of rooms cluttered with antiques, where he had his work studio. He received them warmly when he read Rahman's letter of introduction and learned the reason for their visit.

Ali was in his mid-thirties and had studied in Cairo and Jerusalem. He told the teens he was dedicated to the folklore of the region, had studied the origin of the *Book of Wisdom* of Solomon and had a passion for old-world items. "Stuff that predates the Great Meltdown," he explained, gesturing to his vast collection.

"Any chance you could share a few stories with us, Ali?" Zeina asked. "I'm kind of a collector myself," she added shyly.

"Absolutely," said Ali excitedly, adding, "The stories I'm translating now are traditionally attributed to Solomon, but they're actually from a body of ancient wisdom written by an anonymous author who, we believe, was from North Africa. This is why your friend Professor Rahman and I are working together."

Ali took the teens to a room that contained an ancient copy machine from the early twentieth century, called a "roller copier." Shuffling through a stack of papers next to the machine, he finally found the ones he was looking for. He inserted them through the two rollers, cranked the handle and produced a new copy.

"Here they are," said Ali, blowing on the papers to dry the ink. "All I ask in return is that you pass these stories on. Fewer and fewer people read these tales, and if we don't keep them alive, they'll disappear from human memory, just like the animal species that have gone extinct by the thousands."

"That's exactly what I intend to do—keep the stories alive," Zeina said.

The roller copier wasn't the only antique in the studio. Jamal was most interested in a collection of weapons that were kept in a glass display case. Ali explained that they were from the Mameluke dynasty, as he fumbled with a cluster of small keys on a keychain. When the old case was opened, Jamal immediately reached for an oddly shaped tube attached to a curly cord and put it to his ear. The cord was attached to a boxlike apparatus, from which extended another cord that would have once plugged into a socket in the wall.

"Hard to imagine our parents and grandparents making

phone calls with something like that, isn't it?" Ali said to him. "Come, take a look at this. The newest in my collection." He pulled out a long sword with great care.

Ali and Jamal spent some time comparing the shapes and uses of various swords and daggers, until Zeina joined them from the other room.

"Our taxi is outside waiting," she said, peering down at the street through the big windows. "Thanks so much for the stories, Ali. I hope we can stay in touch somehow."

"And where are you going now?" Ali asked, putting the sword back in its case.

"Turkey," said Jamal. "We need to pick up another passenger in Antalya."

"A beautiful city. There's a bookstore there that has a great collection of old books. It bears the name of its owner, a man named Deniz. Everyone knows him. Apparently he has some real treasures hidden away—in case you want to buy something. If you tell him why you're interested in stories, maybe he'll offer you a good deal." Ali walked the two teens to the door. "Well, good luck!"

"The coast is clear," Jamal said to Zeina as they left the building.

The taxi ride wasn't a long one, and they were relieved when they arrived back at port. They knew they should tell Omar and Mirta what had happened that day, because the man who had tried to lure them into his car had mentioned Omar by name. That couldn't have been a coincidence.

"Look, Zeina, let's not say anything for now, okay?" Jamal said. "We'll do it later. I have a better plan for the next port."

The black-feathered birds, perched on the pier's pylons, spread their wings and gazed hungrily into the water.

Once on deck, Zeina put the manuscripts on a table and then took off her headscarf. Suddenly a gust of wind snatched up the papers, and in an instant they were swept over the rail. Zeina flung herself at them, open-armed and screaming like a bird. As she stood at the rail watching the papers floating on the water below, several cormorants swooped down to investigate and peck at them.

"No!" she cried, her eyes filling with tears. As the cormorants poked at the papers, she walked back to her cabin and stayed there until Mrs. Piscarelli called her to help with dinner.

After dinner and Omar's words of welcome for Antonio, Zeina was asked for a story.

She stood up and said, "I just learned one about a bird."

Jamal looked up, surprised. "But you didn't even read them!" he whispered as the passengers settled themselves down for the tale.

"Shhhh, I read one quickly while you guys were looking at the weapons," she replied. And then she began.

The Bird's Advice

King Solomon relates that there was once a man who went into a forest to hunt birds. Seeing a very fat one hopping from branch to branch distractedly, he threw a net over it. The hunter lowered the net, very satisfied with his catch. He was about to stick the bird into a cage when he heard it say, "Tweet, tweet, please don't kill me!"

"Well, well! A talking *bird!" said the man. "But why shouldn't I kill you?! I was thinking of taking you home so that my wife could use you to flavor a plate of* pilau. *What do you think?"*

"I'm a magic bird," said the creature, "and if you set me free, I'll give you three pieces of advice."

"Bah! I don't need advice," said the man. "Instead of three pieces of advice, why not give me three wishes, like other magical beings?"

"Because," said the bird, "wishes without wisdom are worthless."

"Hmmm ... that does sound quite clever. Well, let's have these three pieces of advice, then. We'll see what kind of wisdom a little sparrow has to offer!"

"As you will," said the bird. "I'll give you the first piece of advice now: If you lose something, no matter how important it is to you, don't be sorry."

The hunter thought about this.

"Now comes the second piece of advice, assuming you'll permit me to jump up to that branch," the bird said.

"Go, then. This is quite amusing," said the man, releasing his captive.

"Secondly," said the bird as it perched on the branch, just out of the man's reach, "never believe anything that sounds ridiculous, unless you have proof."

"That seems like good counsel, although it's a bit simplistic," said the hunter, "because everyone knows that!"

"And now the third piece of advice," the little bird continued, flying to a higher branch. "Don't try to do anything you're not prepared for."

"That's not very deep," the hunter observed, but nevertheless, he repeated the third piece of advice to himself.

"What a foolish man you are!" said the bird from

> *high up in the tree. "If you had taken me to your wife to flavor a dish of* pilau, *she would have found a huge diamond in my stomach, and you would have become rich. Rich! Rich! Forever!"*
>
> *"Come down from that tree, little bird! You tricked me! Let me get my hands on you. I'm going to pluck you here and now!" shouted the man. He started to climb the tree. Every time he lurched higher, the bird flitted up to a higher branch. Finally, the man reached a branch too thin to support his weight. When it snapped, he plummeted to the ground with a tremendous yell, breaking more branches as he fell.*

Jamal threw himself onto the ground, pretending to be the hunter floundering under the tree, and the smaller children jumped up and down in their seats, shrieking with laughter.

> *"Twee-hee-hee," the little bird laughed, "what a foolish man you are! Have you already forgotten the three pieces of advice I gave you? First of all, if you lose something, no matter how valuable you think it is, don't be sorry. You were sorry for having lost me and the diamond. Secondly, I told you that you should never believe anything that sounds ridiculous, unless you have proof. How could there be a large diamond in a stomach as small as mine? What's more, birds eat insects and seeds, not diamonds. Humans are the only animals that admire stones."*

"You lied to me!" screamed the hunter, struggling to his feet.

"Thirdly," the bird continued, "I told you that you should never try to do something you aren't prepared for. You should never climb a tree as high as this one without first losing a few pounds! Isn't that right, my friend?"

The hunter looked down at his round belly.

"You can see now that all the diamonds in the world won't make you happy if you lack wisdom," said the bird.

And with that, it flew away until it reached the top of a mountain, laughing more loudly than ever.

8: Tartus, Syria

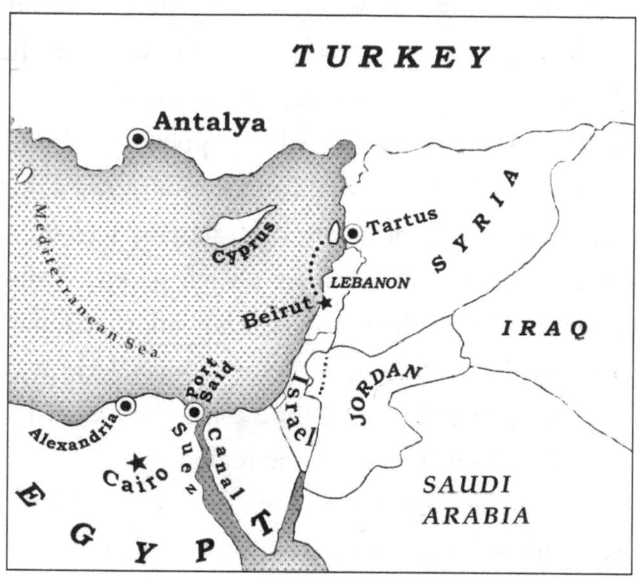

Dement had been smart enough not to tell his boss in advance about the attempted Beirut kidnapping, in case it failed—which it had. So he just left a message now, saying that *The Dreamer* had arranged to dock in Antalya, Turkey, and that he would give instructions to the captain of *The Concordia*.

"The Spaniard will be passing to the east of Cyprus and arriving that night," Dement told Wulandar. "Board his ship seventy-five miles south of Antalya. You should arrive a couple of hours earlier, since they're traveling slowly."

"Don't worry. We'll get them sooner or later," the captain assured him.

That morning, all the boats in the area received news that an unidentified submarine had destroyed the communications cables that ran along the bottom of the Mediterranean Sea. All global transmissions to that part of the world, including connection to the UNet, depended on those cables.

"Something like that was bound to happen sooner or later!" said Omar. He consulted his coordinates and verified that *The Dreamer* wasn't far from where the sabotage had occurred. He and the other crew members all felt a certain disquiet at having to navigate these waters, knowing that something dangerous might be lurking far below. Omar decided that it would be prudent to let some time elapse before setting out again, until things were safer in the region.

So he left a message via satellite phone for Tiryaki, an engineer from Istanbul who was waiting for them in Antalya. *The Dreamer* would be delayed. The Syrian port of Tartus was a few miles from the ship's current location.

"Tartus!" Omar thought. He and his parents had left Syria in 2011, and the prospect of returning there unleashed a flood of memories and emotions. Although Syria had expelled him and his family a quarter-century ago, he mused, today its ancient port would be a safe harbor.

Soon *The Dreamer's* passengers saw the forest of masts on the Syrian coast. The ship tied up between fishing boats and navy vessels. The crews on the neighboring ships looked curiously at *The Dreamer's* tricolored striped flag.

Igor counted the travelers as they disembarked. When Zeina walked past, he almost didn't recognize her. She had changed her jeans and school T-shirt—with its *Institut Espagnol Ochoa* logo—for a simple blouse, a long skirt and a *shayla* that covered her head and fell over her shoulders.

Jamal had also changed his appearance somewhat. He wore a *keffiyeh* that belonged to his father, and a pair of dark sunglasses. These made him look older. After reviewing the strange things that had happened to them, he and Zeina had devised a plan: From now on, when they visited a port, they'd go "incognito."

Mirta and Omar took the two teenagers with them as they walked through the city. It was the first time Omar had set foot in his homeland since he was eleven, and his heart beat hard in his chest. He wanted to show Tartus to his family, but the city was spread out and didn't have an RAA fleet. By noon they decided to turn back and head to the ship via public transportation.

"Would you mind if Jamal and I returned on foot?" Zeina asked. "It feels so good to stretch our legs after being on the ship." Tartus was a quiet town, so neither Omar nor Mirta objected.

The two teenagers walked down a boulevard lined with scraggly palm trees that indicated years of drought and neglect. At a picnic table in a small plaza, three young men wearing virtual glasses were waving their arms in the air, interacting with a game that was visible only to them.

Near a tiled fountain surrounded by benches, a man in a wheelchair was selling balloons. Zeina was still on edge from their last adventure and kept looking around with a worried expression on her face.

"Stop looking so suspicious," Jamal said to her. "Nothing's going to happen to us here."

They approached the balloon seller, and Jamal greeted him in halting Arabic.

The teens asked the man about the city and its people, and Jamal explained, with Zeina's help, that Syria was his father's homeland. The balloon salesman was an ex-soldier, and he spoke of the war that had taken place three decades before, of the people who had gone away and returned, and of those who hadn't come back but had remade their lives in far-off places. And also of those who hadn't survived. Jamal was thankful that his family was among the fortunate ones.

After a while, Zeina asked the balloon seller if he knew any storytellers.

"An odd request," the former soldier said, "although it wouldn't have been so strange back when I was a boy. But everything has changed around here." Glancing at the young men and their virtual goggles, he added, "Syria's culture has been lost. Or maybe it's hidden, buried somewhere, waiting for someone to dig it out." He paused and looked around with bleary eyes, as if fighting off bad memories. "I'm no storyteller, but I have one that's always been my favorite, if you'd like to hear it."

"We'd love to!" Zeina said enthusiastically, sitting on the bench near him. The man smoothed his mustache with one hand, cleared his throat and began.

The Hidden Treasure

Many years ago, in the Iranian city of Tabriz, when that country was called Persia, there was a man named Kamran. He started off poor, but thanks to years of hard work, and because of his astuteness and his austere lifestyle, he was able to accumulate a small fortune. However, so deeply ingrained were his habit of accumulating and not spending, and his fear of what might happen in the future, that instead of enjoying his wealth, Kamran spent all of his time thinking about how to protect it. He had no confidence in bankers and didn't think any hiding place in his house was secure enough; so, after pondering long and hard, he decided that the best way to safeguard his treasure would be to bury it far from his home.

One dark night, Kamran left his house with a chest full of money and a shovel, taking care that no one saw him. Eventually he reached a faraway place, where he buried the chest under a tree. That tree would always mark the spot where his treasure was buried.

One day, however, Kamran found himself in need of money, and that night he went to his hiding place with a shovel in order to withdraw some of his savings. He dug and he dug in the place where he knew his treasure was, but it had disappeared!

Kamran was in shock. For several days he wandered the streets of Tabriz in a state of turmoil, without anyone to turn to. Time passed, and he had to work very hard to support his family, until one day he came up with the idea of consulting an old wise man, a friend of his late father.

Rather ashamed, Kamran told his story to this man, without omitting any details. "It's impossible that anyone could know where my hiding place was! No one was there that night, and there was no place nearby for anyone to hide!" Kamran lamented.

"Let me think about your case," said the sage. "Maybe something will occur to me."

Days passed, and Kamran heard no news. Again he visited the wise man, who begged his pardon for not having solved the mystery.

However, a young boy who was working in the old man's household heard the two of them talking about the lost treasure, and said, "Master, permit me to interrupt. I have an idea."

Kamran thought this strange. "If an ancient sage like the sheikh *can't come up with a solution," he exclaimed, "how could a mere boy like you?"*

"He's a smart boy," said the sage. "Let him speak."

"What kind of a tree was it, sir?" the boy asked.

"A jujube," said Kamran after reflecting for a moment.

"I'll bet I know what happened, sir," said the boy. "I think you should ask the doctors of Tabriz if any of them prescribed jujube root for a patient. Surely the person who looked for jujube root is the one who found your treasure."

Impressed with the boy's intelligence, Kamran and the sheikh went to interview all the doctors in Tabriz. Sure enough, they soon found one who had prescribed root of jujube for an asthma patient. They spoke with that patient, who acknowledged having found the treasure and, being an honest merchant, returned it to its rightful owner.

Kamran rewarded the boy for his intelligence and willingness to help. Still, he wondered aloud how a boy could know more than an adult.

"I don't know," the sheikh replied. "I only know that the ways of Allah are mysterious."

"As indeed they are," said the ex-soldier, by way of ending his story.

"I agree, sir!" Zeina said. "Great story! I've noticed that in these old tales, often it's a child, or a slave, or an old woman, or a poor immigrant who surprises us with their wisdom at the end."

"That's true, my daughter. Sometimes what we neglect can be important, and what seems important can be trivial. The world seems upside-down, doesn't it?" said the war veteran.

"It sure does," said Jamal. Thanking the man, he bought a few balloons for the kids back on *The Dreamer* and checked the time. They had to return to the ship.

The two teens had walked for barely ten minutes back along the boulevard with the ragged palm trees, when they heard quick steps approaching them.

Jamal turned his head. "Run, Zeina!" he shouted, seeing two men rushing toward them from behind.

The teens took off, trailing the balloons behind them. Zeina lifted her skirt to her knees, much to the disapproval of an old man standing in a nearby doorway. Glancing at him, she didn't see a raised edge on the concrete sidewalk, and so she tripped on it and stumbled, twisting her ankle and letting out a deep groan. Jamal turned back to help her, grabbing her arm so she wouldn't fall. She limped to a stop, unable to continue.

The two pursuers rushed by without paying them any mind, eyes glued to a figure up ahead. "Thief! Grab that thief!" one of the men shouted, pointing to a young man slipping between two cars, a briefcase under his arm.

Zeina, who was obviously in pain, leaned on Jamal's shoulder.

"Sorry, Zeina, I was sure they were coming after us!" Jamal said.

"Yeah, and you said *I* was too suspicious!" she said, rubbing her ankle.

As Jamal helped Zeina limp down the boulevard, he said, "I was thinking about what that old soldier told us about the people who left this country and never came back. My father was a boy when he left Syria, so he adapted quickly to life in Europe. But for my grandparents, I think it was a real shock."

"I'm sure it was. My mother sometimes felt really homesick," Zeina said. "She missed her country and her people so much! But you know what, Jamal? At least immigrants know what they're missing. Other people feel nostalgia and don't know why. Does that ever happen to you?"

"Hmm," said Jamal. "Actually, it does sometimes. My father often says that we're *all* exiles in this world. Maybe he's right."

As they made their way slowly into the port—Zeina holding onto Jamal's arm as she limped along, and Jamal still holding the balloons—they were glad to see *The Dreamer*. The ship was now their home.

The next day, at sunrise, their home sailed for Antalya.

9: Antalya, Turkey

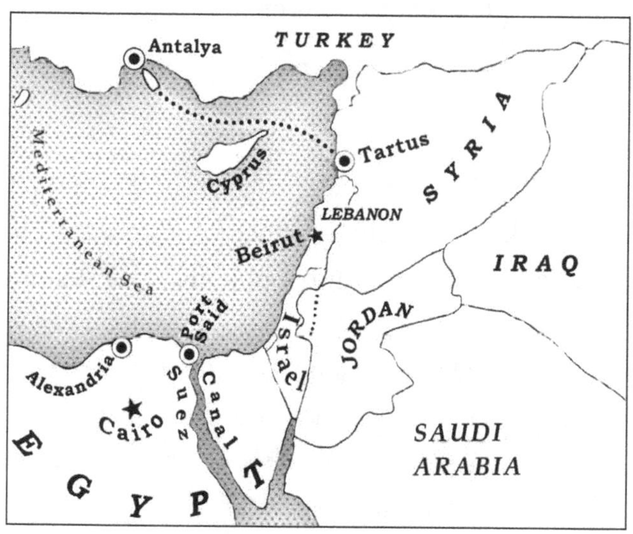

The Concordia had waited for hours off the Turkish coast, but never saw the scientists' ship. The monitor had showed every craft sailing within a wide radius, but *The Dreamer* wasn't among them. Captain Wulandar assumed—correctly—that Omar had been scared away by the attack on the underwater cables and had taken refuge in another port.

Wulandar's suspicions were confirmed when Dement phoned to inform him that *The Dreamer* had just left Tartus and was on its way to Antalya. The latest instructions were to sail back, southward. Based on the routes of the two ships, they should nearly run into each other.

As for the boarding plans, they were unchanged. "Be

sure to keep the capsule in a cool place," Dement had said. "Don't forget that the bacteria are live, and any increase in temperature could activate them prematurely."

At nine o'clock in the morning, *The Dreamer's* children were already on deck, where Zeina—armed with a piece of chalk—was marking their progress in broad jumping, a skill she had recently taught them.

On *The Concordia,* the members of the crew were waiting for the time when they could board *The Dreamer.* Dement monitored *The Concordia's* movement via his holophone. They couldn't fail this time.

"Have you already given our man from Eritrea that shot of pseudo-probiotic 0101?" Dement asked.

"Yes, and it worked just as you said," replied Wulandar. "He's got a swollen lump the size of a lemon jutting out from his belly—which he isn't too happy about."

"It's just a fake hernia—only phantom symptoms, nothing real," said Dement. "The pain will be gone by tomorrow, and so will the lump."

"Sure. Not the first time he's done that," commented Wulandar. "It's the way some Eritrean guys escape the military draft, you know."

By 9:30 a.m., the two ships were just a couple of nautical miles apart. *The Dreamer* was moving northwest at thirteen knots, while *The Concordia* bore southeast and was already slowing down. On board *The Dreamer,* the children were cleaning the deck after their games, while Tapio played his violin, accompanied by his father on the *kantele.*

On *The Concordia*, a crew member was preparing to carry out his mission. In one pocket he concealed a gun, which he hoped he wouldn't have to use, and in another pocket he stashed a tiny refrigeration unit that contained a small capsule.

At 9:45 a.m., the SSB radio announced the arrival of an international task force charged with repairing the underwater transmission cables. Soon, helicopters would be circulating overhead, and naval vessels from various countries would be converging on the area to secure it.

"Damn it!" roared Captain Wulandar on *The Concordia* when he heard the news. Plainly, they could not intercept and board *The Dreamer* with helicopters circling like buzzards overhead.

For their part, Omar and John decided to leave the area as quickly as possible. They disconnected the ship's electric motors and fired up the gas engine.

In less than an hour, *The Dreamer* neared sheer cliffs overlooking the tranquil waters of the Gulf of Antalya. On the heights, the ancient city stood among Roman monuments and Islamic minarets glistening in the sun. In the background, the ship's passengers could see the vague outline of the Taurus Mountains, shrouded in blue haze.

Tiryaki had been waiting in Antalya for three days. He saw the ship coming from afar and waved his arms high in greeting.

The bookstore Jamal and Zeina sought was located in the Kaleici district, not far from the port, but with the orthopedic boot that Dr. Roble had given her, Zeina could barely walk. Mirta had even suggested the teens stay on board for Zeina's sake, but Jamal was insistent.

"There's a famous bookstore here, Mom," he had said. "Everyone's heard of it. We have to go!" His mother couldn't really say no, although she had never known her son to be so interested in bookstores before. She chalked it up to Zeina's good influence.

Tiryaki, a man in his thirties with wild black hair and a thick mustache, immediately offered to help Zeina and Jamal. With Omar and Mirta's permission, he arranged for a car to take the two teens to the bookshop and bring them back. After a short discussion, *The Dreamer's* financial committee agreed to give Zeina a book budget, in case she and Jamal found anything worthwhile. The adults had grown to respect her as the ship's storyteller, and they trusted her opinion.

The bookstore was on the first floor of a beautifully restored house that had been built in the Ottoman era. Deniz, the owner, was about sixty years old, with white hair, a shaggy mustache and a good-natured expression. He was alone when Jamal and Zeina arrived, and he greeted them warmly.

"I don't know any storytellers in Antalya," he told them. "But luckily I have some priceless volumes. Why don't you see if something catches your eye?"

Deniz invited the teens to browse through his precious collection. The wooden floor of the old bookstore creaked under their footsteps, and the whole place smelled of old paper, leather and wood—an unusual combination in a world where everything was electronic.

"These are books about the imperial powers that governed Turkey," said Deniz, pointing with his cane to a shelf of leather-bound tomes. "The Persians, the Greeks, the Romans, the Ottomans. Modern Turkey inherited something from all of them. And here's the collection of traditional stories."

Zeina ran a hand across a row of books. She had never seen so many volumes together.

"When digital books became common here in Turkey, many booksellers put their hard-copy collections up for sale, but not me," said Deniz. "I decided to keep them, because you never know what the future holds. Did you hear what happened to the UNet yesterday? Printed books are still valuable, my friends. The ones you're looking at have increased in value because of their scarcity, of course, although I'll give you a good price if you find something you like."

Jamal chose books based on their illustrations, but Zeina followed her intuition—picking up books, reading the title and a few beginning paragraphs, and turning the old pages with care.

It was the best single-client sale the bookseller had made in years. With a huge grin on his face, he removed a book from its place on the shelf, blew the dust off and presented it to the teens. It had an intriguing cover with an image of a sailing ship leaning into the wind as sailors threw a coffin into the sea.

"I especially recommend reading this story, because it happened here, on these seas," Deniz said. "Take it as my gift—no extra charge! Have you been to the island of Lesbos? Have you heard of the city of Mytilene?"

"Mytilene … sounds familiar," said Jamal. "I think my dad mentioned that that's where the immigrants from Syria, and maybe from Iraq and Afghanistan, landed in Greece when he was a kid. That was a few years after he left Syria with my grandparents, at the beginning of the conflict there."

"That's right," said Deniz. "The refugees sailed along Turkey's east coast to Lesbos, in Greece. But not everyone arrived. So many small boats and rafts went down, and so many immigrants perished! Interestingly enough, the story in this book took place in the same waters and on the same island, but some thirteen hundred years earlier."

"In the same place?" Jamal asked.

"Yes, and in other places, too," continued Deniz. "Like Tyre, which nowadays is in Lebanon; and Tarsus, not far from here; and Antioch and Ephesus, which are now Turkish."

"Tonight we'll read this book to everybody on board. I bet your dad will appreciate it," Zeina said to Jamal, and she thanked Deniz for the gift.

"If you stop in Jeddah when you're passing through the Red Sea, visit Walid. He works at the Petroleum Museum, but he has an interest in Arabic tales and can tell you some good ones."

The ship's children had gone to visit ancient ruins with their families and now returned clutching pebbles they were sure had been touched by Roman gladiators. Jamal and Zeina, lugging a big box, got back from the bookstore and set the newly acquired books on the shelves of *The Dreamer's* library, in a special section they had labeled "Stories of the World."

As the sun set in a brilliant splash of color, the young passengers gathered at the starboard rail, watching as the beautiful city of Antalya receded into thc distancc. Then they were called for dinner.

After the meal and some words of welcome for the new passenger, Omar invited Zeina to begin her story.

The Book of Apolonio

About two thousand years ago, the small city-state of Tyre, on the east coast of the Mediterranean Sea, was ruled by a young king named Apolonio.

He was kind, courageous and intelligent. He was also good at solving riddles and brain-teasers, a common pastime among his people, and uncovering the truth behind appearances.

But Apolonio inadvertently made an enemy of a wicked king named Antioch, who reigned over a much larger neighboring kingdom that shared its ruler's name.

You see, in the course of solving a particular mystery, King Apolonio discovered something shameful about King Antioch and his family. When Antioch found out that Apolonio knew his secret, he swore to hunt Apolonio down and kill him.

Because Antioch was much more powerful, Apolonio chose to flee in order to prevent an attack on his city. Leaving his kingdom in the hands of a trusted minister, the young king boarded a ship with a small group of his best men.

Shortly after setting sail, a terrible storm blew up, sending the boat to the bottom of the sea and casting Apolonio onto the shores of an unknown land. As he was lamenting his misfortune, he saw someone walking toward him. It was a fisherman, who, seeing the castaway naked and shivering with cold, ripped his own mantle in two so that he could share it with the unfortunate king. Then the fisherman led Apolonio to his humble house, where the young man could rest and regain his strength.

Once he was fully recovered, Apolonio decided to set out on foot, and eventually he found himself in the city of Pentapolis, which was ruled by King Architrastres. Apolonio decided to settle here for the time being.

One day, as luck would have it, he was invited to a banquet at the royal palace. It was on this happy occasion that he met Princess Luciana, the daughter of

King Architrastres. Apolonio and Luciana immediately recognized one another as soulmates and declared their love for each other.

To protect himself, Apolonio had decided not to reveal his true identity to anyone, so the marriage between the princess and a supposed commoner might have been a problem. But Luciana was the light of her father's eyes, and he consented to the match. And once he discovered that Apolonio was well-versed in the affairs of state, the king offered his son-in-law the title of Royal Counselor.

And that's how Apolonio went from king to shipwrecked sailor, and from shipwrecked sailor to king's counselor.

But destiny is unknowable, and fortune is a wheel on which happiness alternates with sadness—now one, now the other. And nothing is permanent.

One day, months after the wedding, with Luciana expecting her first child, a boat from Tyre sailed into the port of Pentapolis, bringing news of the death of King Antioch, Apolonio's old archenemy. "This is very good news," thought the exiled king, and he decided that now he could reveal his identity and return to his own city.

The day of departure arrived. Since the baby was due to be born after the royal couple arrived in Tyre, they decided to bring along Licorides, Luciana's former nursemaid, to take care of the new princess.

A huge crowd bearing flowers and gifts for the

travelers gathered at the port. Architrastres and Luciana shed many tears, and everyone was saddened by their separation. In those days, journeys were long and dangerous, and a departure could mean many years of absence.

Finally, to the sailors' shouts of "Ho-hooo, ho-hooo!" the sails unfurled, the anchors were drawn up and the ship sailed off under a brisk wind that soon pushed it far from the coast. Everyone waved. Those on board waved toward land, and those on shore waved seaward, until the boat became a tiny speck on the horizon and then disappeared.

But the travelers were happy, and the crew sang and celebrated the favorable winds that bore them forward so swiftly.

They had been sailing for several days when enormous clouds appeared and obscured the sun, turning the sky a dark gray. The sea—no friend to Apolonio—became turbulent. An icy wind suddenly whipped up, threatening to tear sail and mast apart. Tossed about on the waves, the boat groaned from every plank.

Luciana, who was frightened by the violence of the storm, suddenly realized that the baby was about to be born, and was swiftly carried to her bed. Between the roar of the waves and the howling of the wind, the gasping cries of the newborn child were scarcely heard. Luciana had given birth to a beautiful baby girl.

Then tragedy struck. Fragile and weakened by the voyage, Luciana lost consciousness. All the color drained from her face, her pulse faded away, and she fell into a death-like state.

Seeing no sign of life, those around her began to shout: "Oh lady, dear lady, don't die now! Look at the beautiful baby girl beside you! Oh, woeful the hour we embarked! What are we to do?"

Apolonio was desperately trying to help his crew trim the sails, when he saw Licorides approach with a baby in her arms. But the good lady's expression didn't convey happiness. Between sobs, she let it be known that Luciana had died the moment his daughter had arrived in the world.

"Look, Apolonio," said Licorides, "this is your daughter, the daughter of your deceased queen. You must keep the baby safe!"

Words could not express Apolonio's profound sorrow at hearing this news. As soon as he was able to talk, he said, "Oh gods! Why do you cause us to love the creatures of this world, only to rip them from us, never to be seen again?"

Some of Zeina's listeners wiped tears from their eyes. She kept on with the story.

The waves and wind continued to slam the ship. Now, in those far-off times, sailors believed that delivering a body to the ocean's depths would make a tempest abate. Apolonio, knowing how strongly his crew clung to this superstition, realized that nothing would convince them otherwise.

So he ordered that a coffin be swiftly constructed out of light wood and caulked with lacquer and pitch inside and out to make it totally watertight. This casket was perfumed with sweet-smelling oils, lined with the richest satin and rubbed again with other natural fragrances.

"Ah! Such a sad bed you must rest on now, my love!" Apolonio said. "Without light, without fire, in this hostile sea! And I can't bring you with me! Where is your soul now? Crossing the River Styx toward the kingdom of Hades? Oh, Licorides, bring me my writing instruments and my treasure chest and jewels. Go quickly, before I lose what strength I have left!"

So the great treasure chest was brought to Apolonio, who took out various jewels and put them in a corner of the coffin. Then, on a metal plaque, he engraved Luciana's name and lineage, and the circumstances of her death. He also engraved a request—in case anyone found her—that she be given a proper burial, so that her soul might reach the Island of the Blessed.

Closing the coffin and tying it with thick nautical rope, the crew slowly and with much sorrow lowered it into the water. The disconsolate Apolonio wept as he watched it drift away, until it disappeared behind the rough waves that carried it inexorably on its voyage of no return.

"What a sad story," whispered Liyang.

"If my mama were to die, I wouldn't let anybody throw her into the sea," said Kimiko.

"Wait a minute, kids, the story isn't finished," continued Zeina. "As I've said before, sometimes what looks bad is really good, and what looks good can be bad."

As the afternoon waned, the wind blew the clouds away. The crew raised the sails, and Apolonio ordered a change of course toward Tarsus, the closest harbor, where the baby could be cared for by the family of his old friend, Governor Estrangilo.

Now, as you know, the world is full of surprises, and the hand of destiny sometimes intervenes in unexpected ways—and can change what once seemed immutable.

On the following day, the wind blew gently. Little by little, the waves carried the coffin, with its precious cargo, to the coast of Ephesus. There it happened that a wise doctor who was walking by the sea came upon the mysterious box and, without further ado, carried it home and summoned a locksmith to open it. Imagine the doctor's surprise when he found a beautiful woman inside, luxuriously dressed and still warm.

Taking her pulse and placing his ear over her heart,

he said, "Ah, I think they've been too hasty in throwing this young woman into the sea! She has only fainted, and if we act quickly, she may regain consciousness."

A great bustle of activity began. Dry wood was brought in and a fire started. The woman's body was anointed with a warm balsam and wrapped in a woolen mantle. Then a bottle of smelling salts was opened under her nose. The vapors worked immediately, and the beautiful Luciana sighed deeply, as if her soul had returned to her body.

Meanwhile, in the city of Tarsus, Apolonio left the baby and her nursemaid under the care of Estrangilo and his wife, Dionisia. The couple, who also had a newborn girl of their own, gladly accepted the charge. Apolonio left a large sum of money in gold and silver, in case he couldn't return quickly, for he wanted to ensure that his daughter received the very best education.

"And what's the little one's name?" asked Estrangilo.

"Tarsiana," said Apolonio, "in honor of the city of Tarsus."

With a broken heart, Apolonio decided to journey to Egypt, where he had friends. He told himself he wouldn't return until he had found a future husband for his daughter—a normal preoccupation among royal fathers in those days.

Licorides wept when her master, sad but determined, set sail once again.

Years passed. Tarsiana grew into an intelligent, kind

and beautiful girl—and more so with each passing year. Of her parents, she was only told that her mother had died and that, since her father's circumstances had prevented him from looking after her, she had been left in Estrangilo and Dionisia's care.

Over the years, none of the letters sent by Apolonio to his daughter ever reached her or Licorides, because they were intercepted by Dionisia, who hid them away.

At the age of seven, Tarsiana began to study under the finest tutors, to learn all the arts in addition to grammar, arithmetic and geometry. By the age of twelve, she had learned to sing, dance, recite poetry and play various musical instruments.

Tarsiana was no less advanced in the sciences. She knew the positions of the stars and constellations, and she was well versed in the texts written by wise men past and present. At age fourteen she could speak as an equal with the philosophers of the court, although she always spoke with modesty.

Tarsiana found pleasure in things that other children found tedious. She was so curious about everything that she was reluctant to miss even one day of learning. When her lessons were over, she would rush to the public square to listen to the storytellers there. Afterward, she would recount the stories to her friends without missing a single detail.

Although her stepsister received a similar education,

she didn't take advantage of it in the same way— either through laziness or lack of innate talent. So she seemed slow and uninterested beside the brilliant Tarsiana, who was admired and loved by all.

Well, not quite by all. The marked difference between the two girls made Dionisia very jealous. She thought that if she could only get rid of Tarsiana, her own daughter would receive more attention and praise. Thus did a silent, blind hatred for Tarsiana grow in Dionisia's breast until, like a ravening monster, it consumed her. She then came up with a plan to kill Tarsiana, and bided her time while she waited for the right moment.

The faithful Licorides, who had cared for Tarsiana like a mother for fourteen years, fell ill one day and died shortly afterward. But on her deathbed she told Tarsiana the story of the girl's true origin.

"Listen closely, Tarsiana," Licorides said. "Apolonio of Tyre is your father, and King Architrastres is your grandfather. His daughter, Luciana, whom I've spoken of so often, was your mother! Your father went on a long journey, but he'll come for you one day. He's a strong and courageous man. Now you must be strong and courageous, too. Keep this knowledge in your heart. You'll know when the time is right to reveal the truth."

The good nurse was buried in a cemetery overlooking the sea, and from that day onward, very early every morning, Tarsiana would go to the tomb with a sprig of flowers, a candle and some incense, to pray and meditate.

Dionisia, seeing that this presented a perfect opportunity to carry out her plan, one day summoned her slave. She could barely contain her excitement as she explained what she wanted him to do, promising him a large sum of money in addition to his freedom.

"Go to the cemetery tomorrow morning," ordered Dionisia. "Arm yourself with a good dagger. Seize your opportunity when Tarsiana is alone and at prayer. Kill her and throw her body into the sea. And don't come back without having done what I've told you, or you'll regret it to the end of your days!"

Even though the servant was repelled by the task, the pay was too high to refuse, plus he feared Dionisia's wrath. So the following day, he got up at dawn, sharpened his knife and went to the cemetery.

"Heavens! Is my freedom worth a maiden's life?" he asked himself again and again. But, as often happens with people, slave or otherwise, his self-interest and desire to obey were stronger than his principles.

Tarsiana had lit her candle and incense and had begun to pray. The servant found her kneeling beside the tomb. When he drew near her from behind, ready to grab her by the hair, she sensed his presence and turned around. Immediately, she understood what he was about to do.

"What are you doing, Teofilo?" Tarsiana asked in fear. "Why do you wish to kill me? What crime have I committed against you or anyone else? Please, I beg you...."

"You are innocent," replied the servant, "but I must obey my mistress."

"Dionisia? I have never offended her. What does she accuse me of?"

"My orders are not to discuss the reasons for your death, maiden, but to make it happen."

"If there's no hope, at least give me a moment to pray," Tarsiana pleaded, sobbing.

"Do it, but quickly," said the assassin. "The gods don't need many words."

Tarsiana began to implore the gods, her words coming out in a fear-fueled rush.

"Heavenly gods! Why should I have to die? I've never done evil to anybody, nor even killed so much as a mouse or fly! Once I stepped on a worm by accident, and I cried over it!"

The servant was about to commit the abominable crime. His hand trembled as it reached for the weapon in his belt. He knew this would be the most horrible act he would ever commit.

"I am a bad man," he thought. "No, I am a weak *man, a slave, one who cannot say no when given a mission like this. Or am I just a greedy man?"*

Then he raised his eyes to ask pardon for his moral weakness. The wretched man knew very well that the heavens had eyes with which to observe the actions of mankind!

Just at that very instant, he noticed an ominous-looking galley with black sails, anchored just off the coast. On the beach in the distance, a group of fierce pirates, brandishing their swords, were running toward him, clearly intending to attack.

Without further thought, the terrified servant released Tarsiana, dropped his weapon and fled, forgetting heaven and earth, knife and victim, and leaving the girl at the mercy of the pirates.

They lost no time and, realizing they wouldn't be able to catch the slave, seized Tarsiana instead.

Some minutes later, the girl found herself in the hold of the pirate ship, setting sail for who knows what new city, where she would be sold as a slave.

In a state of great agitation, the unsuccessful assasin rushed to the home of his mistress and told her that Tarsiana was dead. He had such a frightened expression on his face that Dionisia did not doubt him.

"Now," she ordered, "put on mourning clothes, and go weeping into the street. I'll do the same and will tell the people that Tarsiana has died of some sudden illness."

The people believed Dionisia, who even staged a false funeral.

Meanwhile, locked in the dark, dank belly of the ship, Tarsiana thought about the strangeness of her destiny. Something that could have been a terrible misfortune had saved her life.

"Okay, that's it. We'll finish the story tomorrow," Zeina concluded.

The children went to bed, grumbling at being unable to persuade Zeina to continue. She promised them she would finish the tale at breakfast.

After their active day, the gentle rocking of the ship lulled the children into deep sleep. But the adults stayed awake, discussing the voyage.

"Speaking of pirates," said Igor, "tomorrow we sail the most dangerous seas yet."

"But pirates are only after important cargo, right?" Jamal asked. "We aren't of any interest to them, are we?"

"You never know," said Mr. Chissano. "Kidnapping is one of their most profitable businesses."

The thought of their children being kidnapped sent a chill down the parents' spines. Little by little, they went off to their cabins, leaving Omar and John to navigate a dark and unknown sea.

On *The Concordia*, Wulandar faced another problem. In front of him, the Eritrean tossed and turned in bed, in agonizing pain. Something had gone wrong, and the lemon-sized bump on his abdomen had doubled in size.

"The probiotic dose was too strong," said Wulandar.

"No, captain, that's not possible," his second-in-command said. "We followed the instructions to the letter. He must have had something already, and the probiotic just made it worse."

"Whatever it is, this guy's out of commission. We'll have to leave him in Port Massawa. Better for him and us if he dies at home rather than aboard our ship. Call that Somali fellow we'd been considering. Tell him to meet us in Port Berbera in forty-eight hours."

Wulandar considered his next move. He knew that the scientists' ship would be stopping in two more cities to pick up passengers. By then he'd have the Somali trained for the mission. Wulandar was also interested in knowing if *The Dreamer* was armed, just in case things didn't go as planned. A drone would be able to determine that.

10: **Port Said, Egypt**

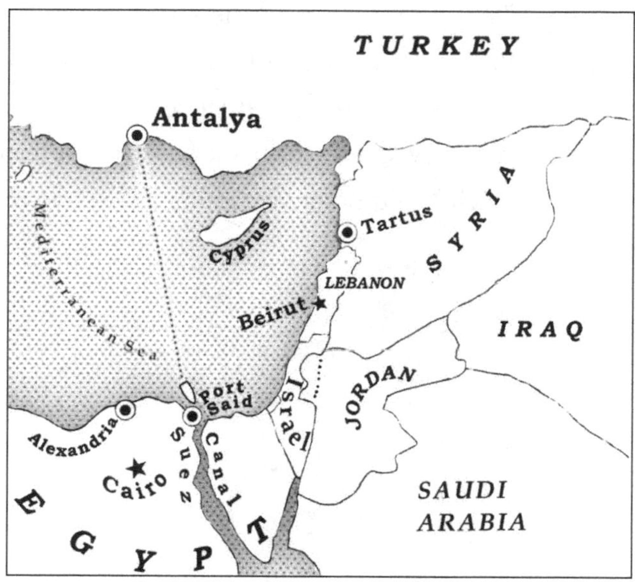

Shafts of hazy light shone through the portholes of *The Dreamer*. It was early morning on a sweltering Sunday, and John announced that the ship was within an hour of Port Said. The children appeared one after another in the dining room, gathering unceremoniously around Zeina. They begged her to finish the story of Apolonio.

When everybody was present, she opened the book to the last page she had read from. The children looked on expectantly, so intent on the story that the delicious French toast Mrs. Piscarelli had painstakingly prepared for them could have been boiled turnips and they wouldn't have noticed.

"Does anyone remember where we were?" asked Zeina.

"She was on the pirate ship!" came a chorus of voices.

"That's right," continued Zeina. "The pirate ship arrived at the city of Mytilene, on the island of Lesbos."

"So that's where it sank!" exclaimed Jamal.

"Jamal, you haven't even read the book, and you're inventing things already!" Zeina said before resuming her narrative.

The Book of Apolonio - Part Two

In Mytilene, Tarsiana was sold to Leno, a slave merchant who intended to offer her favors to as many men as cared to enter his establishment. The poor girl wept bitterly at her fate. What could she do to escape her bleak future as a slave? She searched and searched in her mind for a possible solution, but every door seemed to be shut.

Suddenly she remembered what her nursemaid used to say to her when she was very young. "My pretty child," Licorides had advised, "when you have a problem, don't despair. Use your intelligence and your experience. Use what you know, because knowledge is your weapon and your treasure."

This memory restored Tarsiana's strength and inspired her. And then she had an idea. She told her new master that she was an artist and a storyteller, and that he'd earn far more money by sending her to the marketplace to entertain the public than he'd earn by offering her to men.

The master allowed himself to be convinced by the girl's persistence and grace— although in truth, he was also swayed by the idea of having a more respectable source of income. In a voice loud enough for everyone to hear, he exclaimed, "An intelligent man should diversify his investments." Then, to Tarsiana, he said, "Well, child, let's try an experiment. Tomorrow you'll go and play your lyre in the public square. If things go well, I'll let you keep your new ... eh ... profession, and nobody will bother you around here."

That afternoon, the slave merchant returned to

his house with a tambourine and some old stringed instruments, plus a beautiful new dress, some cheap jewelry and a tiara of flowers, so that Tarsiana could adorn herself.

And so the next day, scented with perfumes and dressed like springtime, the girl set off to the public square, where she sat down on a bench and began to play and sing softly.

There were few listeners at first. Some children who were running and playing in the square stopped and then, intrigued by what they were hearing, drew near to Tarsiana. As she began to gain confidence, other passersby stopped to listen as well. Soon she was singing in a strong voice, dancing gracefully and telling marvelous stories. Each time she finished one, the audience applauded loudly. Tarsiana's debut was a huge success!

That night, she returned to the slave owner's house with a purse full of money and a radiant smile. Her master rubbed his hands together with satisfaction, and his eyes glittered like gold coins. He ordered her to go to the public square to perform every afternoon from then on, without fail. He relished the idea that soon he might be known as "the protector of the arts of Mytilene," and from then on began to treat the girl with greater consideration.

A year passed. Tarsiana would go each day to the

square to play and sing or to dance to the rhythm of the tambourine. When a song ended, she would tell a mystery tale, or one of Aesop's wise fables, or a joke. She had heard so many of them in the public square of Tarsus! When the people who were gathered around grew tired of laughing, one riddle after another would put them in a reflective frame of mind. If their heads began to hurt from too much thinking, a love story would soon bring tears to their eyes. If they became too sentimental, she would tell them something funny. No performer in that place had ever received as much applause as she did.

But what the public most admired was Tarsiana's knowledge. On clear nights she would point to the sky and talk about the planets, or speak of Egypt and other strange places, or recount the feats of Alexander the Great in Persia and India, or explain the significance of numbers and the harmony of the universe. Tarsiana had read the most important books of her age and had committed them to memory, guarding the knowledge they contained as she would a precious treasure. Now she generously shared that knowledge with her audience.

In this way, Tarsiana saved herself from being abused and humiliated, which was the sad fate of other slave women. Everyone loved her, and no one as much as Antinagoras, the governor of Mytilene. He was Tarsiana's most fervent and devoted admirer.

Having heard about her talent and wisdom, he began to visit the public square daily and became her protector. Every night, Tarsiana returned to her house accompanied by an armed guard. Meanwhile, she made sure she followed Licorides' counsel, and never revealed her own story. It was better to remain silent and follow her destiny.

One day, King Apolonio decided it was time to return to Tarsus to be reunited with his daughter. All this time, he had been traveling through North Africa, without a fixed address for receiving letters. He knew nothing about Tarsiana's life but imagined her living like a princess, knowing he loved her and reading the letters he always sent.

When Apolonio finally arrived in Tarsus, he hastened to the mansion of Estrangilo and Dionisia, weighed down with exotic gifts and anxious to see Tarsiana. He planned to take her with him to the city of Tyre. How delighted he was at the prospect of seeing his daughter again!

But when he arrived at the door of the great house where he had left Tarsiana, he was greeted by the hypocritical Dionisia, who was dressed in mourning clothes. Shedding crocodile tears, she told him, between theatrical sobs, that his dear little daughter had passed away.

"She died of heart failure, poor thing. Here one

minute and gone the next!" Dionisia said with feigned sadness. "We've marked her grave with a monument."

Knowing that the girl's father would one day return, the woman had indeed had a tomb built. But it was, of course, empty.

Devastated, Apolonio, went to visit the grave. He wanted desperately to embrace the stone, even though it was cold and hard. Strangely, however, when he knelt beside it, he wasn't able to shed even a single tear. His intuition told him that his daughter wasn't there, and that he should leave the city immediately. Feeling even more desperate, as well as guilty and confused, Apolonio gathered his men, ordered his ship to be readied, and embarked once more, this time for an uncertain destination.

But his spirits were low, and he soon sank into a deep depression. He even thought of throwing himself into the sea, because the world, and all that it contained, seemed so hateful to him.

The sea had never seemed to be a friend to Apolonio, and this voyage was no different in that regard. While they were sailing, a great tempest arose, and the rain and wind lashed at his ship for several hours. As night fell, the sea became calm, but the boat was badly damaged. Rudderless and with a broken mast, it drifted for several days at the mercy of the wind and currents. Apolonio's grim thought was that his life, too, was without direction, and he let himself be carried away on a tide of despondency.

And so King Apolonio lost himself to grief. He fell silent, refusing to speak with anyone and gesturing that he was not to be spoken to. So deep was his sadness that he didn't even notice when, one morning, the damaged vessel floated into a harbor.

His men joyfully lowered the anchor, giving thanks to the gods for this good fortune. They raised a shout to let Apolonio know it was time to go ashore, but they heard no reply. So they went to look for him and finally found him lying still, wracked by sorrow, in the darkest cabin of the ship. Not even the good news of having made land—and at a harbor, no less—could cheer him.

Now, it happened that this harbor was none other than the port of Mytilene. When Governor Antinagoras heard of the arrival of a foreign ship, and of its strange commander-king who refused to speak, he decided to go and see this man, wishing to help.

The sailors told Antinagoras that their captain was Apolonio, King of Tyre, but that he didn't wish to receive visitors. However, Antinagoras insisted, so they allowed him to go on board.

Upon seeing poor Apolonio in such a sad state, his beard grown long and matted, his hair tangled, his gaze absent, the noble governor was filled with pity and wanted to offer his friendship and counsel.

"May the gods be with you always, King Apolonio!" said Antinagoras by way of greeting. "I've heard of you and would like to speak with you."

But he was unable to get a word out of the king.

"May the gods preserve you, noble Apolonio," persisted Antinagoras. "I'm the governor of this place, and if you'll come out of the shadows, I'll take you to see my city and my palace."

"Whoever you are, go in peace," Apolonio murmured. "My heart is broken, and life is no longer important to me."

When he heard this sad declaration, Antinagoras decided to send for the young storyteller Tarsiana, who was famous for being able to lift people's spirits. The girl came immediately with her kithara*, accompanied by another slave woman.*

Antinagoras said, "Tarsiana, there's a king here who's in a state of profound melancholy. If you can't cure him, no one can! See what you can do to help him, I beg you!"

Tarsiana found herself intensely interested in the poor, sorrowful stranger. She said she could ease his suffering if she was left alone with him.

Seating herself near him in that dark room, Tarsiana greeted the stranger in a low voice. Then she gave her kithara *a soft strum and began to sing sweet songs of happy times. But though her music was beautiful, the king appeared to ignore it.*

She then asked if he would like to try to solve some riddles.

Surprised by this strange challenge, Apolonio looked directly at Tarsiana for the first time and immediately forgot his oath of silence. The girl was the very image of his dear dead queen! He began to answer Tarsiana's riddles correctly, one after the other and without hesitation. But after some minutes, haunted by the memory of Luciana, he shouted, "Enough silliness! Begone!" And he rudely pushed Tarsiana to the side.

Sadness had made Apolonio blind. He, who had easily solved each of Tarsiana's riddles and had been the only one to discover the nature of King Antioch's secret—which he had also accomplished by solving a riddle—was incapable of working through his own problem, even though the solution was right there before his eyes.

Feeling hurt and scorned, Tarsiana began to weep, saying, "Oh, Eternal Architect of the Heavens! Have pity on me in my affliction! Born on the tempestuous sea, and greeted by death the moment I arrived in this life! My mother died upon giving me life, and instead of being buried on land, she was thrown into the sea all alone, in a floating coffin!"

With each phrase the girl uttered, Apolonio grew more and more amazed.

"I was the ward of the governor of Tarsus," continued Tarsiana, "whose wife plotted to kill me when my nursemaid died. Then I was kidnapped by pirates, who sold me to a dealer in women! And now I, daughter and granddaughter of kings, am an orphan and a slave! Is this not a greater pain than your own, sir?"

In these few words, Tarsiana had told Apolonio her life story, something she had hidden from the people of Mytilene.

Hardly able to control his agitation, Apolonio began to question her, speaking quickly.

"Who is your father? Who is your mother?"

Tarsiana told him that her father was the king of Tyre, and her mother the princess of Pentapolis.

"Can she have heard my story from others?" Apolonio asked himself. And he continued questioning the girl.

"And what's the name of your stepmother?

"Dionisia, sir."

"And who was your nursemaid?"

"Licorides was her name."

"Oh! Is this an illusion cooked up by my crazed brain? Or has a cruel god sent a vision in order to play a joke on me?" exclaimed Apolonio, raising his arms skyward. Suddenly he fixed his gaze on the girl and asked, in a voice that was almost breathless, "And who are you?"

"My father named me Tarsiana."

Then Apolonio stood up and called his men. "Come, come! Look at this creature and tell me if she's really flesh and blood, or if she's just an apparition!"

Tarsiana indignantly exclaimed that she was no phantom. Extending her hand, she told Apolonio that he could pinch her—lightly, of course—and then, seeing his expression, she said, "But my good sir, why do you weep? Do you still believe I'm deceiving you?"

"Quickly, Helicanus! Bring me the smelling salts," ordered Apolonio, suddenly overcome with joy. "Look, everyone, this is my daughter, this precious girl, Tarsiana, a princess. Yes, a slave no longer! Because I'm her father, Apolonio, king of Tyre, who no longer feels pain, because I've found her! Oh, my daughter! My soul! It was for you that I was dying! Come here, my child—born on the sea, buried in Tarsus and found again on the sea!"

Mrs. Kim took out a handkerchief to wipe her tears. Zeina sipped her tea and continued.

"Yes, my little one. I'm Apolonio, your father," he said.

The girl thought she was dreaming. She clutched her chest to calm a heart that seemed as if it would pound its way out of her body like a bird breaking out of its cage. She opened her mouth, and for the first time the eloquent Tarsiana was at a loss for words.

Finally, now that they recognized one another, father and daughter shared a long and tender embrace. Then, turning to his men, Apolonio said, "And you, my friends, listen! I am well again! Prepare for a celebration!"

Tarsiana recounted every detail of her adventures, describing to her father how she'd been saved from a miserable life by using what she'd learned as a child, and how the education he'd ensured for her was the best legacy he could have given her.

When the festivities were over, Tarsiana, whose heart was generous as always, immediately busied herself freeing the merchant's slave girls, setting them on the road to another way of life.

Soon afterward, father and daughter embarked for the city of Tyre, where Apolonio had wished to return for so long. But in the middle of the journey, the king heard a mysterious voice whispering to him to change course and head toward Ephesus on the Aegean Sea. A vision of the city's temple came to his mind, and Apolonio obeyed the voice.

As soon as they reached Ephesus, they made straight for the famous temple. When Apolonio entered its main hall, which was supported by beautiful tall marble columns, he went to the altar and approached the statue of the goddess Diana-Artemis. Kneeling at its feet, he said a prayer before identifying himself and telling the story of all that had befallen him since first leaving Tyre.

Dressed in a diaphanous blue-and-white tunic, a beautiful woman—whom Apolonio thought must be the incarnation of Diana herself—appeared from behind the altar.

She was Luciana.

We need not pause here to describe their encounter. Suffice it to say that the king thought he was seeing a mirage, until Luciana kissed him very sweetly.

After holding his dear spouse for a very long time, he said, "Luciana, this is Tarsiana. She's our daughter, who was born at sea."

"I knew, my beloved daughter, that we would meet again one day!" said Luciana. "I saw it inscribed in the flight of birds. I heard it in the whisper of leaves in the breeze. I read the signs of your arrival in the traces the waves leave on the sand. The oracles did not lie!"

With eyes full of tears, Luciana opened her arms, and Tarsiana at long last rushed into her mother's embrace.

Zeina placed her hands on the open book and paused long enough to let her audience take in the emotional scene. Then, looking at the rapt faces, she slowly began to tell the remainder of the story from memory.

A little later, when the afternoon light no longer streamed through the high temple windows, and the planet Venus had emerged on the horizon, damsels lowered chandeliers from the temple's ceiling and lit the candles, and soon the hall was bathed in warm light. Luciana called for abundant food to be served, and the family shared a meal for the first time.

The following day, Apolonio thanked and richly rewarded the doctor who had rescued Luciana, and then the family departed for Pentapolis.

But first the ship stopped at the spot where Apolonio had come ashore after being shipwrecked many years before. Disembarking, he sought out the fisherman who had attended him when he sat, cold and miserable, on the beach.

"Good man," Apolonio said, "do you remember me? I'm the castaway to whom you gave half of your mantle. Take this, which I now return to you in one piece, because my search has come to an end." And thanking him again, Apolonio put a priceless, gold-embroidered mantle over the fisherman's shoulders.

Now the family could return home to Pentapolis, where Luciana's parents were still waiting for them, and then to Tyre, Apolonio's homeland.

Apolonio composed a book about his adventures and sent it to the library of Ephesus, and that's why we have it today.

"Great character, that Tarsiana!" Mirta observed. "Another woman who, like Scheherazade, changes her destiny by telling stories."

"What a story! Why isn't it more widely known?" somebody else asked.

Mrs. Piscarelli, a lover of plays, noted that she recognized a Shakespearean version of the story, which was entitled *Pericles, Prince of Tyre*.

Jamal looked at his father. Omar had turned to the map and, with a touch of nostalgia for a place he had only imagined but had never seen, lightly brushed his fingers over the island of Lesbos and the city of Mytilene.

The Dreamer was nearing Port Said, located on the northern tip of the Suez Canal, which had widened with the rising seas. While the wider canal was a blessing for shipping companies because it meant shorter waiting times for boats wanting to pass through, the rising seas were a calamity for coastal communities, which were flooded by the salt water. The canal was now open in both directions simultaneously, and in the morning *The Dreamer* sailed through its calm waters and into the Gulf of Suez.

When the ship entered the Red Sea, some of the passengers noticed the silhouette of a boat that seemed to be trailing them. Omar radioed the vessel but received no response. Then it disappeared. Soon after, a message arrived with the news that pirate ships had been spotted prowling the waters between Sudan and Ethiopia. Precautions were urgently advised. Everyone was on high alert.

"That's what I was afraid of," said Taro Wang.

"Wouldn't it be better to get out of here as fast as we can?" suggested Mrs. Ullakko, anxiously peering out to sea through binoculars. She saw a boat coming toward them and handed the binoculars over to Omar, who swore quietly under his breath at the sight. The boat was approaching fast—the radar showed that it was flying across the open sea at eighty knots per hour.

John sounded the alarm, and over the intercom Omar sent the families to the hull, while he and a few others stayed in the control room. He took out the satellite phone, which was more reliable than the holophone when offshore, and dialed their base in Cádiz. A couple of technicians there had been hired to monitor *The Dreamer's* journey twenty-four seven, in case of an emergency.

"We can't be sure, but it seems that a pirate boat may be pursuing us," Omar told Cádiz.

"Stay on the line. I'll communicate with the patrolmen."

"Hurry up. The boat is already near!"

Omar ordered the cameras on the towers to be turned on. John had already engaged the second gas engine, and *The Dreamer* sailed on at full speed.

Omar had already thought of a plan of action to take if an emergency like this arose. He had money set aside and would use it to negotiate with the pirates. He'd also tell them that his ship was on a scientific mission, and that they'd be in big trouble if they interfered with its progress. A cold sweat ran down his back, and a flood of grisly images cascaded through his mind as he heard the next message.

"Captain Gomes here, from UWF. No cause for alarm. It's a rescue operation. Take a look off your bow."

The small party on *The Dreamer* looked off the bow. A strange lump was floating in the water.

"It's a whale," said Mr. Chissano.

"No, maybe a deflated rubber boat," replied Taro Wang. "There might be a castaway."

"Neither," said Omar, who was peering through binoculars and could see, stamped on the side of the object, the words "Universal Wi-Fi," which they now realized was what "UWF" stood for. "It's one of those balloons that carry the WorldNet to remote places where there aren't any towers. Seems this one's fallen from the stratosphere." He breathed a sigh of relief.

"I'm glad it didn't fall on our heads!" said Jamal, who had disobeyed the orders to hide in the hull with the others. His father looked at him disapprovingly.

"Not likely," Tiryaki explained. "They have a short lifespan, like butterflies. And when they're out of service, they're brought down very precisely, in places where there aren't any people."

The speeding boat passed them and slowed down as it reached the balloon, which several crew members quickly secured to their vessel with rope. *The Dreamer's* passengers, who had been told they could leave the hull, watched the towing operation in astonishment. Trailing the enormous balloon behind it, the rescue boat signaled *The Dreamer* with a high, piercing horn and was soon out of sight.

"Wow, that was scary!" said John, visibly relieved.

Omar was somewhat embarrassed. But it was better to be an alarmist than overconfident, he thought, because in those waters anything was possible.

By the time the rescue boat's wake had dissolved in the waves, the silhouette of another boat—the same one they had seen upon entering the Red Sea—was once again visible on the horizon.

"John, get us out of here!" Omar said, and called the border patrol in Saudi Arabia.

The Dreamer sailed eastward at full speed and stayed a short distance from the Saudi coast. Then a couple of fast border-patrol speedboats escorted it to Jeddah, the nearest port.

Not everybody was happy, since Jeddah was roasting hot, even in the fall. But Zeina and Jamal were thrilled.

11: **Jeddah, Saudi Arabia**

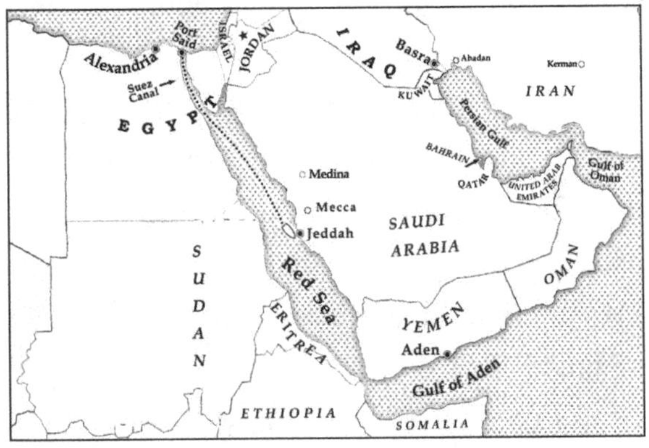

The city of Jeddah was impressive, with open avenues and tall buildings, but its wealth from the days of the petroleum boom was long gone. It had survived because it was the main port of entry for Mecca, whose pilgrims and visitors paid the high prices Jeddah's merchants and proprietors demanded. But, although Jeddah was bustling with visitors, many of its better-off inhabitants had abandoned the Arabian Peninsula and migrated to other countries, in order to escape the suffocating heat.

"Mom, can Zen and I visit the Petroleum Museum here?" Jamal asked. "It's supposed to be really good."

Mirta looked at her son sideways, wondering what he was up to. "Since when have you been interested in museums?" she asked with a sly smile. She'd already guessed that he and Zeina wanted to explore the city on their own.

"Come on, Mom. How could I not be interested in the history of petroleum? It's what got us into this mess in the first place," Jamal said, the note of mild sarcasm in his voice indicating that she was, in fact, right.

"Okay, but how about taking some of the younger kids with you?" she said teasingly.

"No way! As if I'm not stuck with them often enough as it is. Besides, there's no way they'll want to come."

"True. And their parents won't let them go anyway," Mirta thought. "Let me talk to your dad," she said, turning to seek him out.

Mirta was surprised at Omar's response. He'd been to Jeddah before and told her that crime and dissent were dealt with very harshly there, with police and cameras on every corner—which meant that the kids would be fine. Plus, the museum was supposed to be really great.

Returning to Jamal and Zeina, who were waiting expectantly, Mirta told them, "OK, but be back by five!" Then, remembering Omar's instructions, she added, "Zeina, I've got a *hijab* and *abaya* in our cabin. Go get them and put them on. And Jamal, you need to wear your *keffiyeh*. They've got very strict rules of decorum here, so you need to make sure you follow them."

The teens took off, thrilled to be off the boat and free. Cops were everywhere, so there was no need to be afraid of thieves or kidnappers, real or imagined—which was just as well, because Zeina would have found it difficult to run in her *abaya*. Besides that, her ankle, though less swollen than before, wasn't yet back to normal. She still limped a bit, so she and Jamal had to walk slowly.

The Petroleum Museum was at the end of a sun-drenched avenue. Walid worked in the book and photography section, and Zeina, who asked for him in her perfect Arabic, was able to find him easily. After introducing herself and Jamal and mentioning Deniz, she told Walid that she was on a mission to find as many storytellers as she could, in order to collect little-known wise tales for the ship's "Stories of the World" collection.

"A very commendable project," Walid said. "I'm not a storyteller, but in my free moments, I like to study traditional tales. It's a bit of a hobby."

Jamal noticed that the man was wearing a long yellow tunic—an uncommon sight in this country.

"Ah, yes, it's to differentiate myself from the clerics, who wear white robes," he said when he saw Jamal looking at his tunic. "I carry God in my heart, not in a tunic or rosary. I try to hear His voice, rather than the voice of the clergy. . . ."

Walid had been speaking with energy, but as he lapsed into silence his expression became sad.

"But if you're looking for good stories, I have one that you can take with you. I think it's a very important tale." He picked up a manuscript from his desk and handed it to Zeina. "It was sent to me by a woman named Noora Al-Jamil. She said I'd like it, and she was right! Noora's a very smart lady. She directs the Cultural Center in Basra, which I recommend visiting if you ever get the chance."

The visitors would have liked to stay longer, but they didn't want to interrupt Walid's work any further. They thanked him for the story and his time, and left.

Zeina put the sheets of paper in her purse. This time, she promised herself, she wouldn't lose them to a gust of wind.

Jamal wanted to check out the city, but the heat was stifling, the distances enormous and public transportation nonexistent. With Zeina's ankle still hurting, they decided to head back to port.

Along the way, her ankle grew worse. Jamal put his arm around her waist and had her lean on his shoulder. The port was just a few blocks away.

Halfway there, they ran into a group of five men in white robes and *shumagh*, the red-and-white-checkered headdress typically worn by Saudi men. With their matching outfits, long beards of the same length and dark glasses, the five looked like identical quintuplets. They stood in front of the teens, blocking their way.

"Let her go!" one of the men said, extending his arm and poking Jamal's chest with an incriminating finger. "You're under arrest!"

"What are you talking about?" Jamal answered defiantly.

One of the men pointed to a badge he wore. Zeina's heart jumped when she read the letters on it: CPVPV, which she recognized as an acronym for Saudi Arabia's Committee for the Promotion of Virtue and the Prevention of Vice.

"Religious police," she told Jamal quietly, in Spanish.

"We're foreigners," said Jamal in his halting Arabic. "And

I can't let her go, because she's hurt. Don't you see? She's limping! Zeina, show them your ankle!"

"I can't. I can't show my ankle to these men," Zeina said softly.

One of the men pointed to a parked flying car and, with what looked like an electric stun cane, motioned to both teens to get in. When Jamal protested, he was threatened with the cane. Before he or Zeina had time to send a message, the police took their HWatches away and turned them off.

Scared, the teens got into the eight-rotor passenger drone. Although it was designed to hold no more than two people, the skinniest of the men squeezed in beside Jamal while the four other men got into a car. The drone soared up over the city and in a few minutes landed on the helipad of the detention center.

Jamal was taken straight to a cell. Zeina was left sitting on a wooden bench in the anteroom for two hours, until someone—she couldn't tell if it was a judge or a police officer—called her in.

By five-thirty p.m., Jamal's parents were beginning to worry. It wasn't unusual for the teens to be late, but it wasn't like them not to respond to messages. Jamal's HWatch had allowed Omar and Mirta to track his movements, so they knew where his last stop had been, but they didn't know where he and Zeina were now. So Omar decided to go to the museum.

There, the staff informed him that two young people had been in to talk to Walid. But Walid told Omar that the teens had left hours ago. Omar called the police from Walid's desk, and was put on hold for nearly twenty minutes before finally being told that the two unaccompanied minors had been taken to the detention center.

Although Omar had to pay a fine to have them released, he was overjoyed to find them both uninjured—but he was furious when he found out the charges. The religious police lectured Jamal and then told a judge to issue an order deporting the boy.

Zeina, whose purse had been searched, was asked who had given her the manuscript. She replied that she had found it in the street. Since it was considered subversive literature, the police confiscated it and told the judge to deport her as well.

"Don't bother with the paperwork," Omar said to them rudely. "We'll all be leaving at dawn."

When the police gave the teens back their HWatches, Jamal noticed that the GPS in both had been disconnected. Had this been done merely to scare the parents and teach the kids a lesson, or was there a more sinister reason? He'd never know the answer.

That evening, at the usual time, Zeina announced that it was story time. The manuscript might be burnt to a crisp by now, she thought, but she'd read it through while waiting on that hard bench in the detention center, and she remembered the story perfectly, in all its detail.

The twenty-seven passengers on board were ready to listen.

They had no need to scan the horizon or watch the radar. They were in a safe harbor, and they were perfectly fine—as long as they didn't venture into the city.

Zeina began the tale.

The Travelers and the Elephant

A long time ago, when sailing vessels were fragile and prone to accidents at sea, a ship was navigating near the coast when a terrible storm blew in. The crew were all cast into the sea, but by swimming with the current, they managed to reach shore.

Among them was a man named Ibrahim. He was just as afraid as everyone else, because the place was entirely unknown to them, and there were no villages around, or even trails by which to find their way.

A few days went by without the crew finding a way out. They knew their circumstances were so dire that they would all die in that desolate place unless they found food and water soon. One of them proposed that each man make a promise to do something good, so that God might hear it and save them.

One man promised to pray several times a day. Another said that he would make a pilgrimage on foot. Another, that he would fast; yet another, that he would make charitable donations. And so on and so on, each man promising to do something worthy.

When Ibrahim's turn came, he said, "I promise not to eat elephant meat."

"But what kind of sacrifice is that? Do you think this is a joke?" asked the others.

"No, I said it without thinking," said Ibrahim. "And I swear, I can't even explain it to myself. I was just trying to think of something good to promise, and that's what came out of my mouth!"

The men then decided that it would be best if they all went off in different directions to hunt for food and then returned to the same place at an appointed time, to share whatever they'd found.

And that's what they did. But as it happened, none of the men found anything to eat—that is, except for one, who found a baby elephant and brought it to the group.

Everyone agreed that the elephant would provide them with sufficient nutrition to continue traveling, and that this would be better than dying of hunger. So they killed the animal and cooked its meat over the fire they managed to light. Then everyone ate—except for Ibrahim.

"Come on, Ibrahim, eat. Here's your portion," the others urged him.

"But don't you remember my promise? How can I break my oath?" he said. "What good are promises if a person breaks them?"

His companions had no answer and continued eating in silence. Then they stretched out on the ground to sleep.

A little while later, they heard the furious trumpeting of an elephant drawing closer and closer. The animal stopped when it reached their campsite, where the men lay paralyzed with terror. Then, using her trunk, the mother elephant began to smell the breath of each man, one by one. Whenever she detected the scent of elephant meat, she stomped the offender to death with a single blow from her huge foot.

When she came to Ibrahim, however, she sniffed at him several times while he, in mortal terror, remained motionless, just like his unfortunate comrades. Finally, she lifted him up with her trunk and, depositing him on her back, carried him off.

The elephant bore him away at a fast trot for a day

and a night, until they came to a village. Kneeling, she allowed Ibrahim to dismount, and then she turned and trotted off in the direction they had come from. Safe and sound, Ibrahim soon found people who helped him return to his homeland.

As the appreciative audience talked about the story and its possible deeper meanings, Zeina approached Mrs. Piscarelli and spoke to her quietly. Soon the two were in the anteroom of the bigger bathroom, with the girl sitting in a chair, her shoulders wrapped in a towel, and Mrs. Piscarelli wielding a pair of scissors. The heavy mass of long, dark began cascading to the floor like a waterfall. Zeina sat there stoically, as the sharp scissors cut away until the job was done. Then she removed the long bandage from her ankle and wrapped it tightly around her chest to flatten her breasts. She'd already asked Tapio, who was tall for his age, to lend her one of his long, white shirts. A beret was the final touch.

When Zeina emerged for breakfast the next morning with her new look, some of the children giggled, while the adults looked at her with curiosity and amusement.

"Zeina, what on earth have you done?" Mirta asked, smiling and already suspecting the answer.

"Just want to blend in," Zeina explained, acting like her sudden change in appearance was no big deal.

"Well, I suppose I can understand why, after your episode in Jeddah," Omar responded.

Jamal, a big grin on his face, pointed out one big problem:

Zeina still walked like a girl. So with his guidance, she started to practice walking like a boy—much to the delight of the younger children.

12: **Aden, Yemen**

With the pirate threat diminished—at least, according to the authorities—*The Dreamer* sailed away from the skyscrapers lining the port of Jeddah, but kept near the coast. Finally leaving the Red Sea, it passed through the Strait of Mandeb and entered the Gulf of Aden.

The atmosphere on board *The Dreamer* was festive. Ming-Jung and Tapio made Chinese, African, Mayan and Polynesian masks—most of them fierce-looking warrior faces—under the artistic direction of Mrs. Chissano. The masks would be used to decorate the walls and ceilings of the dining room and bathrooms.

Peering down at the ocean through the safety netting that encircled the ship just above the deck railing, other children were mesmerized by the choreographed zigzags, pirouettes and straight-ahead darting of entire schools of fish. Numerous other vessels could be seen sailing close by and in the distance.

From the Darwin deck, Ada and Leia were the first to hear the sound. As they looked up, what had appeared to be a bird in the distance suddenly headed straight for their ship. Changing course at the last minute, it nearly hit the mast and antennas, then began circling the ship while emitting a strange purring sound.

"Dad! A UAV is buzzing us!" shouted Jamal from the upper deck, where he was fiddling with the antennas to improve the reception.

Omar ordered the children into the dining room and ran for the satellite phone to call the base in Cádiz, which responded instantly.

"We're getting buzzed by a drone!" he shouted into the phone. "And it's taking photos!"

"Okay, we have your position on screen. We'll call the Yemeni authorities. You head to the port of Aden and file an official complaint," was the advice from Cádiz.

Omar radioed a message through open channels to whomever was in the vicinity. "This is *The Dreamer*, Captain Omar Homsi speaking. We're getting buzzed by drones. I repeat, we're getting buzzed by drones, which is against international nautical law. Anyone with any information, please contact us immediately."

Someone from a ship flying the British flag responded, "This is *Dover White* to *The Dreamer*, Captain Eyre speaking. I repeat, this is *Dover White* to *The Dreamer*, Captain Eyre speaking. Unfortunately, drones are legal in this part of the world, as long as they remain within sight of the people who launched them."

This meant that the drone came from one of the nearby ships, or else from a vessel farther out, where somebody was flouting the law. But why send a drone at all? "Thanks, Captain!" said Omar.

He turned to the monitor and began scrutinizing the data from the other vessels. The profile of one of them, *The Altromondo*, suggested it was the very same ship they'd seen in the Red Sea. But it had a different name and flew a Jamaican flag rather than the Panamanian flag the other had flown. Omar knew that didn't prove anything, because pirate ships changed names and origins the way people changed underwear.

The Dreamer's arrival in Aden was announced over the ship's loudspeaker. Although some of the buildings closest to the water were no longer habitable because of the rising sea level, the city was nevertheless surviving all the same. The population had spread upward toward the mountains, building flat white houses that nestled against rocks of the same color. Located in the crater of an extinct volcano, the old port continued to operate as it had for centuries.

Omar spoke to the port director, who'd already received news about the drone and said the Yemeni Intelligence Service planned to investigate. It was possible, the director pointed out, that no law had been violated. His advice was to await further notice, so most of *The Dreamer's* passengers left the ship to explore the city.

Ancient Aden, or what was left of it, lay nearby. The marks of war and postwar chaos were evident everywhere: in the expressions of suffering on nearly every face, in the legions of orphans living in ruined buildings, in the hostile stares directed at anyone who looked foreign. The country's wounds were a long way from being healed.

Some of *The Dreamer's* passengers stopped at a teahouse to eat *luqaymaat*, a favorite Middle Eastern dessert. The owner quickly pushed together enough tables to accommodate everyone.

A flower vendor moved from table to table. "One huuundred riaaals for a rose!" he sang out. "Fiiiifty riaaals for a poemmmm!"

Some youths carrying on at a table in the corner threw an empty soda can at him. The atmosphere wasn't exactly family-friendly, and the passengers from *The Dreamer* were thinking about finding another place to eat, when Omar asked the flower vendor, in fluent Arabic, "Are the poems yours, my friend?"

"Peace be with you, stranger," said the Yemeni. "No, they're poems from our greatest Arab poets, and I know them by heart. Would you like to hear one?"

Omar considered how difficult it would be to translate an Arabic poem for his fellow passengers.

"And do you also sell stories?" asked Mirta.

"Saleem sells anything! Even the clothes off his back!" jeered the boys in the corner.

"Yes, but I don't sell this!" the flower vendor shouted, putting a hand on the hilt of the knife that was in his belt. "I use it!"

The owner of the place turned red as he glanced, clearly embarrassed, at the long table.

"I'll tell you what, my friend. I'll give you two hundred rials if you tell us a good story," Omar said in an attempt to ease the tension. "Do you know one?"

"As a matter of fact, those goons in the corner remind me of a story about animals. Would you like to hear it?"

"Yes—if it's appropriate for children, of course. I'll translate for them."

"It's a story for everyone," said the flower vendor, sending a sharp look at the corner table.

The owner sighed with relief. The flower man smoothed his tunic—which at some time must have been white—adjusted his belt and took his position at the end of the table. He scanned the children's faces, scrutinizing each one, and said at last, "Do you know anyone who understands the language of animals?"

"No!" shouted some of the children after Omar translated the question. "Yes!" cried a few others. The rest sat staring at the Yemeni's wide belt with its sheathed knife.

"Well, some people *do* understand the language of animals, even though most of us don't. Now, the man in our story didn't understand a word of it, and he thought it would be useful to learn. But it wasn't."

"Is this a sad story?" interrupted Leia.

Saleem paused to think about the question, while Omar translated.

"No, it's a wise tale," the flower vendor replied.

The Language of Animals

Once upon a time, there was a farmer who kept several different kinds of animals.

One morning he woke up with the idea of going to

Moses, who knew the language of animals, and asking to learn this art, because animals were part of creation, and to know their language would bring the farmer closer to God, the Creator of all beings.

After listening to the farmer, Moses doubted that such knowledge would be useful to him. But after consulting the Most High, Moses agreed to the farmer's request and taught him now to communicate with animals.

As soon as the farmer had learned how to do it, he decided to test it out, and went to the hen house. There he overheard a conversation between the rooster and the dog, and to his delight and amazement he could understand what they were talking about.

The rooster was saying to the dog, "Guess what! The horse, poor fellow, is about to die!"

At first the farmer was saddened by this news, but it wasn't long before he decided to sell the horse as soon as possible, before it died. And so he did. After all, he'd worked hard to earn the money to buy that animal. Let someone else lose such a prized possession!

Sometime later, as he was returning to the barn, the farmer heard the rooster telling the dog that the mule was going to die soon too. So of course, the man made haste to sell the mule. He felt extremely self-satisfied as he realized that his new knowledge was working to his economic advantage.

That afternoon, when he returned to the barn, he heard the same rooster telling the dog that the farmer's slave was also about to die. Without a second thought, the farmer brought his slave to the market and sold him to the first buyer he encountered.

By this time, some of the other diners had formed a circle around the travelers' table and were listening with rapt attention. The flower vendor continued:

But that very night, the farmer heard the rooster saying, "Know what, dog? The man, our master, is going to die very soon."

In a panic, the farmer ran to Moses as fast as his legs could carry him, prostrated himself on the ground and asked what he should do. Then he heard Moses' voice saying, "Quickly! Go to the market … and sell yourself!"

The adults sat quietly thinking about the story, while some of the youngest children argued about the ending.

"Thank you, Saleem," said Omar as he handed him two hundred rials. "That's a great story, one we all should think about."

"And that lot in the corner, too," added Zeina, sending the boys a dirty look from under her beret.

Saleem pocketed the money together with some coins offered by other diners, left a rose on the table and, with a sorrowful but dignified air, strode out of the restaurant.

Later that afternoon, a Yemeni police official informed Omar that the drone he'd seen buzzing his ship was the work of some teenage boys, the sons of the few rich families left in the country, who liked to use their high-tech toys to scare people. Omar's irritation at the inconvenience the drone had caused was balanced by a feeling of relief.

The men on the fishing boat flying the Jamaican flag were also relieved. The photos taken by their drone showed that *The Dreamer* had no heavy weapons mounted on its upper deck, and no armed personnel visible anywhere. All that could be seen were a bunch of children playing happily on the decks.

Cabdull, the Somali hired to carry out the covert operation, was happy to know there would be no armed confrontation, but the presence of children left a bad taste in his mouth.

"The world is unfair," he tried to reason with himself, "and I'm just a man trying to survive. Anyway, they're the children of rich people, privileged ones"—as if all of that made any difference. Still, the knot in his stomach wouldn't go away, although he did his best to ignore it.

By holophone, Dement said to Captain Wulandar, "Our guys in the area say *The Dreamer* is already sailing toward the Persian Gulf. So the Strait of Hormuz is the perfect interception point. There's no other way out of the Gulf, right?"

"Right," answered Wulandar. "But there are lots of ships out there—the water's crawling with them. The most practical thing would be to wait until *The Dreamer's* in the Arabian Sea, where there are fewer patrol boats."

Dement paused for a moment. "Okay, but don't let them out of your sight."

The Dreamer bore eastward and then northward toward the Gulf of Oman as it rounded the Arabian Peninsula. After sailing for so long, it would finally reach the heart of the Middle East.

"Civilization took a turning point here," Helka Ullakko explained to the children during a lesson. "The people learned to farm on a scale large enough to feed those who weren't involved in agriculture, and this transformed society by freeing them up to develop things like art and science. They even developed the first non-pictographic writing system." Looking at Zeina, she added, "and maybe even some of the stories we've been listening to since we began our voyage."

In Oman, on the southern coast of the Gulf, the city of Muscat came into view, stretching from the high mountain of Al Hajar all the way down to the water. From *The Dreamer's* decks, its passengers saw the dikes that kept the sea from flooding miles of precious reclaimed land. They saw the silhouettes of tall buildings—now practically empty, standing in mute testimony to a former time of abundance—and, on the city's outskirts, the rusting petroleum refineries.

"Those refineries are all relics now," Helka said.

The passengers also noted scores of solar panels shining in

the sunlight, and vast wind farms where white turbine blades rotated slowly in the breeze.

John had set a course for Basra—or "Balsora," as it was called in the old books.

"Basra is a legendary city," Helka said during the children's geography and history lesson. "It's said to be the actual site of the Garden of Eden."

"Mrs. Ullakko, what's the 'Garden of Even?'" asked Ming-Jung.

"The Garden of *Eden*, Ming-Jung. It's a place described in the Bible, which was written for the Jewish people thousands of years ago," said Helka. "Basra is also where Sinbad the Sailor came from."

"Who is Sinbad the Sailor?" Tapio asked.

"He's a character in a story from *The Arabian Nights*, which is also called *One Thousand and One Nights*," Helka replied. "The story goes that Sinbad lived in Basra but liked to travel. He made seven wonderful trips and had amazing adventures. I'll bet Zeina could tell us some of those stories. She probably knows them better than I do."

Night was falling. *The Dreamer's* lights shone on the Shat Al-Arab estuary, and John took advantage of the high tide to sail in. As they drew near the city, the lights of the houses, towers and minarets twinkled through the palm leaves on both banks. A nonstop chirping of crickets mingled with the sound of traffic. Basra never slept.

13: **Basra, Iraq**

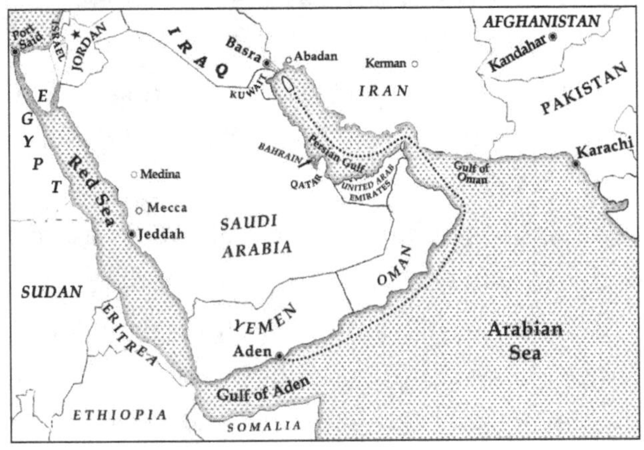

Had *The Dreamer* been a larger boat, it would have been impossible to dock in Basra, because the river, though wide, was shallow. By midmorning, the travelers were walking down the gangway and into the city. At noon, Omar and Jon Kim went to meet Ramanujan, the Indian passenger they'd come there to pick up.

Jamal suggested to his mother that she and the other families head to the Cultural Center, because Walid, from the museum in Jeddah, had said that it was worth visiting, and that they should ask for the director, Noora Al-Jamil, who had a great collection of literature. The building might even be air conditioned, Jamal added, because the heat in town was unbearable.

He and Zeina, meanwhile, wanted to head to the bazaar.

Mirta came up with all kinds of objections, reminding him what had happened in Jeddah.

"But Mom," replied Jamal, "now it's different. We're just two boys. Nobody's gonna notice us. Look at us! Do we look like foreigners? Or rich kids?"

"Zeina, you can hardly walk with that boot!" said Mirta.

"I don't need it anymore. Dr. Roble says I'll be okay with normal boots. They're hot but much better than the orthopedic kind," Zeina said, pulling up her pant legs to show off her new footwear.

Mirta was still hesitant.

"Mom, have you seen all the police, armed vehicles and cameras everywhere? You can't take a step without being watched. It's safer than Cádiz!" Jamal argued.

"That's what we thought about Jeddah!" Mirta said, exasperated. "But fine, go! As long as you promise to be careful and keep in touch! I want you back on this ship by five sharp. Not a minute later!"

The Cultural Center was a remarkable building. Its curves made it look like an open book. Mirta and other members of the group were soon lost in its maze of ramps and staircases, until they found the director's office, where Noora Al-Jamil received them cordially.

She was in her forties and wore a long purple-and-white

shayla over her head, one end hanging in front and the other cast over her shoulder, and a tunic in the same shade of purple. Calling for tea, she invited her visitors to make themselves comfortable.

"Our story collection is at your disposal, and we'll help you make copies of anything you like," she said.

The collection included *One Thousand and One Nights* and *The Assemblies of Al Hariri*, both of which Noora recommended to anyone interested in classical Arabic literature. "They're each interesting and funny," she said.

"How can the city afford to maintain this center in such difficult times?" Mirta asked tactfully.

"Indeed, the government has its priorities, and we're not one of them," Noora explained. "So we rely on private donations."

Mirta took a mental note.

Meanwhile, in the bazaar, Zeina and Jamal walked past the market stalls, asking their usual question. They had almost given up, when they found a man in a black turban, who told them that not far from Basra lived the best storyteller in the country.

"And how can we find him?" asked Jamal.

"If you like, I can take you there," the man said.

Jamal was about to accept the offer, but Zeina jabbed him in the ribs with her elbow.

"Thank you, but that's not necessary. Could you just give us directions, or the address?" Zeina said, opening up a map of Basra and the surrounding area on her holophone.

"It's here," the man said, pointing to a spot in the marshlands outside the city. "This is the East Hammar Marshes. You have to take a bus that goes to Marsa al Zawareq. There you'll find a small dock. Ask a rower to take you to Jassim Al-Asadi's house. Do you have passes for the bus? If you don't, they sell them over there." He pointed to another stall in the market.

They thanked the man for the information, bought bus passes for that day, and left.

"Better to go on our own," said Zeina, relieved.

"Aren't you being a little paranoid, Zeina? We were the ones who approached him!" Jamal answered.

"Paranoid, no. Cautious, yes. And don't call me Zeina in public! I'm Mahmet!"

They bought two bottles of water and walked to the bus stop.

After an hour's ride, the bus let them off in the middle of nowhere, in front of a building that bore an Arabic name Zeina translated as Center for the Restoration of the Iraqi Marshlands. It was quite imposing, in sharp contrast with the humble houses nearby, some of which were made of cinderblock and others of straw. About ten feet away was a small pier, at the end of which a lone boat floated in the green water of a canal that ran through a sea of reeds. Other boats were leaving or returning, laden with bales of straw.

Jamal asked the boat owner if he knew how to find Jassim Al-Asadi's house. The man nodded and quoted Jamal a price.

Within minutes they had entered another canal so narrow that it only allowed one boat to pass through at a time. In the middle of that canal stood a water buffalo that refused to budge until the boat owner hit it with a long reed.

"Are you foreigners?" the boatman asked after a long silence. Of course they were, and because of their accents there was no way they could deny it.

Some oil towers that had fallen into ruin appeared on the horizon.

Zeina wanted to know who owned the marshlands, and whispered the question to Jamal. When possible, she avoided talking, finding it too difficult to speak like a boy. Jamal asked the boatman as best he could but didn't get a clear answer.

"It depends…" said the man. "The tribes, the government, the families. When my ancestors were alive and there was plenty of water here, the marshes belonged to the tribes. The people made their living by fishing. In my grandfather's time, the government drained the marshes, because it didn't want us here, and my people had to leave to find work in Basra. When my parents lived here, the marshes were again filled with water, thanks to restoration work that had been done. Some families returned to take possession of whatever they could, but now the water is very salty."

The man scooped up some water with one hand, brought it to his lips and then spat contemptuously.

"We've arrived," he said shortly after that, pointing up the slope.

"Could you come to pick us up in an hour?" asked Jamal.

"All right," said the man.

Back at the Cultural Center, while Mirta and a few other adults were busy selecting books to copy, Noora Al-Jamil invited the rest of the party to a room where a volunteer, a young woman named Leila Mansur, was telling stories to a group of schoolchildren. As they entered, Leila began to narrate a new story in Arabic, but switched to English for the benefit of the foreigners, since her students all studied English.

"And to end our evening," said Leila, "I'll tell you a story that's very well known in the West. I'm sure our visitors have heard it. It's called 'The King's New Clothes.'"

The King's New Clothes

Once upon a time, there was a king. He lived in a small city and loved to dress well. This king spent a fortune on jewels and clothing and liked to show off a new outfit on every occasion. He would mount his majestic horse and parade through the streets like a peacock, basking in the applause and praise that were showered on him by his subjects.

One day three strangers arrived in the city. They traded in trickery, conning people into handing over their money. Soon after they arrived, these charlatans became intent on carrying out their most audacious plan ever: to deceive the king himself!

Knowing that the monarch had a weakness for luxurious clothing, the three men opened a shop in the market. They filled it with looms and magnificent fabrics, and announced to the town that they were the best weavers ever to set foot in the kingdom. In reality, none of them even knew how to thread a loom, let alone how to use one.

When the king heard that new weavers were in town, he invited them to the palace in hopes of being offered the most precious robe in the world. So the three impostors dressed up in their finest clothes and presented themselves at court.

"Your Majesty," they said, "our specialty is a highly unusual fabric, one that can only be seen by those who really are what they think they are. It cannot be seen by those who are not what they believe themselves to be."

This idea fascinated the king. Right away he began to think that this would be a good way to test his subjects and courtiers, so as to find out which ones were who they said they were and which ones were liars and impostors.

"I want you to make me a robe of this marvelous cloth," he said. "You'll be most generously compensated."

"As you wish, Your Majesty," the three impostors murmured in unison, bowing deeply.

The king issued a command that a special salon in

the palace be set aside for the weavers to begin work on the marvelous garment, which required a great many bobbins of the finest silk together with a king's ransom in gold and silver thread. Of course, the so-called weavers hid all of this away for themselves.

After several days of merely going through the motions of weaving from dawn to dusk, the three swindlers announced that the fabric was finished and ready for His Majesty to inspect.

The king had no doubt at all that he would be able to see the cloth but, just in case, decided to send his most trusted minister to render an opinion first.

Entering the room, the minister got the biggest shock of his life. Try as he might, he couldn't see any cloth! But he pretended he could, cocking his head and peering from various angles at the empty space the impostors were gesturing toward. "What's going on?" he thought. "Am I not really the legitimate heir and scion of a most noble family, and worthy of the post I occupy?" As fear overcame him, sweat began to pour from his brow.

"Well, Mr. Minister, what do you think of our work?" the impostors asked.

"Er … mag—magnificent!" the minister stammered, bluffing as best he could, to hide his dismay. "What a wonderful design! What glorious colors!"

"Come closer and feel the softness of the cloth yourself. What do you think?" the swindlers said, while

pretending to show him the cloth that was supposedly hanging from the loom.

The minister made a show of passing his fingers over the cloth while continuing to sing its praise. But he sweated profusely all the while, and on his way back to the king, he rehearsed what he was going to say.

"And the fabric, my dear minister, how was it?" the king asked anxiously.

"Splendid, splendid, Your Majesty! Stupendous!" the minister answered, retiring to his chambers as soon as he could get away.

One of the little boys in the audience couldn't contain himself any longer and exclaimed, "What a bunch of liars! What a dumb king!"

"Shhh! Be quiet," said the other children. "Let the lady tell us the rest!"

"Actually, he really *was* a foolish king," Leila said.

The king sent others to the fake weavers' salon. But everyone came back with the same story. "The cloth is a work of art. The cloth is worthy of kings!" they all reported, even though an astute observer would have noted that each one was pale with fright.

The king finally decided that the time had come to see the cloth for himself. When he entered the weaving salon, he met several courtiers, who were exclaiming enthusiastically at the beauty of the fabric and describing the design, the vivid colors and the unrivalled smoothness of its texture.

"Enchanting!" said one.

"Excellent work!" said another.

The king, naturally, could not see anything, because there was nothing to see. He asked himself how it was possible that he was not a legitimate king. Was he not the son of his father, a king who had also inherited the crown? "If this isn't true, my reign is finished!" the king thought. He immediately began to praise the fabric to the skies as the others had done, repeating what he had heard about delicate designs, beautiful colors and wonderful quality.

Very discouraged by what he saw or, more accurately, did not see, the king nonetheless harbored some suspicions. He went to a cleric who, as a religious man, inspired total confidence. But this cleric, fearing the loss of his reputation, also reaffirmed the existence of the precious fabric and praised its extraordinary weavers—even though he, too, had seen absolutely nothing.

"It's the most marvelous thing in the whole wide world!" he told the king emphatically.

So the day came when the fabric was declared finished, and the king asked that a sumptuous robe be made for him out of it. A celebration was organized, with the people invited to come out in the streets to see their monarch riding by in his new royal garment. By this time, the entire city had heard of the magical fabric and believed that only those who were not who they thought they were would be unable to see it.

The next morning, the "weavers" presented the king with his robe, wrapped in fine—and quite visible—cloth. They opened the cloth and proceeded with great ceremony to hold up the supposedly magnificent garment it contained. Then they asked the king to disrobe.

After he'd undressed, the weavers—with gestures of exaggerated respect—pretended to place the garment over his body. The celestial robe was so light, they assured him, that he would not even feel its weight on his skin.

"Doesn't it look good on me?" the king asked, pacing and turning so that they could appreciate every aspect of the robe's glory.

"Fantastic!" they shouted.

Thus assured that he was wrapped in the most glorious of robes, the king mounted his horse and headed onto the principal avenue of the city, followed by a procession of courtiers. The people crowded the sidewalks, mouths agape. The king attributed their expressions to wonder at the sight of his amazing garment.

Of course, the very opposite was true. No one saw anything but a naked king waving to the people and beaming from ear to ear. Yet nobody had the courage to speak the truth.

Nobody, that is, except for one little boy. As the

procession passed in front of his house, this boy, who was sitting on the stoop, turned to his mother and shouted, "Mama, why is the king naked?"

The king heard him and was greatly confused. He shot a reproachful glance at the poor mother, who tried to cover her child's mouth, but just then another little boy shouted out to the entire silent throng, "It's true! The king isn't wearing anything but a crown!"

The people began to look at one another, and their murmuring grew louder and louder, until all finally had to admit that they saw nothing more nor less than a king as naked as his horse. It was very difficult for them to suppress their laughter.

By the time the king and his courtiers realized they had allowed themselves to be tricked, the weavers, of course, were long gone.

Meanwhile, in front of a thatched hut in the marshlands, Jassim cooked food on a grill that was set up on the ground, with fish and flatbreads lying nearby. The grill was made of reeds, and Zeina noticed that instead of coal or wood, the fire was fueled by dry buffalo dung. Her grandfather had cooked the same way in Mauritania decades earlier, her mother had told her. Jassim's hens were fighting over a few grains on the ground, and ducks rummaged for worms on the banks of the canal.

When Jamal told Jassim the reason for the teens' visit, the storyteller invited them into his house. It was strange to see the walls and even the furniture—a few chairs and a cot in the corner—made entirely of reeds. Everything was yellow and brown, as if life had been paused forever in perpetual autumn. The dirt floor was partially covered with faded oriental rugs. Jassim lived there alone.

"I know many stories," he said. "I learned them from my great-grandfather. There was a time when my house was filled with people who came to hear them. But not anymore, because so many have left these marshes."

"Because of the lack of water?" Zeina ventured.

"Because of the lack of *good* water," answered Jassim. "Today the water is very salty, and even the buffalo milk isn't fit for the children to drink, because the grass and reeds are no longer the same. I'm one of the few who are still here, collecting the reeds and selling them in Basra to people who make baskets. But enough about sad things. I'll tell you a story that I'm sure you'll understand, because I see from your eyes that you're perceptive young people."

Jassim shooed away a duck that was about to enter the house and began his tale.

The Cadi, the Poor Man and the Lady

There was once a poor man named Mansur who had managed—after much work and sacrifice—to save a small amount of money.

One day he needed to travel, but he worried that thieves might break into his house and steal his savings while he was away. So he thought he would ask the cadi *to keep the money for him until he returned. Mansur knew the* cadi *charged a small fee for that service, but it would be worth it to have peace of mind. And there was no risk involved, because as local magistrates,* cadis *were considered honorable men.*

But what Mansur—who automatically thought highly of all titled people—didn't realize was that reputation isn't always reality, and that sometimes a good reputation is nothing more than a facade. So it never even occurred to him to ask the cadi for a signed contract when he handed over a box containing all of his savings.

When Mansur returned from his journey and went to retrieve his money, the cadi played dumb and asked, "What box of money are you talking about?"

"The one with a hundred gold coins that I left with you for safekeeping."

"I don't know what you're talking about," the cadi replied. "You must be dreaming!"

Mansur tried and tried to make the cadi recall their verbal agreement, but the latter turned a deaf ear.

"I beg you, honorable sir, try to remember!" Mansur implored.

"Stop bothering me, madman! Get out of my house!" the cadi finally said. "I've never seen you before in my life, nor have I ever accepted your money for safekeeping!"

Since Mansur kept insisting, the cadi summoned two burly servants, who each grabbed Mansur by an arm and threw him into the street. Landing headfirst in a mud puddle, he began to weep and lament.

"Years of hard work and sacrifice, all lost!" he

moaned. "And all because I was naïve enough to trust that rotten thief of a cadi*!"*

An older woman who knew a great deal about human nature happened to be passing by at that very moment.

"Why so sad, sir? What happened?" she asked Mansur.

Through his tears, he told her about his misadventure with the cadi*. "God knows the sacrifices I made to save that money," Mansur added, beating his chest in sorrow at having been such a fool.*

"Calm down, my good sir, and let me give this some thought. I might be able to help you," said the woman. A short time later she turned to Mansur and said, with an air of quiet confidence, "Come with me. I have a plan."

They walked to the woman's house, where she disappeared into her bedroom and emerged a few minutes later dressed in the finest of garments and carrying a box full of old odds and ends. Asking one of her servants to carry the box on his shoulders and another to follow behind, she announced, "We're going to pay the cadi *a visit. I know where he lives." To Mansur she said, "You'll wait outside the* cadi*'s house. When you see a front window being closed, knock on the door and, once you've entered, enter the room with the window and, as calmly as you can, ask the* cadi*, once again, to return your money. But be sure to ask for* double *the amount he owes you."*

At the cadi's *house, the old woman entered with the first servant, while Mansur remained outside with the second servant.*

Seeing an elegantly dressed lady accompanied by a servant carrying a box that seemed extremely heavy, the cadi's *eyes lit up with greed.*

"And what have we here, my good woman?" he asked.

"Honorable cadi, *my husband has gone on a journey, and I don't feel safe keeping this valuable hoard of gold in the house while he's away."*

"Of course, good lady. You may leave it in my custody with confidence. It will be safe here, and you'll be able to sleep peacefully, without any worry."

"Thank you! I knew I could place my trust in you," said the woman. "How much will you charge for keeping my box for one week?"

"One percent of its value, good lady. And how much did you say is in here?"

"About five hundred gold pieces, plus various precious stones. You'll count everything before signing a receipt, won't you?"

"Yes, we always do business in the most transparent manner."

"Then it would be best to close the window, honorable sir, as we'll need privacy."

"Of course!" exclaimed the cadi, *hastening to close the window that faced the street.*

At this signal, Mansur knocked on the door and, after

being admitted by one of the cadi's servants, entered the room and calmly said: "Gracious and honorable cadi, I've come for the two hundred gold coins I left with you for safekeeping."

"Two hundred?" exclaimed the cadi. "But you only left one hundred gold coins with me, don't you remember?"

"Oh, right, excuse me! That's true, it was only one hundred gold coins. Thank goodness you have such a good memory!"

The cadi's face reddened with fury, but he knew that what he had just done was necessary to prove his honesty in front of the old woman. After all, she was entrusting him with far more than a hundred gold coins!

"Of course, my friend, how could I not remember? Let's see. Here's your box, all intact. You're welcome to open it and confirm that all the money is there."

Turning to the woman, the cadi said, "As I said, my lady, your fortune will be in good hands with me, and you can retrieve it whenever you wish."

Mansur opened the box, counted its contents and confirmed that everything was still there. With a light bow, he thanked the cadi for his services, gave him one gold coin as payment and left as fast as he could, carrying the box on his head.

At that moment, the woman's second servant, who was also following her prior instructions, entered the *room and said, "Madam, your husband has come back from his trip early. You must return home right away."*

"Oh, wonderful!" she exclaimed. "Excuse me for bothering you, cadi, *but it seems that I won't need your services after all. Thank God my husband has come back safe and sound!"*

And so saying, she asked the first servant to hoist the box once again onto his shoulder, and he and the second servant followed her out into the street, leaving the cadi *open-mouthed and unsure just what to think of the woman, of Mansur and of his own stupidity.*

"Thank you, Jassim," Zeina said when he'd finished. "Traditional stories seem to favor the use of ingenuity over brute force, don't you agree?"

"Yes, they often illustrate how wise people solve problems indirectly," Jassim said while checking the fish. "Ah, the food is ready!"

Jassim invited Jamal and Zeina to share the meal with him, which they did. Afterward, Jassim and Zeina exchanged some stories, and the girl confessed that she wasn't really a boy. Then the teens heard a shout, indicating that the boat had returned to pick them up. Jamal left some money for Jassim and thanked him for his hospitality. Then Jassim accompanied the teens down the short path to the small dock.

But the man waiting in the boat was not the one who'd brought them there.

"Where's the boat's owner?" Jamal asked.

"He's sent me to pick you up," the man replied.

Zeina and Jamal eyed him nervously, and Jamal discreetly asked Jassim if he knew the man.

"I don't know him well, but he's from around here."

The teens climbed into the boat and waved goodbye to Jassim, saying they hoped to meet again. Jassim waved back and said he hoped so too, but reminded them that fate was unpredictable.

Zeina and Jamal only had two hours to get back to the harbor at Basra. The buffalo was in the very same spot as before, once again blocking their way. The teens expected the rower to use a stick or an oar to get the animal to move, but instead the man turned in to a canal that was almost hidden in the thickness of the reeds. It was narrower than the boat itself, and the oarsman had to push through with force.

"He's finding another way, I think," said Jamal to Zeina, in Spanish.

"At this rate, it would have been easier to move the buffalo out of the away," Zeina whispered irritably.

"Zeina, he knows better than we do!" Jamal responded.

"Mahmet!"

"Sorry!"

The boat approached the bank of the canal by a clearing, where a trail led into the reeds. Another small boat had been hauled onto the beach, and two men who were clearly not locals stood on the shore, watching the teens' boat approach.

"Get out here," the rower said in a quiet voice.

"This isn't the pier!" Jamal said, surprised.

"Come on, get out!" said the taller of the two new men.

"What do you want?" Jamal asked angrily.

The other man pulled out a gun and pointed it at the teens, while the boatman remained motionless, keeping his eyes on the water. Zeina groaned and started to get out of the boat.

"Mahmet! Don't get out!" Jamal yelled in Spanish.

"They have guns, Jamal. Come on," she said quietly, reaching for his arm.

"Keep your mouths shut and do what I say, kids. HWatches off," the man with the gun said in a calm voice as they climbed out. The taller man threw their HWatches into a bag before patting Zeina and Jamal down. As the boatman rowed away, Jamal glared at him and angrily gritted his teeth. Zeina was stiff with fright. When the man searching her suddenly smirked, she was fairly sure he knew she was a girl, despite her hair and outfit.

The men marched the teens at gunpoint along the path through the reeds, until they came to a small cinderblock building. The taller man opened its door, signaling them in. Jamal considered grabbing Zeina's arm and making a run for it, but the man with the gun kept it leveled at them, with his gaze fixed on them, the whole time.

"Assholes!" Jamal shouted as the door closed.

"Cowards!" Zeina yelled, not caring what her voice sounded like anymore.

The only sounds from outside were the click of a padlock and the soft footsteps of the men walking away. From a small hole in the door, Jamal saw one of them disappear into the reeds, while the other man stood guard by another small building.

In the semidarkness, Zeina slumped to the floor. "What just happened?" she asked, putting her head in her hands. Everything had taken place so fast that they hadn't had a second to think. Some light came through a small window just below the ceiling, and her soft voice echoed off the cement walls. "Do you think they know who we are?"

"Probably," replied Jamal. "If not, how could they hold us for ransom?"

"Think that's what they're after?"

"Most likely."

"Think they have anything to do with those guys in Beirut?"

"I don't know, Zeina, but they're probably after more than a few bucks. They didn't take our money, just our HWatches."

Zeina was silent for a long time. After a while, Jamal tried to cheer her up.

"Don't worry," he said. "My parents will give them whatever they want. We're no use to them dead." He grabbed the water bottles they had brought with them, handing one to Zeina. "Drink some water. It's hotter than hell in here." The ceiling was made of metal, and the heat was becoming unbearable.

Outside, the silence was punctuated by a single shrill note of what they hoped was just a benign wetland insect.

As their eyes adjusted to the dim light, Zeina screamed.

At the Cultural Center, students were restoring old books. Noora approached them and asked for a few volunteers to help the visitors make copies and show them how to use the bookbinding machine. One of the students put sheets of paper in the machine's tray, and in less than a minute, the pages came out as a beautifully bound book. It was entitled *Tales for THE DREAMER*, and for the cover, the group had chosen a picture of Sinbad the Sailor in his boat.

"Are you going to your island from here?" asked Noora.

"We still have to stop in Karachi," Mirta said, "to pick up the last passenger. Do you know anybody there who works with traditional stories?"

"Actually, I do. You'll want to speak to my friend Nasim. He's a writer but also an avid reader of the old tales. I'll give you his number."

The visitors thanked Noora, who wished them a safe journey.

Upon leaving, Mirta used her phone to tap into the UNet and send a donation to the Cultural Center, care of Noora.

At five o'clock that afternoon, as the new book sat in a prominent place in the Stories of the World section of *The Dreamer's* library, Omar appeared with the ship's newest passenger: Ramanujan, an electrical engineer.

By five-thirty, with no sign of Jamal and Zeina, Mirta began to worry, so she tried calling first her son and then Zeina, but got no answer. Even more troubling was the fact that their devices seemed to be turned off. Something was obviously wrong.

When the sun began to set, concern turned to despair. At six p.m., Omar called the police, who said the teens hadn't been missing long enough to warrant an investigation. Omar told the officer on duty that they were both responsible kids, and that if they were this late, they were definitely in some kind of trouble. The officer promised that the police would take action as soon as they could.

By eight p.m., Mirta sat on the deck crying, hoping desperately to see Jamal and Zeina suddenly appear. Omar and Ramanujan ran frantically from police station to police station, asking for help. John was on the alert for any communication that came through on the ship's radios and monitors, while Helka spoke with the base in Cádiz in the hopes of coming up with a plan. Urho Ullakko, Jon Kim, the Robles, the Wangs, Antonio Mercado and Joaquim Chissano paired up and went into the city with holograms of Jamal and Zeina, looking for anyone who might recognize them. The rest of the voyagers stayed on the ship to care for the children and keep Mirta company.

Back in the marshland, Zeina's scream echoed through the small room. "One crawled up my leg!" she shrieked, jumping up and brushing at her thigh. The room was infested with scorpions!

Jamal tried to squash one the with the tip of his shoe, but soon more scorpions were clinging to it. Zeina found a piece of cardboard in the corner and slid it under the ugly creatures, pushing them out, one by one, through the narrow space under the door. It was slow work, and in the dim light it was impossible for the teens to be sure they'd gotten them all. Jamal noticed some sandbags against the far wall. It was clear that the room was used to store construction material. He pushed a few of the bags up against the space under the door, to prevent the scorpions' return.

The heat had diminished, but fear took its place. The water was gone. How long would they be locked in there? Would they die of thirst before they were let out? Or from the venom of a scorpion they hadn't managed to catch?

In a coffeeshop in the center of Basra, two men were conversing in low tones.

"Good news, buddy. They've got the kids. The father's going crazy."

"Good job, Bruno."

"He won't leave Basra until he finds the kids. And he won't find them. So that's the end of his trip, my friend. *The Dreamer* will miss the deadline!"

"That's the plan. Cheers, Bruno—to the mission!" said Dement, holding up a glass of soda.

Surreptitiously, Bruno Beremolto extracted a small flask of whiskey from a pocket of his shirt and poured a good serving into his own glass.

"*Salute, compagno*," he said in his native Italian, taking a few gulps. "Glad we don't have to board that damned boat. Too risky," he added, wiping his mouth with a sleeve.

"And the Somali?"

"I'm sure he'll be paid for what he's done so far."

"How long will it take for the guys at the Ross Dependency to grant us permission to take possession of the island?" asked Dement.

"According to the contract, if the scientists don't get there within three months, they lose their chance, and it goes to the next in line—which is us!"

"Perfect! Time for a vacation, Bruno! Let's give the boss the good news," said Dement. "Your turn to call."

Beremolto downed the remaining contents of his glass. "Alert! Alert! High alcoholic content!" his HWatch warned.

"*You'd* better do it," he grinned.

"Want to try and sleep, Jamal?"

"Can't. Thinking."

For a long time, the teens could only hear the rhythm of their own breathing. Jamal could have sworn that his heartbeat was loud enough for Zeina to hear, but he didn't want to ask. They hadn't heard the man outside for some time, and finally Jamal stood up and looked through the small hole in the door. It was dark out. He put his ear against the hole, but all he could pick up now was the monotonous chirping of a lone cicada.

"I think that guy went into the other building," Jamal said. "Might be sleeping." He left the door and, as quietly as possible, piled up a few sandbags under the small window near the ceiling. It was circular, and a bright moon shone through the glass, next to which dangled a thin chain. Jamal pulled the chain, and the window pivoted open on its horizontal axis, squeaking loudly. He froze, but no sound came from outside. The half-circle opening was far too small for the teens to squeeze through. He grabbed the windowpane and tugged hard, but the metal rod through its axis held it firmly in place.

"I'd kill for a screwdriver!" Jamal finally said, climbing back down.

"For your loose screws?"

"Not funny."

"I've got one in my boot," Zeina whispered.

"What?" Jamal almost shouted. "Why didn't you tell me?" he hissed.

"Why should I?" the girl said as she fished out a small multi-tool. "Borrowed it from Tapio. That boy loves taking stuff apart. It's got a little knife on it, too, and with everything that's been happening to us lately, I just thought it might make me feel better."

"Holy crap! And those creeps didn't notice?" Jamal said, flicking out the different tools.

"Nope. But what are you going to do with it?"

"Well, not even you can squeeze through that opening, right?" he said, climbing back up the sandbags. "But if we take out the metal rod, I think the whole windowpane will come out. See how it's fastened with screws?" He pointed to the hinges on the top and bottom of the central rod.

Wielding the screwdriver in the moonlight, Jamal removed the screws one by one. Zeina perched precariously next to him and grabbed the window before it fell to the ground. Together they laid it carefully down, making sure to be as quiet as possible.

"I'll go first," Jamal said, "and I'll make a pile of reeds for you to land on. Be careful of that ankle!"

He put his head through the opening. The moon, now behind a thin cloud, spread its soft light over the reeds. No one around. The distance to the ground on the other side was slightly less than ten feet. A considerable distance for most people, but not for him or Zeina, both of whom knew how to jump from great heights without breaking any bones. Jamal landed on the soft soil and quickly began to gather reeds. Zeina landed with a soft thud and, after rolling to absorb the impact, got up unscathed.

Guided by an instinct that emerges in times of danger, they crawled toward the trail. From there they continued with pounding hearts, stooping wherever the reeds weren't high enough to conceal them, until they reached the narrow channel through which they'd arrived that afternoon. In the vast darkness of night, they slid silently into the water. The moon reappeared from behind the cloud, casting a ghostly white light on the water. The crumbling oil towers silently guided them in the right direction. They sloshed through the salty thigh-high water for an hour, thankful that it was still warm outside, and arrived at the pier just before dawn, when the first bus arrived to take the locals to their jobs in Basra. Zeina and Jamal showed the driver their passes, got on quickly and hurried to the last seat by the emergency door, just in case their kidnappers decided to go to Basra by bus too. Although that seemed improbable, the two teens nevertheless tried to make themselves invisible—which, wet as they were, was easier said than done.

At five a.m., several policemen were standing in front of *The Dreamer.* Omar was filling out paperwork, while an exhausted Mirta answered questions as best she could. Zeina and Jamal were so filthy they were hardly recognizable as they approached the ship, but Mirta gave a sharp yell as she saw them, and ran toward them. As they embraced, a strong smell of swamp enveloped them all.

The teenagers apologized profusely, and told their story. The policemen promised to keep the family informed about the progress of their investigation into the incident, but Omar saved them the trouble. "No need, officers," he said. "We're leaving Basra this second."

Jamal apologized again to his parents but reminded his mother that she had told them to be back at "five sharp," and that it was, in fact, five o'clock.

But Mirta was in no mood for joking and sternly sent them to shower and change their clothes.

Omar made it clear that from then on they were absolutely prohibited from going into any city or town—or swamp—unless they were accompanied by an adult.

John plotted the route to Pakistan, where they would pick up Farooq, *The Dreamer's* last passenger. They hoisted anchor and sailed once again through the green waters of the Shat El Arab, this time heading downstream. The lights of the boats, bobbing between the waves, glistened like floating stars.

14: **Karachi, Pakistan**

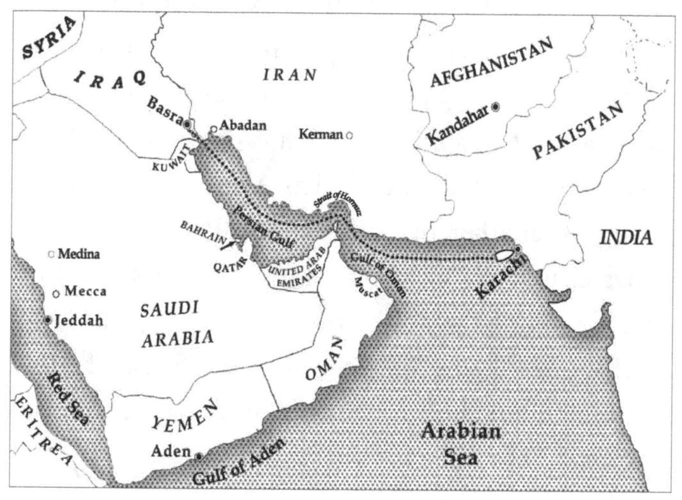

Jamal was fast asleep, his dreams ebbing and flowing like waves lapping on sand. When he finally rolled out of bed, got dressed and walked out onto the ship's Galileo deck, he saw the coastline slipping past, as *The Dreamer* emerged from the bluish gloom of the early hours, and the miracle of dawn revealed the Iranian port city of Abadan.

"Where are we? What country is that?" he asked, still half-asleep.

"We're in the Persian Gulf," Urho Ullakko told him, "and what you see to our left is the east coast of Iran, which was formerly known as Persia. That's how the gulf got its name."

Jon Kim was showing his son, Ming-Jung, the ship's position on a holographic globe. *The Dreamer* was crossing a storm zone, but, for the moment, the waters were calm under a cloudless topaz sky.

Zeina and Mrs. Piscarelli were preparing lunch. The other children were busy cleaning up—until they discovered the masks that had been hung in the dining room several days before. Joãozinho, grabbing one that caught his fancy, became the Mayan god of the Sun, Kinich Ahau; while Ming-Jung, snatching up another mask, became a Polynesian god. The two boys chased the girls, who shrieked and ran, all of the children forgetting their chores.

The ship passed smoothly through the Strait of Hormuz and the Gulf of Oman before finally reaching the Arabian Sea once again.

Stationed in the strait, *The Altromondo* received a radio signal from Luxembourg as its crew watched *The Dreamer* glide through the water. *The Altromondo* followed at a discreet distance, with Wulandar, its captain, keeping the Spanish boat in his sights. Dement and Beremolto had both been fired in the wake of the teens' escape from the marshland. Captain Wulandar was now in direct contact with Palvo.

Although Basra was a vibrant city, the megalopolis of Karachi surpassed it in diversity. Crowds jostled in the streets, rich and poor sharing space among the bicycles, rickshaws, carts, automatic cars and buses—as well as electric motorcycles and scooters, whose drivers zipped through traffic with amazing skill.

As in Basra, the travelers from *The Dreamer* found themselves enveloped in the fragrant smoke from street-food vendors, who sheltered under colorful umbrellas and white awnings. But the people roaming the streets of Karachi seemed poorer than in other cities, or perhaps just more disoriented, as if they were foreigners who didn't know where to go.

The presence of armed soldiers was even more noticeable here than in other cities. They guarded the banks, mosques and schools, and were posted on street corners and at bus stops. Military police in armored vehicles wore the sleek jetpacks that were becoming popular with civilians in Western countries but were still a rarity in the East. When one of those policemen jetted through the air in pursuit of a fleeing suspect, everyone watched in amazement.

Nasim, the writer who'd been recommended to *The Dreamer's* travelers by Noora at the Cultural Center in Basra, was waiting for them in a restaurant well within walking distance, but the younger children begged to ride one of the colorful city buses. When they got off, they saw a street vendor running pomegranates through a manual press. He offered them a small cup of the scarlet juice.

"Try some, kids! Only fifty cents! Very good, very good!" he urged.

From the other side of the street, Nasim saw *The Dreamer's* travelers approaching and crossed to help them negotiate the unruly traffic. The strong smell of curried fried fish, as well as other less-identifiable aromas, filled the air.

"Welcome to Karachi!" said Nasim amiably. He was thirtyish, wore his hair in a ponytail and had an intense gaze. They sat down in a corner of the restaurant, where they'd been given a long table to accommodate them all.

Omar remarked on the tremendous crowds in the streets.

"This year, the winter monsoon began in September," Nasim explained. "And to make matters worse, nowadays the high tides in the Arabian Sea subside more slowly than before. So the Indus River between Pakistan and India is in flood stage and wreaking considerable havoc. That's why we have so many internal migrants here. It's a nationwide catastrophe."

The waiters served a meal of *biryani* rice with vegetables, and *karahi* chicken for those who wanted something spicier.

"I very much admire your adventurousness," Nasim said. "Unfortunately, I know nothing about environmental science, although I gather you're on an important mission—and an enviable one."

"As a writer, you also do important work, Nasim," Mirta said. "You create stories, and stories are vital to humanity. We were told that you get many ideas from traditional tales. We'd love to hear some."

"Well, it's true that stories from olden times inspire my own writing, because they have so much to say about the human condition, don't you think?"

"Certainly!"

"But it's not necessarily an easy profession," said Nasim, referring to several unfavorable articles that had been written about him. "Do you know the story of the father, the son and the donkey?"

"No, but we'd love to hear it," said Mirta.

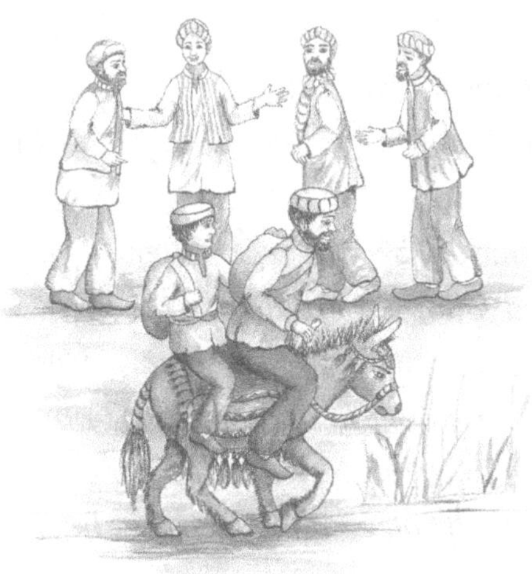

The Critics

One day a man and his son went to the market to buy some tools. They had a donkey with them to carry their purchases, and, as it was a beautiful day, they decided to walk, so they arranged themselves with one of them on either side of the animal.

After they'd been on the road for a short while, they

came upon some men going in the opposite direction. The two groups exchanged the usual greetings and then continued on their way, but not before father and son heard the other men murmur, "What a strange pair! To be walking when their beast is carrying practically nothing! What a waste of energy!"

When they had walked a bit farther, the father asked his son, "What do you think about what those men said about us?"

"Maybe they're right, Father."

"Well then, you get on the donkey, and I'll continue walking."

The son did as he was told. After a while, the two encountered another group of travelers, who, after greetings, could be heard to comment, "How shameful! Such a strong young man, who could obviously walk miles without fatigue, lets his poor father travel on foot while he himself rides a donkey! Never have I seen such a worthless son, nor a father of such weak character!"

"I agree with them, Father," said the son. "I should be the one walking—not you, who are older. It's only right."

So the father climbed on the donkey, and the boy trotted along behind.

They soon met a third set of travelers, who, after seeing the father mounted and the son on foot, said, "Just look at that father! What a heartless man! Still strong and accustomed to hard work, but comfortably mounted on a donkey while that poor boy has to huff and puff just to keep up!"

When these men were out of earshot, the father again asked the son for his opinion.

"Father, I think we should both ride."

"Well, get on behind me, then," said the father. And so they continued on their way.

The next group of travelers they met exclaimed, "What a sight, and how stupid! Two adults breaking the back of that skin-and-bones donkey! It won't live long with treatment like that!"

This time, the father did not ask for his son's opinion. He already knew from the boy's look that he had understood. They both dismounted and walked along the road, one on either side of the donkey.

"I see why you like that story," Omar said to Nasim and then laughed.

"You know, I read the very same story when I was in high school, back in Spain," Mirta said. "It was attributed to Don Juan Manuel, a Spanish writer from five hundred years ago."

"I believe it," Nasim replied. "Stories travel with people, and they belong to everyone. This one was told to me by a storyteller from Afghanistan, a man with an inexhaustible supply of tales."

When the time came for the travelers to depart, Omar said, "It was great to meet you, Nasim. Here, I'd like to give you something on behalf of *The Dreamer's* party. I bought this ring in Basra. It has a phrase written on it in Urdu, but I don't understand it."

Nasim took the ring and read the inscription.

"It refers to the story of the king's ring," he said. "Do you know it?"

"I don't," Omar replied.

So Nasim told the story.

The King's Ring

A certain king asked a wise man to come up with something that could make a happy man sad, and a sad man happy. The wise man withdrew to contemplate the king's peculiar request and, after a time, returned with the solution. He gave the king a ring on which the following words were engraved: "This, too, shall pass..."

"I'll try to remember that, my friend," said Omar.

Zeina, who hadn't talked during the whole conversation, discreetly typed "afgh?" and sent the abbreviated HWatch message to Jamal.

Jamal felt the buzz on his wrist. "And who's the Afghan storyteller you mentioned, Nasim?" he asked a few seconds later. "Where does he live?"

"His name is Mohsin, and he lives in Kandahar."

"Could we visit him?" Hussain ventured.

Mirta glanced at Jamal and Zeina as if to say, "Don't even think about it!"

"Of course you can," said Nasim, "but he speaks only Pashto. Do you have an automatic translator, one of those tiny things that fit in your ear?"

"Yes, but we left it on the ship," said Jamal. "We haven't needed to use it so far, with Zeina around. You know, she speaks Arabic."

"Wonderful!" said Nasim, looking at Zeina with admiration. "But here we speak mostly Urdu, besides English. And in Afghanistan they mainly speak Dari or Pashto."

"Whatever you have in mind, Jamal," said Omar, "the answer is *no!*"

"Dad, I thought maybe you could come with us."

"Me?"

15: **Kandahar, Afghanistan**

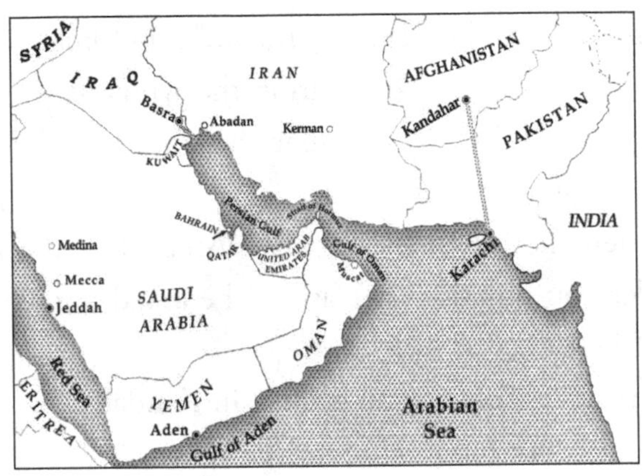

Four hundred and seventy miles from Karachi, Kandahar was not just around the corner. Omar was told that to get there would take at least twelve hours by car, plus time spent at the border.

"It's out of the question, Jamal," he said. "With all of that driving, it'll take something like three days just to find the storyteller—not to mention the time spent visiting him. No way! Maybe you can send him a letter. Nasim might have his address."

"A letter? Dad, how about sending a message by carrier pigeon?!" Jamal replied sarcastically.

"I'm not joking, Jamal. I don't see any other way. Post offices still exist, you know. We're not going to delay the trip for three days."

"Dad, have you ever been to Afghanistan?" Jamal asked.

"Never."

The truth was that Afghanistan held a special attraction for Omar, but he'd never had the opportunity to go there.

"Okay, how about we do this?" proposed Jamal. "I have my savings. I'll buy three round-trip plane tickets so you won't need to use our expedition funds or delay the trip for more than one day. I'm sure there are flights all the time. We can leave in the morning and come back at night. What do you say, Dad?"

Omar was surprised by Jamal's commitment to what he and Zeina called their "story-discovery mission." Jamal was obviously taking it very seriously. Omar could see how proud his son was whenever Zeina came back with a new story, as if she were bringing a newly found treasure to the ship. In the end, Omar didn't want to disappoint the teens. After all, this would be their last opportunity to see another country before they reached Antarctica. He consulted his wife.

"Let Jamal use his own money. It'll make him feel good," Mirta said.

The streets of Kandahar's oldest bazaar were full of salespeople sitting on piles of carpets or on sacks of wool, cotton, grains or tobacco. There were mounds of dried and fresh fruit all around. Between the stalls, vendors of high-tech products were everywhere, competing with one another in strident voices as they offered all kinds of gadgets: mini-drones for domestic use; holographic phones, skin implants to hide wrinkles and create a false impression of youth, virtual goggles, chip-implanted Legos for assembling into electronic toys, and all the other digital paraphernalia that inundated the world's cities at relatively low prices.

They found Mohsin in one of the many craft stalls, where he was hammering out a brass plate. He stood up to greet them. The storyteller was a tall man, and as thin as a wheat stalk. His white shirt seemed too large for his slender body, whose muscular arms—developed from years of wielding his hammer—seemed out of place. Mohsin called for a boy to serve tea.

After speaking of their mutual friend, Nasim, and asking a few questions about metalworking, Omar let his son talk.

"Nasim told us you're a great storyteller, a specialist," Jamal said, "and that you have a story for everybody. We're travelers and adventurers. Do you have one for us?"

Mohsin laughed, revealing a couple of missing teeth. His eyes were a bright shade of blue, and contrasted with a face tanned by Kandahar's merciless summer sun.

"Specialist? My only specialty is trusting my intuition, which tells me which story to tell, and to whom," Mohsin said. "Or which path to choose at a crossroads, for example. Would you like to hear a tale about that? It's also one about travelers."

"Yes, please," Zeina answered for them all.

"It's also a story of travelers, and it's called...

The Three Travelers and the *Naan*

Three companions set out on a journey together. They decided to pool their funds, since, separately, their resources were too meager to buy much of anything. Their combined funds were sufficient to purchase one small piece of naan, *a delicious flatbread. Instead of eating it immediately, they proposed to leave it for the next day, and they went to sleep by the side of the road.*

The sun was already high in the sky when they awoke the next day. They were all very hungry.

"Come to think of it," said the first man, "this naan *is too small to satisfy any of us. We'll all go hungry."*

"Very true," said the second man. "I propose the following: Let's tell each other our dreams, and the one who had the most interesting dream gets to eat the naan*."*

They all agreed and began to recount their dreams.

The first man said, "I dreamed that I was on top of a magic mountain, and that I was so high up I could see God and the angels. It was extraordinary. It was the most marvelous vision a man could have." He looked at the others, sure that they wouldn't be able to come up with a more amazing dream.

The second man said, "I dreamed that I traveled on a magic carpet to a place where I could see not just God and his angels, but all of creation, below the Earth and above it. In a word, I was able to see the entire universe." He looked at his companions, sure that his dream was the winner.

When it was the third man's turn, he said, "I dreamed that a marvelous being came to me, who was none other than the Invisible Guide, and he said to me that, as I was a humble man, I deserved the entire naan*. He told me to get up and eat it. I could not, of course, disobey such a command. So I opened my eyes, got up and ate all of it."*

Upon hearing this, the other two hastened to see if it was true, and, unfortunately for them, it was. As you may imagine, they became quite angry at first. But they finally realized that the third man's dream had, indeed, been the best, so he deserved the naan.

Mohsin told other stories as well, and at lunchtime led the travelers to a bakery where, he said, Kandahar's best *naan* was made. Then he took them to visit the city's fabled Red Mosque, before sending them on their way back to Karachi laden with gifts.

Back on the ship in Karachi, Zeina and Jamal told the other passengers about their meeting with Mohsin, and that evening everyone gathered to hear the story of the three travelers and the *naan.*

"What do you think?" Zeina asked when she finished the story. "Do you think the third man deserved the treat?"

"Yeah, 'cause his idea was the best!" said Ming-Jung.

"Or maybe because he was the humblest," Tapio suggested. "Or at least, that's what the Invisible Guy told him, right?"

"The Invisible *Guide*," Zeina corrected.

"I think it was because he woke up!" said Liyang. "If the others hadn't been asleep, the third man wouldn't have eaten the bread."

"If it had been me, I would have stayed awake all night!" added Leia.

"I think he deserved it because he was the only one who heard a voice telling him what he should do," said Mirta.

"Wish I could hear a voice like that!" Zeina thought.

Afterward, Urho Ullakko approached her. "At first I thought you were here just to entertain the children. But I must confess, dear Zeina, that we *all* love your stories! You always seem to choose ones that resonate with something deep inside us."

A warm feeling spread through the girl's chest. She realized that the more stories she heard, the more other stories emerged from deep within the hidden folds of her memory—tales she'd heard as a child but hadn't thought of in years. And now they were all filling that place inside of her that had been left so empty when her mother died.

"I'll be the guardian of the wisdom that these stories contain!" she said to herself. "Well, at least among the population on our island in Antarctica." If she could do that, she'd be happy, she thought.

"Farooq's arrived!" announced Igor, the agronomist, who had been watching the cars coming to the port.

A few minutes later, a man with a clear and radiant expression got out of a car. He was very young, perhaps twenty.

"Too young to be a scientist," Igor commented to Omar as they went to help with Farooq's luggage, which included a heavy chest. Omar reminded Igor that Farooq was one of the young quantum computer geniuses.

"I know of your interest in traditional stories," Farooq said as he climbed the ramp, "and I brought you something." After showing him his quarters and setting down his bags, a small group of passengers showed Farooq to the dining room. As he placed the old chest on the table, a cloud of dust rose from it.

"What's in the chest?" Ada asked, standing close to her twin sister.

"Gifts!" Farooq said, unfastening the iron latches and revealing the contents with a flourish.

"There are more books here than there are hairs on my head!" Joaquim Chissano, the biochemist, exclaimed.

"And in English!" added Igor.

"When you were in Kandahar," Mirta said to Omar, "Farooq called from Kabul. We were talking about books, so he went straight to Islamabad."

"Islamabad has the biggest bookstore in the world," explained Farooq. "Bigger even than any in the United States! The store has millions of books! But now, I'm flat broke," he said, making a big show of pulling out his pockets so Ada and Leia could see they were empty.

"Well, you won't need money where *we're* going!" Jamal said.

Zeina couldn't keep up with so many titles. As the other passengers filtered in to meet Farooq, the group at the long table unpacked the chest, chatting excitedly. There were books of all sizes and for all ages—some light and thin, some heavy; some leather-bound with gold lettering; some colorful. There were even coloring books, much to the younger children's delight. There seemed to be storybooks for everyone.

Zeina thanked Farooq with a shy smile, and he melted like a snowflake in sunlight.

Hours later, the members of *The Altromondo's* crew began preparing for their imminent mission. *The Dreamer's* movements were being monitored in Luxembourg by Fernández, the newly hired chief of operations. "Sir, *The Dreamer* already left Karachi and is heading south," he informed Palvo. "Wulandar doesn't want to get too close, so as not to raise any suspicions. In my opinion, he shouldn't lose sight of them. Finding a ship in the Arabian Sea is like finding a needle in a haystack."

"I trust you're bringing me a solution, not just the problem," Palvo said caustically.

"We have two alternatives," said Fernández. "One, we can send out another drone, one of those that are equipped to collect phone signals and determine the exact position of the ship as well as its speed. But that would only work if someone on *The Dreamer* actually used a phone."

"And the other alternative?" Palvo asked.

"Contact Orbitall, the commercial satellite company that offers espionage among its services. It's pricey, but quick and certain. They'll send the information directly to *The Altromondo*. I mean, *The Tranquility*."

"That seems simpler and less risky," Palvo said. "You're in charge, but make sure everything is completely confidential and can't be traced."

"Not a problem. I'll have answers tomorrow."

16: **Indian Ocean**

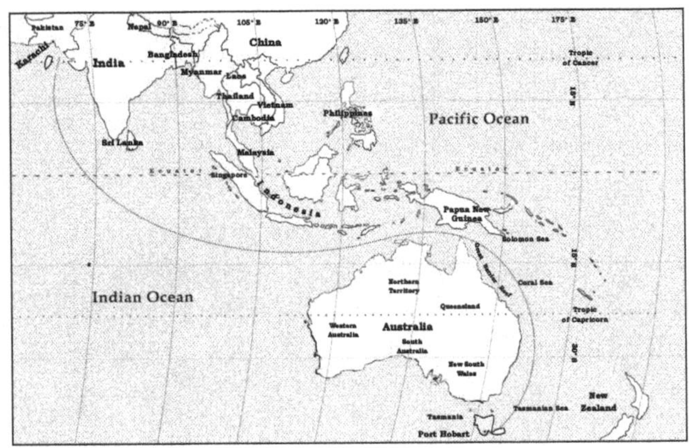

"We've just crossed the Tropic of Cancer," Omar informed the Cádiz base.

"So you've finally left the Gulf! You had us worried, Omar. Now we can get some rest!" came the reply.

The Dreamer sailed under a cloudless, crystal-blue dome. From the ship's bridge, Omar saw a small vessel approaching. Its Jamaican flag was barely visible through his binoculars. A few minutes later, an SOS call came in to *The Dreamer*.

"This is Captain Almora of *The Tranquility*. Do you have a doctor on board?"

"This is Captain Homsi of *The Dreamer*. Is this an emergency, Captain?" Omar asked.

"Yes. We have a sailor with an abdominal hernia, and we believe it's strangulated. He's in intense pain, has a high fever and is vomiting. If your doctor confirms that it's urgent, then we'll call for a helicopter immediately."

"Registration number, Captain?" asked Omar.

"Five-nine-four-eight-six."

Omar checked the registration number and the name "Almora" on the electronic registry, and then the name of the vessel. *The Tranquility* was registered as a fishing boat. Name and license were in order. He consulted with Dr. Roble, who suggested that they put the man on camera for a remote diagnosis. Moments later, a sailor's abdomen appeared on the infirmary screen. The swelling was evident, but not its cause. Dr. Roble would have to examine the man personally.

"Send the patient over in a skiff," said Omar. He didn't want to make a ship-to-ship transfer directly. It would be better to maintain a certain distance from the other boat. Better to be safe than sorry, especially on the high seas.

"Yes, of course, Captain."

Omar didn't consider it necessary to raise the tower screens and show the weaponry they concealed. There were tasers and lasers, as well as cannons and machine guns. However, he did activate the cameras to record the encounter, in case there were complications.

Once the two ships were within sixty feet of each other, *The Tranquility* lowered two men in a skiff, which arrived alongside *The Dreamer* in less than a minute. John Wood and Joaquim Chissano then lowered an inflatable boat into which the sick sailor was transferred and lifted up to the deck. His companion remained in the skiff, awaiting the results of the examination.

The sick sailor looked terrible and was taken right away to the infirmary.

"Sit down, please," said Dr. Roble. "What's your name?"

"Thank you, Doctor. My name is Cabdull. I hope you don't send me to a surgeon!"

"We'll see. We won't do anything hasty," Dr. Roble assured him. "Let's take a look at that abdomen of yours."

"Doctor, my stomach's in knots. Can I use your bathroom first?"

"Of course. Down the hall, second door on the left."

Cabdull found the door in question, opened it, turned on the light and discovered he was in a bathroom. Scanning it for cameras, he noted two portholes, but because of their location no one could see him from the outside.

With trembling hands, he extracted a small package from his waistband. In all his years as a mercenary, he had never done anything like this before. He would have been more comfortable relying on his old friends, firearms. The weapon he had brought with him this time was invisible and treacherous. He recalled what Captain Wulandar—or Almora, as he was now calling himself—had told him: "There's no risk. You don't even need a protective mask—just gloves, if you feel the need for them." That reassured Cabdull, who took the capsule out of the case and looked at it. It was still quite cold, although it had thawed out a bit. So far, so good.

Suddenly Cabdull thought he heard a voice from the other room and started to feel nervous. He put his ear to the wall. A woman was talking about a mission of some sort. "Whatever!" Cabdull thought. He brought his attention back to the task at hand and looked for the ventilation duct. According to the boat's blueprint that his boss had obtained from the man in Liverpool, the duct was behind a door and down low near the floor. At last he saw it.

Cabdull knelt by the duct, quietly removing its screen. The air moved in and out with the boat's movements. It would be a fast, clean operation. The viscous liquid he planned to release into the duct would evaporate, leaving only the bacteria, which would dry out, become airborne and waft into every room of the ship. "Amazing that science can come up with this kind of thing," he thought, looking at the tiny container. "Even more amazing that I can actually make everybody on board sick, or even kill them, with this." A cold, regretful shiver ran down his spine as he thought of his own children.

The air inside the duct was cool. He put on gloves, opened the capsule and was about to place the liquid onto the metallic surface, when he heard the voice again. This time, it was clearer and louder than before. He put his ear to the opening and heard a strong, female voice saying, "The man is about to commit his abominable crime. When he puts his hand to his belt to take out his weapon, it trembles..."

Cabdull's heart skipped a beat, and he replaced the cap on the still-full container. "Could they be watching me?" he thought, looking wildly around.

The voice continued. "He knows that this will be the most

horrible act of his life. 'I am a bad man,' he thinks. 'No, I am a weak man, a slave, one who could not say no when he was given the mission. Or perhaps … just a greedy man.'"

Cabdull pressed his free hand to his chest. The voice resonated in the air duct and in his ears. He remained on his knees, terrified, with his ear glued to the duct, as if an invisible hand were pinning him in place.

The voice continued. "Before completing his mission, he raises his eyes to ask pardon for his moral weakness. He knows full well that the heavens have countless eyes observing the actions of man! And in this precise instant he sees…"

Cabdull raised his head, and an involuntary howl escaped his parched throat as he saw two lifeless eyes looking down on him from a horrid face. Blood raced through his veins, and his vision misted over. Wiping a hand over his eyes in an attempt to clear them, he again saw it: the mask of the Mayan god Kinich Ahau, which Joãozinho and Jamal had glued to the bathroom ceiling days before. Although Cabdull now realized it was a mask, he was sure it had a purpose.

"A hidden camera!" he gasped in a state of paranoia.

The mask's mouth hung open, and scarlet droplets clung to the accusing tongue of the bloodthirsty god. Cabdull covered his mouth with his palm, trembling from head to toe, and shoved the capsule of poison back into its case. As he put the cover back on the duct, the voice seemed to move farther away.

Before leaving the bathroom, Cabdull stuffed the case and

gloves into a pocket and peered down the corridor. With no one in sight, he wiped the sweat from his brow.

In an adjacent room, Zeina continued her story: "*… a ferocious band of pirates, waving their swords, run toward him. Without a second thought, the servant flees in terror, leaving the girl at the mercy of the pirates, who lose no time. Since they can't reach the slave, they grab Tarsiana and carry her off into captivity.*"

Seeing that the hallway was empty, Cabdull made his way back up to the deck. He would need to throw himself overboard and swim for the skiff before he was discovered. His confusion increased as he saw the tall safety netting that had been erected above the railing on all of the decks, to keep the children safe. Was it a trap for him? In a moment of lucidity, he shoved the capsule, case and bag of rat feces through a gap in the railing and watched them fall into the sea. Free of the incriminating evidence, he turned and heaved a sigh of relief. From behind him, he could hear someone approaching. "They couldn't have seen me throw that stuff overboard!" he thought.

"Are you all right?" Ramanujan asked, looking Cabdull directly in the face and seeing it bathed in sweat.

"No … ah … I mean … yes … I just needed some fresh air. That's all."

"Allow me to accompany you to the infirmary."

Cabdull felt trapped. "They can't accuse me of anything!" he thought as he was led down the corridor like a sheep to slaughter. There was nothing he could do but play innocent. Excuses ran through his mind. How would he explain himself when they confronted him with the bathroom surveillance video? "It was my own medicine … Yes … my medicine …"

"You were gone a while! Are you okay?" Dr. Roble asked, guiding Cabdull back to the examination table. "Come lie down here, and we'll have a look."

"Sorry, doctor, I was feeling disoriented and needed fresh air," Cabdull said as he lay back down.

"This swelling may be dangerous," Dr. Roble said a few minutes later, palpating the man's abdomen. "You should be evacuated as soon as possible."

Omar's men lowered the patient to the skiff, and his comrade ferried him, without delay, to the fishing boat.

"Mission accomplished, Captain," said Cabdull as soon as he got on board, still pale and agitated. "They'll all be sick within twenty-four hours."

"And the evidence?"

"I sprinkled the rat feces in the corners of the room."

"Good work, man!" said Wulandar, giving him a slap on the back. Noticing Cabdull's still-trembling hands and shaken look, the captain added, "Relax. Go to the bar and have a drink or two. Looks like you need it."

Wulandar went to the radio and thanked the captain of *The Dreamer* for services rendered, wishing him and his passengers a good trip.

On *The Tranquility*, the crew celebrated a successful mission, fantasizing about the compensation awaiting them in Luxembourg.

Meanwhile, on *The Dreamer*, Zeina continued the story she was retelling by special request: "*The failed assassin hurries home to his mistress in a state of great agitation. Seeing his face, she doesn't doubt his lie that Tarsiana is dead....*"

17: Southern Hemisphere

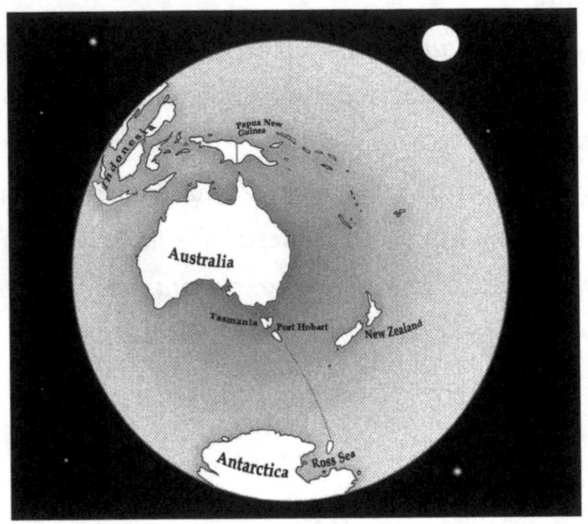

On the evening of December twenty-first, *The Dreamer* crossed the equator. Although it was the winter solstice back home, in the Southern Hemisphere summer was just beginning, and the days would be growing longer. When the voyagers arrived on the island, they'd have three months to accumulate enough solar energy for the winter.

The children darted around the decks under a cotton-candy sky that seemed to reflect the surface of the sea. Little by little, the clouds floated to one side of the heavens like a flock of sheep on the horizon, leaving it awash in radiant orange and red. Then, almost in an instant, the sun sank to the other side of the planet. Jamal was used to the long evenings of Cádiz, but here on the equator, the golden hours of sunset lasted only a few minutes, as the sky went from light to dark so fast that it seemed a feat of magic.

The ship's passengers saw the three stars of Alpha Centauri, home to thousands of Earth-like planets. They saw Polaris and the North Star. And on the opposite side of the sky, hovering over the horizon, they saw, for the first time, the Southern Cross.

Old and young contemplated the infinity of distant suns stretching out above them, as the passengers floated on the immense Indian Ocean, feeling at once insignificant and powerful, humble but also capable. Zeina wondered if pioneers throughout history had shared the same feeling.

Jamal left the book he was reading and went over to Farooq, who was gazing at the stars.

"Do you know what the Infinite is, Jamal?" Farooq asked.

"The universe?" Jamal guessed.

"I've heard that the Infinite is a sphere whose center is everywhere and whose circumference is nowhere," said Farooq.

"It'll take some thinking for me to understand that," said Jamal.

"Take your time."

The days passed peacefully. Jamal, sure he'd travel through the Middle East again one day, continued his Arabic lessons with Zeina.

After a few days, John spotted something unusual. "Look to starboard!" Omar said over the ship's intercom. Everyone came on deck, some with binoculars, which, as it turned out, weren't needed. The huge, rough, grimy patch on the surface of the sea was visible to the naked eye.

"Why didn't our radar detect this before?" Jon Kim asked.

"Not possible," said Urho Ullakko. "These 'great garbage patches,' as they're called, are difficult to see even in satellite photographs, despite their size and density."

Helka pointed out to sea. "You see all that floating garbage?" she said to the younger children. "It's plastic trash. It used to be very common to make bags out of plastic. People tossed them on the beaches, or into the rivers, which carried them out to sea, and the movement of the ocean brought them here to swirl around together forever, because plastic doesn't decompose like paper does. And this is just one of many huge floating garbage patches, where fish and other marine life eat the little bits of plastic and get sick."

"That's terrible!" cried Mrs. Taniguchi. "The sea has given us food for hundreds of thousands of years, and what does humanity give it in return? Plastic!"

"They're called 'oceanic dumps,'" John said. "Some of them have been cleaned up, but not all, obviously."

Mirta sent a message to the scientists at the Foundation, with holographic images, maps and an analysis of the water in various areas around the garbage patch. It was *The Dreamer's* first scientific report from the Southern Hemisphere.

The ship continued eastward and eventually entered the Torres Strait, between Australia and Papua New Guinea. Some of the children huddled in front of the monitor that showed the navigation charts, and watched the ship's trajectory. Tapio, who collected old maps at home, asked John why they couldn't see any of the islands on the monitor.

"There aren't any islands here anymore, Tapio," John said. "The rising seas gobbled them up. The few that remain have become so salty that nothing can grow there anymore."

This close to the equator, the days were intensely bright. The sun beat down with perpendicular rays, and the ship's pool became the most popular gathering place. Helka increased school hours in an attempt to combat the children's growing feelings of boredom and claustrophobia.

As the ship moved farther south, the sun took more time to set. It no longer plunged into the horizon with the same urgency it had in the equatorial latitudes, where night followed day abruptly, almost without warning.

"That's because of the curvature of the Earth, and its tilted axis," Urho said, using an orange and a pencil to illustrate what he was explaining to the children. "The farther we get from the equator, the longer the days will be in the summer, and the shorter they'll be in the winter," he said, pointing at the bottom of the orange to indicate Antarctica.

"But then we'll be upside-down," exclaimed Kimiko, suddenly aware of their position on the globe.

"Sure, we'll all have to wear hats so our thoughts don't fall out," joked Jamal.

"Don't worry, Kimiko. There's no upside-down or right-side-up in the universe," Ming-Jung said, trying to reassure her.

"Or maybe it depends on your per-spec-tive," Tapio clarified, in academic tones.

"That's right, Tapio," Urho continued. "But to return to the sun's rays in relation to the Earth: When you see how long the shadows are on the island, you'll understand why."

On December twenty-fifth, they finally reached the port of Hobart in Tasmania. It was a short stop, just long enough to get a few more supplies, and the next day they embarked again.

The younger children were growing increasingly bored and impatient, and constantly asked, "Are we there yet?"

"We're *never* gonna get there!" was another common complaint.

On one of those occasions, Mirta asked Zeina if she knew the story of Maruf the Cobbler.

"Yes, from *The Arabian Nights*," Zeina said. "The one where a dream becomes reality. It's my favorite! I'll tell it after dinner."

The temperature dropped suddenly that evening, so out came the winter coats. Some were made of plain thermal fiber; others included batteries that generated heat. In spite of the cold snap, the group preferred to sit outside on the deck, bundled up against the sudden chill. Some claimed that if they kept quiet, they could hear the pulse of stars moving farther out into the ever-expanding universe.

Zeina took her usual place in front of the group, and began the story.

Maruf the Cobbler

In the city of Cairo, there lived a cobbler named Maruf. He earned very little money, just enough to provide the simplest food. His wife bitterly complained of their poverty and demanded that Maruf do his utmost to increase his meager earnings. One day the woman became so fed up with the situation that, for better or worse, she moved back to her parents' house, leaving Maruf in peace.

However, despite having been freed from a demanding and ungrateful wife, the cobbler felt humiliated and extremely depressed. To alleviate his sadness, he went for a walk. He walked for a time without any particular direction in mind, until it started to rain, at which point he sought shelter in a ruined mosque. There, the unfortunate Maruf began a litany of prayers and supplications, now recounting his story, now praying to some spiritual being to transport him to a distant place where no one would know him or his story, and where he might find tranquility and hope.

He spent some time in this state of intense emotion, when something extraordinary occurred: A being of unusual appearance materialized out of thin air right in front of him, and said, "I am the custodian of this place, and I have heard your story. It has moved me. Since you're a generous man, I'm going to help you. If you climb onto my back, I'll transport you far away from this place, just as you requested."

Even though he thought he was dreaming, Maruf hopped onto the back of this marvelous being, who immediately flew up into the sky and carried him away as if on a magic carpet.

They flew for several hours through the night air, faster than any bird or even the wind. At daybreak, the amazing creature deposited his passenger on the ground just outside of a city and told him that he was in a Muslim country near the border with China. They had traveled far indeed!

As Maruf walked through the gates of this new city, he was asked where he came from.

"Cairo," he answered, adding that he had left there the previous night.

"What a monstrous lie!" was the answer. "Cairo is in Egypt, and it takes a year to journey from there to here."

To prove his story, Maruf displayed a fresh loaf of bread he had brought along in his pack, but this only served to complicate his situation. People thought he was a madman and began to beat him with sticks and pelt him with stones, just for fun. This commotion attracted the attention of a merchant who happened to be passing. He could tell from Maruf's typical Egyptian clothing that he and the stranger were compatriots.

"You should be ashamed of yourselves. This is not the way we treat foreigners here!" the merchant shouted at the crowd. And at that, the bullies dispersed.

The merchant's name was Ali, son of Sheikh Ahmad of Cairo. Ali informed Maruf that he, too, had arrived poor in the city, but had been able to make progress thanks to his ingenuity. He had discovered that the people in this place had the most respect for those who looked rich, and it was sufficient to merely say and pretend that one was rich for them to believe it!

Ali's story was thus: When he first came to the city, he had gone from business to business in the bazaar, visiting the merchants there, telling them that he had a caravan that was on its way, laden with much treasure, but that he needed a loan to tide him over until it arrived. No one denied him credit. Using borrowed funds, Ali related, he began to buy and sell various and sundry goods at a profit, and since he always repaid his loans on time, he was never at a loss for creditors. It was in this way that he multiplied his capital and actually became a prosperous merchant.

Maruf marveled at this success story. Ali counseled him to do the same and said he would help.

The plan worked well. Maruf collected a sizable sum of money, which he promised to repay when his caravan arrived. But instead of investing his funds in buying and selling, as Ali had done, Maruf distributed them among the poor, because that was his nature.

At first, this didn't bother his creditors. They thought Maruf must be very rich indeed in order to give money away in that fashion. Matters continued in this way for some time, Maruf receiving money on credit and then distributing it here and there to those in need. After two months, however, the merchants began to have their doubts. Was it really true, they wondered, that a caravan was on its way to Maruf?

Eventually, the creditors' suspicions of fraud turned into certainty, and they went to the king to complain. The king, not knowing what to think of Maruf, summoned him to court in order to put him to a test: If he were indeed as rich as he claimed, he should be able to distinguish one precious stone from another.

When Maruf presented himself at court, the king handed him a precious stone and said, "This is a gift for you, Maruf, as compensation for your generosity toward the poor."

But instead of thanking the king and putting the stone in his pocket, Maruf responded, "You may keep it, Your Highness, as this stone is worthless in comparison with what I have in my caravan."

This astonished the king, who thought, "If this man were not really rich, he would have accepted my gift. And if it's true that he has precious stones more valuable than mine, might it not be a good idea to become associated with this man in some way?"

The king decided that the best plan would be to make Maruf his son-in-law. "That's it!" he thought. "Marry him to my daughter!"

The king sent a message to the merchants, saying that Maruf was a respectable businessman, and sent another message to Maruf, offering his daughter,

Princess Dunya, in marriage. This made the vizier furious, as he was sure that Maruf was an imposter. The king was not inclined to listen to this reasoning, however, because he knew that the vizier had always wanted Princess Dunya for himself. Furthermore, the idea of gaining access to Maruf's riches clouded the king's judgment.

Upon receiving the king's message, Maruf informed him that he would have to postpone the marriage because he, Maruf, did not yet have the jewels that he intended to give the Princess, who deserved the very best. But the king, blinded by his greed for the fortune he anticipated, assured Maruf that this would not be an impediment and ordered his palace treasurer to open the treasury doors, so that Maruf could help himself to whatever amount was needed to make him and the princess comfortable.

The wedding was one of unparalleled magnificence: Forty days of celebration, during which all those present, as well as those who were unable to attend, received valuable gifts. When the party was over, however, Maruf began to feel anxious.

Meanwhile, the vizier continued to pressure the king with his suspicions, and even spoke with the princess in an attempt to get her to discover the truth.

One night, Maruf was especially worried and said to Dunya, "I can't ask anything more from your father, because I don't want to abuse his generosity."

"But what are you worried about, dear husband?" Dunya answered. "When your caravan arrives, you'll repay everything."

In a moment of candor, Maruf confessed to her, right then and there, that in reality the caravan existed only in his imagination. He had invented the whole story.

The princess became quiet and pensive and then replied, "You're my husband, and I won't allow you to fall into disgrace. Take this money, flee the country and send me a message telling me where you are. I'll come to you later on, after taking care of matters here." Then she gave Maruf fifty thousand dinars for his escape.

That night, Maruf left the palace under cover of darkness.

The following day, the princess presented herself before her father and the vizier, and calmly said, "Last night, when I was about to broach the subject of the caravan, ten armed slaves came to our apartment window with a letter for Maruf. The letter explained that his caravan had been attacked by Bedouins, and that he had lost a great part of his merchandise, together with many camels and other things. Father, I'm very distressed for my husband's sake! He immediately bade me farewell and hastened away in order to bring back what little his guards were able to defend from the attack."

Glancing reproachfully at the vizier, the king drew

his daughter to him to console her. He had no idea that she had invented the story in order to gain time.

In the meantime, Maruf was riding hard to get as far away from the palace as possible, without any further plan, when he happened to pass a field where a peasant was plowing. Maruf slowed his horse and drew near to greet and converse with the man, who invited him to share some food, which Maruf happily accepted.

The peasant ran to his house to fetch them their lunch. Meanwhile Maruf, feeling grateful for the man's generosity, took up the plow in order to help him. But after a few minutes of working, the plow hit a boulder and stopped abruptly. With a great deal of effort, Maruf lifted the stone and discovered steps leading down to a subterranean chamber. He descended the stairway and found himself in the midst of a vast hoard of treasure. An alabaster slab sat atop an immense pile of precious stones, gold and silver, and on the alabaster was a ring. Recalling the magic rings in old tales that he'd heard, Maruf gave this one a rub. Instantly, an enormous ifrit *appeared before him in a puff of smoke.*

"I am here, my lord and master," said the apparition.

"Who … who are you?" Maruf stammered.

"I am Abu Ak-Saadat, the greatest genie and the commander of seventy-two tribes of lesser genies," said the ifrit *in a thundering voice. "And I am now your slave. Command, and I will obey you!"*

Maruf rubbed his eyes to see if it was all an illusion. But no, the genie was there to serve him and declared that the treasure had belonged to an ancient king, but that now Maruf could do with it what he wished.

Recovering from his surprise, Maruf ordered the genie to carry all the treasure to the surface. Immediately, a small army of genies took the form of slaves and servants and went to work filling chest after chest with gold, silver and precious stones, which they then loaded onto other genies that had materialized in the form of beasts of burden at the entrance of the cave.

When the peasant returned with a plate of lentils and saw the rich caravan, he imagined that it belonged to the king of his country. He excused himself for the humble nature of the meal he'd brought them.

Maruf accepted the lentils, thanked the peasant for his generosity and presented him with a bag of gold. He told the man to come to the palace later, where he would be received with honors.

Maruf sent the caravan ahead to meet his father-in-law, and the genie Abu Ak-Saadat went along too, in the guise of a messenger. The king's joy at seeing the caravan arrive was beyond description. The princess, however, didn't know what to think. Perhaps, she told herself, her spouse was, in fact, rich and had lied to her in order to test her loyalty. The merchant Ali, for his part, concluded that it was all the work of the princess, who wished to save her husband. The other merchants, open-mouthed with astonishment, hastened to declare in unison, "I knew all along that he was not an imposter!"

But the vizier still had his doubts. It wasn't possible, he told himself, that a merchant could become richer than a king; nor, furthermore, that he would so generously give away that much money to common people. "This is not the way," he said to himself, "that merchants behave."

The vizier told the king that something very strange was going on, and that he intended to discover the truth. This time, however, he did not approach the princess, but instead hatched a plan that couldn't fail. After dark, he posted himself just outside the window of Maruf and the princess's bedroom, and bent his ear to their conversation.

"My darling wife," Maruf said to Dunya, showing her the ring, "now I must tell you the truth: This is the source of all the wealth that I've brought back. The genie of the ring is at my service."

The following day, armed with this knowledge, the vizier pretended to have repented of his attitude toward Maruf, and invited him to lunch at his table. Taking advantage of a moment when Maruf was distracted, the vizier poured a sleeping potion into his guest's water glass. Within moments, Maruf was asleep, and the vizier stole the ring. Losing no time, he went to his apartments and rubbed it.

The genie appeared in a puff of smoke and declared, "I am Abu Ak-Saadat, the greatest genie, commander of seventy-two tribes of lesser genies! I am now your slave. Command me, and I will obey you!"

The vizier quickly ordered that Maruf be carried off and abandoned in the desert. Then, not content with that act of treachery, he told the genie to carry the king off, too, and to leave him in the same desert, where no food and no water meant certain death.

The ifrit *obeyed these orders.*

Now the vizier not only had command over the genie, but also had usurped the king's power. The next step was to seduce the princess.

But Dunya was not foolish. She put on her most attractive and transparent clothing. When the vizier drew near, she pretended to be pleased with his advances and extended her arms to him in a gesture of acceptance. The vizier lost his head and allowed himself an embrace. Feeling the warm arm of the princess encircling his waist, he did the same to her. It took but a second for the princess to slide her other arm to his waist, take his hand in hers, locate the ring on his finger and rub it.

Lo and behold! The ifrit *appeared in a puff of smoke and offered himself as her slave.*

"Seize the vizier, and make it quick!" she commanded.

Two enormous ifrit *helpers took the vizier in their hands as if he were a mere plaything, lifted him up by the neck and carried him away, kicking and screaming.*

Then the princess ordered the genie to immediately bring her father and her husband back, and in less time than it takes to recount, those two were again beside her in the palace, safe and sound.

Maruf was appointed prime minister, and when the king went to his eternal reward, Maruf and the princess inherited the throne. The two lived peacefully for the rest of their lives.

But one thing must be mentioned: The ring stayed in the princess's power, an indisputably sensible arrangement. Although Maruf was the ring's owner, she was its guardian.

"And that's the end of the story!" Zeina said.

"The genie appeared to Maruf because he was good to the farmer, right?" Kimiko asked.

"But Maruf lied!" Liang interjected. "And lying isn't good!"

"Not all lies are bad," observed Tapio. "Maruf was just imitating something he…he wanted to be!"

"But is that good?" Ada asked.

"Well," said Jamal, "it's like when you just pretend to be a good student and then end up really being one. Know what I mean?"

"I think the story is telling us to have the courage to dream,"

Zeina added. "Because if you think, 'I can't,' or 'I never' or 'That's not for me,' or anything like that, then you'll never get what you want, because you've closed the doors."

"But my daddy says the world is the way it is because we want too much!" Joãozinho commented.

"Your father is talking about material things, Joãozinho—like when you want to buy stuff," Leia explained.

The children's voices mixed with the sound of the waves as the adults listened pensively, their own thoughts drawn in a multitude of directions before trailing off like flecks of foam in *The Dreamer's* wake.

Zeina thought of her mother and how, when she was on her deathbed, she had said to Zeina with great sadness, "Poor girl, I'm not leaving you anything! Just stories!"

"Thank you, Mom," Zeina said now to herself, gazing up into the infinity of stars. "It's the best legacy you could have left me." Zeina's heart, which had been sore and empty before, was now a well of gratitude.

The ocean was flat, gray and foggy.

"We're entering the bottom edge of the Roaring Forties," Omar announced, referring to the South Pacific's fearsomely windy zone between forty and fifty degrees latitude, which signals proximity to the Antarctic Circle.

Suddenly a southwest wind blasted the decks, and everybody rushed inside in a near-panic. *The Dreamer* had entered the Antarctic Convergence Zone, where the cold and dense Antarctic Ocean battles the warmer subtropical waters, creating gigantic waves. The boat began to rock back and forth. The sun disappeared. The children, and many of the adults, couldn't hide their fear. At the sight of waves towering above the windows, everyone had the sensation of truly sailing at the "edge of the world." As, indeed, they were.

The cold wind blasted the ship for two days. Then one morning, as the ship sailed beneath a clear sky, there came a shout: "Icebergs!" Soon *The Dreamer* was wending its way through a labyrinth of floating towers of ice in every shape and size—some of them snow-white, some of them the deepest aquamarine, all of them resplendent and many of them very close to the ship. Awe and amazement showed on everyone's face, as young and old felt an indescribable joy at witnessing such a dramatic example of nature's grandeur. *The Dreamer* was crossing the Antarctic Circle.

By then, night had forsaken them, making darkness a stranger to the sky, which slowly oscillated between degrees of perpetual light.

And then they saw it. Of course, Omar had already seen it pop up on the radar, but he had preferred to let John, who had climbed the mast like a sailor of bygone days, give the shout: "Land ahoy!"

Snug in their parkas and *anoraks,* cheeks reddened by the

glacial air, the thirty passengers of *The Dreamer* turned their teary eyes southward, to an irregular line emerging on the horizon.

"Our island!" Mirta exclaimed. As she spoke, happiness lit every face, and each passenger uttered a silent "Thank you!" Their ocean journey had ended, and a whole new life was about to begin.

A dusting of snow covered the decks, and a petrel, itself as white as the snow, flew over the ship and then settled on a rail, followed by another and another, until soon an entire chorus of avian cries welcomed the new inhabitants of the frozen expanse they quickly named "Isle of the Dreamers."

The New York Times, December 30, 2036

(ANDAMAN ISLANDS) The captain of a ship sailing near the Andaman Islands has been detained along with nine of his crew members, while Interpol investigates a tip that they were planning to raid and poison the passengers of a Spanish ship that's on a scientific mission to Antarctica.

The tip had come from a former member of the detained crew, whose ship, *The Tranquility,* was disguised as a fishing boat. According to a communication from the International Security Service, this former *Tranquility* crew member had been medevaced to a hospital in Cairo from the Eritrean port of Massawa, where he'd been dropped off.

El Mundo, January 1, 2038

(ROSS SEA ADMINISTRATION) A small group of scientists working in Antarctica has just completed its first year conducting research on behalf of the MBG Foundation. The diverse team has already made important discoveries regarding the effects of climate change around the globe.

"The work we're doing will eventually enable us to recommend preventive measures for all countries to take, as well as management strategies to mitigate the catastrophic effects of climate change," program coordinator Omar Homsi said in a holophone interview.

Because of their success, the community of 30 individuals, which includes the scientists' families, will expand to 150 over the next four years, according to the MBG Foundation.

When asked about the challenge of keeping their spirits up in such a desolate, inhospitable environment, Zeina Moura, 17, said "We tell stories."

Glossary of Foreign and Fictitious Words

abaya; also aba a long women's robe that extends down to the feet, used in Arab countries and North Africa.

anorak a hooded, waterproof jacket originally used in polar regions.

banapple (fictitious) a hybrid fruit produced by combining the genes of an apple and a banana.

Berber an ethnic group and language of the indigenous inhabitants of North Africa, who today are concentrated mostly in Algeria and Morocco.

biryani a South Asian rice dish made with a blend of spices, meat and vegetables.

cadi a judge in Muslim countries.

chebbakia a food common in Arab countries and consisting of sweet dough that's fried, twisted and covered with sesame seeds and honey.

cyber (in addition to its usual meaning) a fictitious term for an online school, derived from "cyber school."

fatta a common Egyptian dish consisting of pieces of fresh and stale bread that are fried, mixed with yogurt and chicken, and often accompanied with eggplant and chickpeas.

El Niño the weather conditions associated with a band of warm ocean water in the central and east-central Pacific Ocean around the equator.

Hades in Greek mythology, the god of the underworld.

haj the Muslim pilgrimage to Mecca.

ham radio a type of radio communication that's used by hobbyists, and also by those at sea in emergencies.

Haratin an ethnic group whose members live in the oases of the Sahara in northwest Africa.

hijab a scarf used by females in Islamic countries to cover the head and neck but not the face.

holoconference (fictitious) a teleconference that uses holograms.

holophone (fictitious) a phone that displays holographic videos.

HWatch (fictitious) a combination smartphone/ smartwatch that features holographic videos and images.

ifrit; also efrit according to Arab folklore, an enormous winged creature, either male or female, that's made of smoke, lives underground and frequents ruins.

Interlectorum (fictitious) an Internet search engine dedicated solely to literary works of fiction.

Intertale (fictitious) an Internet search engine dedicated solely to children's stories.

kantele a five-stringed musical instrument traditionally used in Finland.

karahi chicken a dish from Northern India and Pakistan, consisting of pieces of chicken flavored with oil, pepper and other spices.

keffiyeh; also kufiya or shumagh a cotton headdress that's traditionally worn by Middle Eastern men and that features a checkered pattern in white and black or red.

kithara a stringed instrument common in ancient Greece;

precursor of the guitar.

lingua franca a shared language used by the members of a linguistically diverse group to communicate with one another.

luqaymaat a traditional Arab sweet, similar to a fried dumpling.

Maghreb the region of North Africa west of Egypt. "Maghreb" means "west" in Arabic.

Mauna Kea the name of a dormant volcano in Hawaii.

medina the old Arab section of a town or city in North Africa.

Neurocrop (fictitious) a drug that optimizes brain functioning but can be addictive. (The expression "Neuro-crap," used by the character Palvo in *Tales for THE DREAMER,* is a sarcastic deformation of "Neurocrop.")

mutaween Saudi Arabian religious police.

panic button (fictitious) a special mobile-phone button used to make S.O.S. calls in emergencies.

pilau; also pilaf, pulau or pulaw a Middle Eastern dish that consists of spiced rice cooked in broth and that may also include meat, poultry or fish.

Polaris the North Star, which is sometimes used as a navigational guide.

RAA (fictitious) acronym for "Rent an Automatic Automobile."

rial Yemen's currency.

RAB (fictional) acronym for "Rent a Bicycle."

SSB acronym for "single side band," a type of long-distance marine radio.

Sahel the African transition zone between the Sahara Desert in the north and the Sudanese savannah in the south. The Sahel covers several countries and stretches from west to east between the Atlantic Ocean and the Red Sea.

shayla a long, rectangular veil that's common in Middle Eastern countries. It wraps the head and fastens at the shoulders so that the hair is covered but not the face.

sheikh in Muslim countries, a respected male elder or spiritual leader.

shumagh *see keffiyeh*

Southern Cross a group of four stars seen primarily in the southern hemisphere and used by sailors for navigation. Because of their configuration, the four stars are suggestive of a huge cross in the night sky.

Styx in Greek mythology, the river that carries the souls of the dead to the underworld.

taser a weapon that produces a debilitating but nonlethal electric shock.

UAV acronym for "unmanned aerial vehicle," or drone.

UNet (fictitious) the Internet of the future.

Universal Wi-Fi (fictitious) a system of high-altitude balloons that extends the Internet to the remotest parts of the world.

Notes and Bibliography

Throughout these notes are references to the works of the author and educator Idries Shah, who spent more than thirty years collecting hundreds of traditional teaching-stories, mostly from the Middle East and Central Asia, and publishing them for Western readers. For more details on his published works—all of which are available from Amazon—and a complete listing, visit www.idriesshahfoundation.org. Shah's books for young readers are also published by Hoopoe Books (*see website*: www.hoopoebooks.com).

Chapter 1: Cádiz, Spain

Cádiz, one of the oldest cities in Western Europe, is a port on the southwestern coast of Spain. It is the capital of the Spanish province of the same name, in a region called Andalusia.

Many of the environmental problems currently afflicting our planet are due to climate change and are likely to continue for decades. The magnitude of these problems in the future will depend to a large degree on the actions we take in the present. For more information, visit: https://www.sciencenewsforstudents.org/article/climate-change-long-reach.

Omar Homsi's mention of the Chinese having a station "on the other side" of the moon in 2036 was based on actual present-day current events. For more information, visit http://www.techinsider.io/china-plans-mars-moon-landings-2016-4.

For more information on the Earth's spin axis, visit the website https://astronomynow.com/2016/04/11/climate-change-creates-wobbles-in-earths-spin-axis/.

For more information on quantum computers, visit: https://www.youtube.com/watch?v=g_IaVepNDT4.

The Lame Fox

This story was told in 1257 by Saadi of Shiraz, one of the most revered classical Persian poets, in his work *The Bostan* (*The Orchard*). *The Bostan* and another book by Saadi, *The Gulistan* (*The Rose Garden*), are still read and appreciated by millions of people in India, Iran, Pakistan, Afghanistan and other countries of Central Asia, just as Shakespeare is still read and appreciated in the West. In fact, Saadi's writings influenced the *Gesta Romanorum*, a collection of tales and anecdotes that in turn influenced Shakespeare's plays *The Merchant of Venice* and *King Lear*.

The most contemporary translation of *The Bostan* is *The Bostan of Saadi*, translated from the Persian by Mirza Aqil-Hussein, Barlas (the Octagon Press Ltd., 1998); in it, the story of the lame fox is entitled "The Story of the Dervish and a Fox." Also see http://www.iranchamber.com/literature/saadi/books/bostan_saadi.pdf, where the tale is entitled "A Story of a Fool and a Fox."

The same story also appears in two books by Idries Shah: *Learning How to Learn: Psychology and Spirituality in the Sufi Way*, where it's entitled "The Limbless Fox"; and *Seeker After Truth*, where it's called "The Fox and the Lion."

Chapter 2: Tangier, Morocco

This chapter starts out in Mauritania, an arid country in West Africa that, in the present day, has suffered successive periods of severe drought, which have intensified the process of desertification and caused the emigration of many people. In *Tales for THE DREAMER*, Zeina's mother—born in an economically depressed region of Mauritania—was part of a contingent of immigrants who, in the late twentieth and early twenty-first centuries, took the perilous journey by boat from the northern coast of Africa to Spain in search of a better life.

The original inhabitants of Mauritania were dark-skinned nomads. When the Berber tribes came, they brought their own language. In the Middle Ages, as part of the expansion of Islam, the Arabs attacked and conquered the region, introducing the Arabic language and the Islamic faith. The original inhabitants intermarried with the Arabs, forming a group known as the Haratin, or "black Moors." In the early twentieth century, France colonized Mauritania, an occupation that lasted until 1960.

Morocco, in the Maghreb region of North Africa, is another Berber country that was conquered by the Arabs, who again brought their language and religion to the region. Like Mauritania, Morocco is a former French colony.

The Merchant and the Indian Parrot

Zeina tells this story to a group of scientists to introduce an alternative way of thinking and communicating. The tale is included in *The Masnavi*, a book in Persian verse that was written in the thirteenth century by the

Sufi poet Jalaluddin Rumi. Rumi was born in Balkh, Afghanistan, in 1207 and died in 1273 in Konia, Turkey. *The Masnavi* work took him forty-three years to write and is valued so highly that it has been called "the Koran in Persian."

A good contemporary translation of the *Masnavi* is *Teachings of Rumi: The Masnavi,* abridged and translated by E. H. Whinfield (The Octagon Press Ltd., 1979). Here the parrot story is called "The Merchant and his Clever Parrot."

An online version of the same story can be found at http://www.dar-al-masnavi.org/n-I-1547.html, where it's entitled "The Merchant and the Parrot."

The story is also found in *The Way of the Sufi* and *Tales of the Dervishes* (both by Idries Shah), where it's entitled "The Indian Bird."

Chapter 3: Gibraltar

The Iberian Peninsula, which includes Spain, Portugal and Gibraltar, was part of the ancient Roman Empire until the fall of Rome in the year 476. The Visigoths, a people of Germanic origin who had converted to Christianity, ruled the region until 711, when the Moorish general Tariq Ibn Ziyad crossed the Strait of Gibraltar from Africa with his armies and conquered the peninsula.

This first Muslim conquest was the beginning of the Arab occupation of much of Spain, which the Arabs called *al-Andalus*. A long period of Arab rule brought peace—and with it, great scientific and artistic splendor—to the region. Of special importance was the collaboration between Arab, Jewish and Christian scholars, who formed the famous Toledo School of Translators, which was led in the twelfth century by Raymond the Archbishop of Toledo and in the thirteenth century by King Alfonso X (known as "the Wise"). These scholars translated philosophical and scientific books from classical Greek, Arabic and Hebrew into Castilian (old Spanish), and from Castilian into Latin. Because Latin was the language of learning at the time, all of this knowledge soon spread to the rest of Europe.

The Arabs were finally driven out in 1492, when the Spanish Christian forces of King Ferdinand and Queen Isabella laid siege to the walled city of Granada, the last Spanish town ruled by a Muslim (Mohammad XII of Granada, also known as King Boabdil). The Arabs and Jews, who had lived there for centuries and who refused to convert to Catholicism, were expelled. The year 1492 was also, of course, the year the Catholic monarchs sent Columbus to "discover" the New World.

Although the Arabs were eventually driven back to their countries of origin, their nearly eight hundred years of occupation left a deep mark on the language, literature, architecture and—through intermarriage—ethnic composition of Spain and Portugal.

The Maiden Teodor

This story is one of many Middle Eastern tales introduced into Spain by the Arabs. Teodor is one of the heroines known as "wise women." She shares much in common with Scheherazade, the heroine of the *Arabian Nights*; with Tarsiana (see Chapters 10 and 11); with Isonberta, a Spanish-Arabic heroine (*La gran conquista de Ultramar*) who flees into the desert; and with other female protagonists, young and old, who possess knowledge and know how and when to use it.

The version told by Zeina is a retelling of the Spanish "La doncella Teodor." Teodor appears in the tale "The Slave Tawaddud" of the *Arabian Nights,* but the story is probably of Greco-Byzantine origin. As for the questions and answers that form part of the "test" to which Teodor is subjected, this was a common literary device in the Middle East. Similar tests appear in *The Books of Delights* by the twelfth-century Jewish philosopher Joseph ben Meir Zabara of Spain, and also in the Latin Christian collection *Disciplina Clericalis.*

A similar motif is found in the story "The Three Perceptives" in *Caravan of Dreams*, by Idries Shah.

Chapter 4: Oran, Algeria

Algeria is Africa's largest country. Like Morocco and Mauritania, it was originally Berber but was conquered by the Arabs, who brought their language and Islamic faith to the region. More recently, Algeria was a French colony, gaining its independence from France in 1963. Most Algerians are Muslims, although the country has a tiny Christian minority. Oran is the second-largest city, after the capital, Algiers.

After the Spanish overthrew Muslim rule at the end of the fifteenth century, the country's Arabs and Jews who didn't convert to Christianity migrated to the urban centers of the Maghreb—especially Morocco, Algeria, Tunisia and Libya. Much of that migration occurred during the seventeenth century, at the height of the Spanish Inquisition, when non-

Christians in Spain were persecuted and expelled. These emigres brought with them to North Africa their unique variant of Moorish, or *mudejar*, culture, which is why it's not unusual to find in Morocco, for example, arabesque artwork and architecture reminiscent of the beautiful Palace of the Alhambra in Granada and the glorious Mosque of Cordoba.

The Arabs and Jews who came to the Maghreb also brought with them a rich tradition of stories that, from the eighth century onward, travelled from the Middle East to Spain and found their way back five centuries later—transformed, rewritten and edited. As the years passed and populations moved from place to place, these folktales often merged with each other.

One of these is the story narrated by Ahmed, the storyteller of Oran, to Zeina and Jamal.

The Wise Man, the Merchant and the Fish

This is a retelling of "Story XII" from *The Count Lucanor*, by the Spaniard Don Juan Manuel. The full title of his book, which was published in the year 1335, is *Book of the Examples of Count Lucanor and of Patronio*. In it, the story is called "What Happened to a Dean of Santiago with Don Illan, the Magician from Toledo." Virtually all of the *Count Lucanor* stories are of Middle Eastern origin—adapted, of course, to conform with Don Juan Manuel's Christianity.

A similar story, entitled "Revealing His True Nature," is found in Idries Shah's book *The Commanding Self*. This story's motifs of greed and self-delusion as barriers to learning can also be found in the tale "The Magic Monastery," which is included in Shah's book of the same name.

Chapter 5: Tunis, Tunisia

Tunisia, the second country visited by *The Dreamer*, is also in the Maghreb and has the same ethnic and cultural composition as Morocco and Algeria. Here again, Andalusian Arabs left their mark when they emmigrated to these coasts in the sixteenth and seventeenth centuries, bringing with them stories such as "The Tale of Zifar," which Professor Rahman gives to Zeina and Jamal.

The University of Al-Zaytuna (Ez-Zitouna), where Zeina and Jamal found Professor Rahman, was founded in the year 737 and is one of the oldest universities in the Islamic world. Another still-existing North African university dating back to that era is the University of Al Quaraouiyine in

Fez, Morocco, which was founded by a woman named Fatima al-Fihri in 859.

During what's known as Islam's "Golden Age," which lasted from the mid-seventh to the mid-thirteenth centuries, learning was understood to be of greater value than almost anything else. The Prophet Muhammad had emphasized learning; for example, "The ink of the learned is holier than the blood of the martyr" is included in the *Hadith*, a collection of his sayings. During this period, many classic works of antiquity were translated into Arabic and Persian, including manuscripts from ancient Greece, Rome, Persia, India, China, Egypt and Phoenicia. Without Islam's "Golden Age," these important works—which were later translated into Turkish, Hebrew and Latin—might well have become lost.

Abd al-Rahman Jaldun, or Ibn Kaldun, was a fourteenth-century Arab historian, statesman and judge. He is considered a pioneer of social science, demography and economics. His most famous work is *Al-Muqaddinah*, which is about the rise and fall of nations.

The Story of the Knight Zifar

The Book of the Knight Zifar is the first prose adventure story in the Castilian language. It appears in the fourteenth century and contains elements from books of knightly lore, but instead of the customary single masculine hero, the protagonists are multiple members of one family. The Spanish retelling is thought by some historians to have been written by Ferrand Martínez, a priest from Toledo.

The story is based on one from *The Arabian Nights*—where, in *The Supplementary Nights* of the celebrated nineteenth-century English explorer and translator Richard Burton's version (*The Book of the One Thousand Nights and a Night*), it's entitled "The Tale of the King Who Lost Kingdom and Wife and Wealth and Allah Restored Them to Him, Book I."

The theme of the return and reunion of formerly separated family members can be seen as symbolizing the desire to reconnect with our origins in order to understand ourselves. It's a recurring motif in Byzantine Greek sagas of adventure. From its capital, Constantinople (modern-day Istanbul), the Byzantine Empire dominated the eastern Mediterranean region during the Middle Ages. The narrative origins of the reunion-story genre can be traced to the ancient Greek myths, in which the hero often has to cross a body of water to reach unknown territory, where he has harrowing adventures before eventually returning. Students of Greek mythology have pointed out that the journey of the hero can be viewed as symbolic of any individual's life.

Chapter 6: Alexandria, Egypt

Egypt's principal port, the ancient city of Alexandria has been influenced by many cultures over the years. Founded by Alexander the Great in 331 BCE, it quickly became an opulent, culturally Greek urban center with important philosophical schools and a library that had, at its peak, a collection of nine hundred thousand manuscripts. The Jewish School of Alexandria, where the Old Testament was translated from Hebrew into Greek, was also a renowned center of culture in the city.

After its Greek period, the city came under Roman, then Christian and finally Muslim dominion. But many Christians, who belong to the Coptic sect, remain in Alexandria.

This multicultural heritage has had a strong influence on the city's storytellers—who, in today's mass-media world, are an endangered species. But in Alexandria and elsewhere, people have formed cultural organizations that are dedicated to safeguarding the traditional storytellers' presence.

The Monkey and the Gourd

This is an ancient folkloric tale that's also factual—at least, with a baboon and an anthill (see https://www.youtube.com/watch?v=DuAlAN5B0aQ). Idries Shah included a version of it, entitled "How to Catch Monkeys," in his *Tales of the Dervishes*, where he traces the story's written origins to the *Book of Amu Darya* (from the Amu River in Central Asia), an ancient collection of wisdom tales.

The Story of King Yunan and Sage Duban

This tale is told by the fisherman to the *efrit* on the fourth night of *The One Thousand and One Nights* (The Arabian Nights Entertainment, A.L. Burt Co., 1904, New York).

As in "The Merchant and the Indian Parrot" and many other stories, this tale illustrates, among other things, that the transmission of ideas, information and thought is possible using indirect methods.

Chapter 7: Beirut, Lebanon

Situated on the eastern coast of the Mediterranean, Lebanon is culturally very influential, despite its small size. Populated by Canaanites and Phoenicians in pre-Christian times, it later fell under Greco-Roman and then Ottoman rule. With the fall of the Ottomans in 1917, Lebanon became a French protectorate for a short period, then gained its independence in 1943.

These disparate regimes, together with its strategic location at the crossroads of multiple civilizations, forged Lebanon's multicultural identity. Lebanese Muslims, both Sunni and Shia, share the country with Catholic, Maronite and Greek Orthodox Christians, and with several smaller groups and sects, including a Jewish community and the influential Druze. To maintain this cultural diversity, the Lebanese devised a special form of government in which political power is shared equally between members of the predominant religions.

Lebanon's capital, Beirut, is one of the oldest cities in the world, with more than five thousand years of history, and is a principal tourist destination in addition to being a world cultural center.

The Bird's Advice

This story is attributed to King Solomon as well as to an anonymous wise man who lived in North Africa after Solomon's reign. An Ethiopian version, also entitled "The Bird's Advice," can be found online at http://www.ethiopianfolktales.com/en/snnpr/keffa-zone/255-the-birds-advice.

Drawing on Arab-Jewish sources, the twelfth-century Spaniard Petrus Alfonsi, a medical doctor, writer and astronomer who converted from Judaism to Christianity, incorporated the tale into his Latin collection *Disciplina Clericalis* (Story 22, "The Peasant and the Bird," also known as "The Country Man and the Little Bird"). A century later, Rumi included it in his *Mathnavi (Book 4)* under the title "The Bird's Advice." More recently, Idries Shah included it in his *Tales of the Dervishes*, where it's entitled "Three Pieces of Advice."

The imparting of advice is a common feature in "wisdom literature." For example, it can be found in medieval collections such as the Hindu *Panchatantra* (known as *Kalila and Dimna* in the Persian and Arab worlds), and in the many Spanish collections derived from Arab-Jewish sources during Spain's Islamic period.

The idea that lack of proper preparation prevents one from benefitting from good advice—even advice one is anxious to receive—is repeated in teaching-stories from all over the world, as well as in such sayings as "good seed needs to fall on fertile ground in order to take root." The fact that so many traditions hold that it's our own shortcomings that prevent us from developing wisdom would seem to attest to its truth.

Chapter 8: Tartus, Syria

Syria is a vast, topographically rich country with high mountains, barren deserts, fertile plains and ocean beaches. It lies northeast of Lebanon on the Mediterranean coast. Tartus, a beautiful city that dates back to ancient Phoenicia, is a strategic Syrian port that today hosts a Russian naval base.

Among the early peoples who inhabited the region—aside from the Phoenicians—were the Akkadians, Hittites, Egyptians, Babylonians, Assyrians (who gave Syria its name) and Seleucids. With Alexander the Great's conquest in 330 BCE, Syria came under Greek sway and remained so until the year 64 CE, when it became a Roman province. The Muslim conquest of Syria in the first half of the seventh century ushered in a period of great splendor, with Damascus—one of the world's oldest cities—serving as the capital of the important Umayyad dynasty. After many attempts, the Byzantines finally conquered all of Syria by 996, but the country was politically unstable until 1084, when the Seljuk Turks took over, followed by the Ottomans in 1516. Ottoman rule lasted until after the First World War, when the secret Sykes-Picot agreement of 1920 placed Syria under French control and neighboring Iraq under the control of the British.

In 1945, Syria became an independent parliamentary republic. However, this supposedly democratic system didn't prevent the emergence of a dominant group: the Alawites, a branch of Shia Islam and a religious minority in a predominantly Sunni country. The privileges of this ruling class produced resentment among the population, and a peaceful revolt began in 2011, influenced by the movements of the so-called Arab Spring in other Islamic countries. When the Syrian government reacted with ferocity, the country devolved into a bloody civil war.

One of the root causes of that conflict is climate change. Desertification of large areas of Syria, after sustained periods of drought that elicited no aid from the government, left the rural population in misery. At the time of this writing, Syria's civil war has caused half a million deaths and has sent nearly five million desperate refugees fleeing into neighboring Arab nations, to Europe and, to a lesser extent, to the Americas.

In *Tales for THE DREAMER*, Omar Homsi had been part of the first contingent of refugees who came to Europe from Syria.

The Hidden Treasure

This story is of Persian origin, and other versions of it are found in *Folk Tales of Iran* by Asha Dhar (Sterling, New Delhi, 1978), where it's entitled "The Lost Treasure"; and in *The Way of the Sufi* by Idries Shah, where it's included in a piece entitled "Study by Analogy." Shah notes that the story depicts the use of analogy in a learning situation.

Chapter 9: Antalya, Turkey

Bridging Europe and Asia and bordering three seas—the Black Sea, the Sea of Marmara and the Mediterranean—Turkey lies at the crossroads of the East and West.

In 1453, the Ottoman Turks conquered Constantinople, the Christian capital of the Byzantine Empire, and renamed it Istanbul. Five centuries later, the Ottoman Empire disintegrated under the blows of World War I, and in 1923 Turkey became an independent secular republic ruled by Mustafa Kemal Atatürk, who is known as the founder of modern Turkey and is its national hero.

The city of Antalya in southern Turkey, where *The Dreamer* drops anchor for a day, was founded by the Greek Átalo, from whom its name is derived.

The Book of Apolonio

This story is a medieval Spanish verse narrative of anonymous authorship. It was widely known in Spain and elsewhere in Europe in the thirteenth century, and there are indications that it's based on a third-century Greek story whose author is also anonymous.

In style and content, "The Book of Apolonio" belongs to the Byzantine genre, which focuses on the theme of travel as a pilgrimage and learning opportunity. The story's geographical locations correspond to the territory of Byzantium. Apollonius, for example, is from Tyre, on the southern coast of Lebanon. His enemy, Antiochus, is from Antioch (Antakya), in what is now southern Turkey. The city of Pentapolis (Greek for "five cities") was the name given to five urban centers in what is now the Gaza Strip in Palestine. And the coffin that carries Luciana ends up in Ephesus, a city that's known for its temple to the goddess Artemis and is situated on the Turkish Agean coast. In olden times, Ephesus was a port city, but over the centuries, river silt has formed a fertile plain, pushing back the water, so that today the well-preserved ruins of Ephesus lie some miles' distance from the coast.

After the appearance of this story in Spain, many versions gained a wide audience in Europe. In Latin, the tale appears in the *Gesta Romanorum* as well as in the *Pantheon* of Godfrey of Viterbo. In French, it's found in *Le Violier des Histoires Romaines.* In English, it was published as *Apolonious* by Laurence Twine (London, 1576 and 1607) and by Benjamin Thorpe (London, 1834). There were editions in other European languages as well. Shakespeare based his play *Pericles* on this story. An anonymous author introduced one of the versions in this way: "Whoever is prepared to find gold and jewels in the dirt will be a suitable reader of this book."

The version in *Tales for THE DREAMER* is based on a Spanish poem of the same name ("The Book of Apolonio"), which can be found in a modern Spanish translation at http://www.cervantesvirtual.com/obra-visor/libro-de-apolonio--0/html/fedc1e46-82b1-11df-acc7-002185ce6064_1.html.

Chapter 10: Port Said, Egypt

The construction of the Suez Canal in 1869 connected the Mediterranean Sea with the Red Sea. This enabled ships to travel between Europe and South Asia without having to sail around the southern cape of Africa, greatly shortening the maritime trade route between East and West. At the canal's Mediterranean entrance, travelers go through Port Said, a beautiful Egyptian city with many mansions of nineteenth-century vintage.

The Red Sea is not always red, but turns that color with the seasonal bloom of the bacterium *Trichodesmium erythraeum*, commonly called "sea sawdust." This is likely how the Red Sea got its name, although another possibility is the fact that it borders the "red land," which is what the ancient Egyptians called the Egyptian desert.

Extending for one thousand, four hundred miles to the southeast, the Red Sea is connected to the Gulf of Aden by the Bab el Mandeb strait. In recent decades, many vessels sailing in this area have been attacked by Somali pirates—who, when captured, argue that they're forced to resort to piracy because of the depletion of their traditional fisheries by foreign fleets. Although the incidence of piracy has dropped considerably thanks to military patrols, at the time of this writing the practice continues.

Instead of pirates, *The Dreamer* encounters a rescue boat pursuing a stratospheric Internet balloon. Information about a present-day project to bring Wi-Fi connection to all corners of the world using high-altitude balloons can be found online at https://en.wikipedia.org/wiki/Project_Loon.

The Book of Apolonio - Part Two

The second part of this story has as its setting the Aegean Sea (see the Notes for Chapter 9), which laps the coasts of Greece and Turkey. As told in the original poem, Tarsiana is kidnapped and taken to the city of Mytilene, on the island of Lesbos. Today, Lesbos—although just a few nautical miles from Turkish territory—belongs to Greece, which is part of the European Union. Famous as the birthplace of Sappho, the celebrated poetess of antiquity, Lesbos has its capital at Mytilene, which was already a prosperous city in the seventh century BCE.

In 2011, refugees from the war in Syria began fleeing to Europe via Turkey, making the crossing from the Turkish mainland to Lesbos—a flow that continues to this day. Although the distance is short, shipwrecks are frequent, due to the fragility of the overcrowded vessels and the treachery of the waters. As a result, hundreds of travelers, including entire families with children, have perished in the Strait of Mytilene.

The Book of Apolonio is a complex story with many layers of meaning. One of those layers—common in traditional tales from ancient times onward, and represented by the myth of the phoenix rising from its own ashes—is the archetypal idea of metaphorical death, referring to the demise of the false aspects of one's personality enabling the rebirth of a transformed self. In the tale, the first character representing this idea is Luciana, who is taken for dead and buried at sea. The second such character is Tarsiana, who is also taken for dead by the people of Tarsus, although her tomb is fake and she's imprisoned in the hold of a pirate ship. Finally, we see Apolonio, hiding in the belly of his own ship, where he seeks death.

Chapter 11: Jeddah, Saudi Arabia

To the west of the Red Sea are the shores of Africa and to the east, the Arabian Peninsula, a landmass that's larger than western Europe and that hosts several countries: Saudi Arabia, Yemen, the United Arab Emirates, Bahrain, Qatar, Oman and Kuwait.

Occupying the greater part of the Arabian Peninsula's landmass. Saudi Arabia is crossed by the Tropic of Cancer, has a largely desert climate and has historically been the home of desert nomads. The country is also known as "the land of the two holy mosques," since two of its cities, Mecca and Medina, are both places of great spiritual importance in Islam, with Mecca being an important pilgrim destination for all Muslims.

The name "Saudi" derives from the country's founder, Ibn Saud, who in 1932 joined four regions into a single state through military conquest, establishing an absolute monarchy and, in effect, a hereditary dictatorship.

Saudi Arabia today is a country of global importance. There are more than one-and-a-half billion Muslims in the world, and once they've reached puberty they're obligated to face Mecca in prayer at least five times a day, no matter where they may be.

The life and works of the Prophet Muhammad, who was born in Mecca in the seventh century, have made Saudi Arabia the cradle of Islam. After his death, the expansion of this new religion to regions beyond the Arabian Peninsula was astounding. At its height, the Muslim empire extended from China and India, across Central Asia and the Middle East, North Africa, Sicily and the Iberian Peninsula as far as the Pyrenees. Along with their religion, the Arabs spread their language, resulting in diverse Arabic dialects in several of the conquered countries. Classical Arabic remains the language of the Koran, the holy book of Islam.

The second seminal event in Saudi Arabian history was the discovery, at the beginning of the twentieth century, of vast oil deposits there, which quickly gave the country economic and geopolitical importance. Petroleum production brought great wealth to Saudi Arabia and several other countries of the region, although it brought very little wealth to Yemen.

When the Saud family succeeded in conquering all of Arabia, its members established Wahhabi Islam—an eighteenth-century ultraconservative religious movement that grew out of the Sunni branch of Islam—as the national religion under their monarchy. *Sharia* (Islamic law) is strictly applied.

The future of the Saudi Arabian economy, and the other oil-based economies of the region, is uncertain, given the rise of renewable energy sources as well as the discovery of new oil and natural-gas resources.

The Travelers and the Elephant

In *Tales for THE DREAMER,* the oil museum librarian refers to a difference between the official Wahhabi religious interpretation—which enforces approved external behaviour and compliance with rigid orthodoxy—and inner religion or spirituality, which he says brings purity to the heart. To make the distinction plain, he chooses the story "The Travelers and the Elephant," because it emphasizes the importance of listening to the inner voice of intuition.

As with all wisdom tales, this story illustrates more than one point. One could say that the failure to fulfil a promise or intention is a sign of inner falsity, and that to "consume" elephant meat is a sign of looking for the immediate gratification of appetites and desires. Interestingly, the elephant appears as a symbol in several stories retold in *Tales for THE DREAMER.* For example, in "The Knight Zifar," the elephant represents higher perception leading to recognition of something of real value.

A version of "The Travelers and the Elephant," entitled "Elephant Meat," is found in *Seeker after Truth* by Idries Shah, who notes that an early version of the tale was told by Ibrahim Khawas in the tenth century. A century or so later, it appears in Rumi's *Masnavi* as "The Travelers Who Ate the Baby Elephant" (*Book III, Story 1*).

Chapter 12: Aden, Yemen

Located at the southern end of the Arabian Peninsula, the Republic of Yemen was created by the unification of North Yemen, which emerged from the collapse of the Ottoman Empire, and South Yemen, which was under British control until 1967. The two countries were formally united in 1990.

Although Yemen is the poorest country in the Middle East, it has one of the oldest civilizations in the region. The peak of its splendor came during the sixth century BCE, when the queen of the kingdom of Saba is said to have made a romantic connection with King Solomon—a liaison mentioned in both the Bible and the Koran. Today, the ruins of the queen's seat of power in the Yemeni town of Marib shelters several Bedouin tribes and is also an important archaeological site.

It's believed that coffee was discovered in Ethiopia, from where it spread to the Arabian Peninsula. The Yemeni port of Moccha became famous during the sixteenth to eighteenth centuries as a source of coffee. Ships carrying Moccha's "black gold" were dispatched to far-flung markets. Sufi monasteries in Yemen were apparently the first places where coffee was roasted and ground in ways similar to its modern-day preparation.

Civil war broke out in Yemen in 2004 and continues at the time of this book's writing. Traditionally, a Sunni government has ruled the country from its capital, Sanaa, which has, however, fallen into the hands of Houthi rebels, who practice a form of Shia Islam and are supported by Iran. Saudi Arabia, which supports the Sunni government, has subjected Houthi-held areas, including Sanaa, to bombardment, and the violence has spilled over to the port city of Aden.

When *The Dreamer* ties up at Aden for a day, the ravages of war are still evident. The Yemeni who appears in this chapter of *Tales for THE DREAMER* is from a northern tribe. He's wearing traditional costume: a long robe called a *thoob*, which is usually white, and a *keffiyeh*. He sports a dark jacket and has the famous curved Yemeni dagger, or *jambiyya,* in his wide, ornate belt. This dagger serves many purposes but is mainly ceremonial; for example, on occasions such as weddings, Yemeni men use it as a prop for dancing.

The Language of Animals

The ability to understand the language of animals was attributed to the Sufi Najmudin Kubra, who founded the order known as the "Greater Brethren." His miraculous ability was well known sixty years before the birth of St. Francis of Assisi, who is reputed to have had the same gift and may well have studied with the Greater Brethren before establishing the Christian Franciscan order, otherwise known as the "Lesser Brethren."

"The Language of Animals" does not focus on that ability per se, but on the quality of people and the potential misuse of knowledge.

An early version of this story is included in Jalaluddin Rumi's *Masnavi*, where it's entitled "The man who asked Moses to teach him the language of animals" (*Book 3, Story XV*). The same tale (under the title "Saving Oneself") also appears in Idries Shah's book *The Way of the Sufi.*

Chapter 13: Basra, Iraq

The region between the Tigris and Euphrates rivers has been known historically as Mesopotamia, which is Ancient Greek for "the land between the rivers." Considered the cradle of civilization, it was where mankind first began to read, write, create laws and live in cities under an organized government. The earliest of these cities was Uruk, from which "Iraq" is derived. Mesopotamia has been home to successive empires since the sixth millennium BCE. Iraq was the center of the Akkadian, Sumerian, Assyrian and Babylonian empires. It was also part of the Median, Achaemenid, Hellenistic, Parthian, Sassanid, Roman, Rashidun, Umayyad, Abbasid, Ayyubid, Mongol, Safavid, Afsharid and Ottoman empires. For more about the history and culture of Mesopotamia, go online to http://www.humanjourney.us/preAxialMesopotamia.html.

In 539 BCE, the Persian king Cyrus the Great conquered Mesopotamia. Centuries later the region became part of the Roman Empire, and in the seventh century the Arab conquest definitively established Islamic culture and religion there. Baghdad, the Abbasid caliphate's capital, became the main metropolis and center of culture during the "Islamic Golden Age" (eighth to thirteenth centuries). From this important city ruled the Caliph Harun al-Rashid, immortalized in *The Thousand and One Nights*. In the thirteenth century, the Mongols destroyed Baghdad, ushering in the legendary and feared Turco-Mongol military commander Tamerlane ("Timur, the Lame") in the fourteenth century. Following the same path as other Middle Eastern countries, Iraq fell under the power of the Ottomans. In the eighteenth century there was a short period of rule by the Mamelukes (to learn more about these freed slaves who were turned into warriors, visit https://en.wikipedia.org/wiki/Mamluk).

Iraq's modern borders were established by the League of Nations in 1920, at the end of the Ottoman Empire, when the country became the British Mandate of Mesopotamia. In 1921 Iraq became a monarchy, and in 1932 the country gained independence from Britain. Twenty-six years later, the monarchy was overthrown and the Iraqi Republic was formed. It was ruled by the Arab Socialist Ba'ath Party from 1968 until 2003. After an invasion by the United States and its allies in 2003, Saddam Hussein's Ba'ath Party was removed from power, and multiparty parliamentary elections were held in 2005. The American presence in Iraq formally ended in 2011. Basra, Iraq's second-largest city and its main port, lies some 280 miles south of Baghdad.

Images of the amazing Cultural Center of Basra can be seen online at https://www.arch2o.com/basra-cultural-center-dewan-architects-amp-engineers/.

It's in the vicinity of Basra that the garden of Eden, mentioned in the biblical "Book of Genesis," is thought to have been located. The parallels with this and similar origin stories in Sumerian and Greek mythology can be explored online at https://www.humanjourney.us/ideas-that-shaped-our-modern-world-section/post-axial-thought-pathway-to-current-beliefs/common-heritage/.

Also near Basra are the famous Iraqi marshes, where the adventures of the two teenagers in *Tales for THE DREAMER* take place. More information about this unusual marshy region can be found online at https://www.youtube.com/watch?v=EDMlQGPtGp4 and https://www.youtube.com/watch?v=KYefOZh63MA.

The Cadi, the Poor Man and the Lady

The marsh storyteller recounts this tale to illustrate how it's sometimes necessary to devise a trick to escape or expose a painful situation in life or in oneself. His narrative is based on the Tajik version included in *Folk Tales From the Soviet Union* (Raduga Publishers, Moscow, 1986), and also on a Turkish version that can be found online at http://www.uexpress.com/tell-me-a-story/2008/11/2/the-lady-and-the-unjust-judge.

Idries Shah presents a similar story, "The Chest," in *The Commanding Self.*

The Emperor's New Clothes

This story is well known in Europe, thanks to the collection of tales popularized by Hans Christian Andersen. The version narrated at the Cultural Center of Basra in *Tales for THE DREAMER* is a recreation of "Story XXXII" from *Count Lucanor*, where it's called "What Happened to the King and the Tricksters Who Made Cloth." Idries Shah presents the same story in *World Tales*, where it's entitled "The Three Imposters."

Chapter 14: Karachi, Pakistan

At the beginning of this chapter, Urho Ullakko refers to Iran by its former name, Persia. Like its neighbors Iraq, Afghanistan and Pakistan, Iran is home to some of mankind's earliest civilizations. The Persian empires were among the mightiest in the ancient world (see https://en.wikipedia.org/wiki/Persian_Empire#List_of_dynasties_described_as_a_Persian_Empire).

In the sixth century BCE, the religion called Zoroastrianism flourished in Persia and became the state religion of its first empire, the Achaemenid Empire (550-330 BCE), which was ruled by Cyrus the Great. Zoroastrianism had a great influence on the monotheistic religions of

Judaism, Christianity and Islam. For more on Zoroastrianism, visit http://www.humanjourney.us/zoroaster.html.

Many of the most world-renowned poets of the Middle Ages wrote in the classical Persian language, among them Saadi and Hafiz, who were both born in the south-central Iranian city of Shiraz; Hakim Sanai, who was from Ghazna in Afghanistan; Omar Khayyam and Attar, both of whom were born in the Iranian city of Nishapur; Shams of Tabriz, a city in northwestern Iran; Maulana Jalaluddin Rumi, who was born in Balkh, northern Afghanistan; and Hakim Nurudin Abdur-Rahman Jami, who was from Herat, in western Afghanistan.

Following the coast of Iran, *The Dreamer* enters the Gulf of Oman and sails to Karachi, Pakistan. Modern Pakistan is situated on the western edge of the Indian subcontinent, with Afghanistan and Iran to its west, India to its east and the Arabian Sea to the south.

The territory that today is Pakistan has been conquered by numerous empires and dynasties over the centuries. It was part of the Indus Valley Civilisation, which, by 2500 BCE, was the largest civilization in the ancient world, extending over three hundred eighty thousand square miles at its peak, with a population estimated at five million. For more information, visit http://www.humanjourney.us/preAxialHarappa.html

In the eighteenth century, the region became part of British India and remained part of it until achieving independence in 1947, when Pakistan and India split apart. Pakistan became a Muslim nation consisting of two widely separated regions, East Pakistan and West Pakistan, with India in between. But the civil war of 1971 resulted in the secession of East Pakistan, which became present-day Bangladesh. This partition between Pakistan and Bangladesh has had a profound impact, and has caused demographic changes whose geopolitical and psychological effects are still felt today.

Pakistan is ethnically and linguistically diverse, with Urdu, Pashto, Sindhi, Punjabi and Balochi spoken in different regions of the country. Though a Muslim country, it is subject to much sectarian violence from extremists. As the Taliban's attempt to murder Malala Yousafzai demonstrated, this violence is frequently directed against women and girls. Malala's advocacy for girls' education, since surviving the Taliban's assault, earned her a Nobel Prize in 2014.

Karachi is Pakistan's principal port and financial hub, and is one of the South Asian Islamic world's most important centers of higher education.

The Critics

This is a retelling of "Story XXIII" in *The Count Lucanor* and is well known in both Pakistan and Afghanistan. Idries Shah includes a version of this tale in *The World of Nasrudin*, where it's called "What To Do?"

The King's Ring

Both the phrase "This, too, shall pass," inscribed on the ring given to the writer-Nasim by *The Dreamer's* captain, and the story Nasim tells about a ring bearing that same phrase, appear in books by two famous classical Sufi poets, Attar (from Iran) and Hakim Sanai (from Afghanistan). Another version of the story is attributed to King Solomon. Idries Shah included the tale in his book *The Way of the Sufi*, where it's entitled "This, Too, Will Pass."

Chapter 15: Kandahar, Afghanistan

In this chapter, Farooq, the last traveller to embark on *The Dreamer*, gifts the ship with a chest full of books he bought in a particular bookstore in Islamabad, the capital of Pakistan. Although his claim that it's the world's largest bookstore is an exaggeration, it certainly is one of the largest. For more information on that bookstore, visit https://www.nytimes.com/2015/11/25/world/asia/a-storied-bookstore-and-its-late-oracle-leave-imprint-on-islamabad.html.

Like Pakistan, Afghanistan is an ancient and complex country. Part of the Indus Valley Civilisation referred to in the Notes for Chapter 14, Afghanistan has a history that dates back to about 3,000 BCE. For centuries, Afghanistan was a meeting point and a crossroads for trade and migration, and was coveted by a host of invaders: Persians, Greeks, Arabs, Turks, Mongols and, more recently, British and Russians. For this reason, the ethno-linguistic and religious identity of Afghanistan—which is composed of Pashtuns, Tajiks, Hazaras, Uzbeks, Pashais, Balochis, Nuristanis, Brahuis, Pamiris, Turkmens, Gujjars, Aymaqs and members of other ethnic groups that all share the country—has been influenced by many peoples. In pre-Islamic times, Zoroastrianism and Buddhism held sway there, but nowadays Afghanistan is a Muslim country with a Sunni majority.

Afghanistan was occupied in the nineteenth century by the British (who at the time ruled the Indian subcontinent), and in the twentieth century by the Soviets. Both occupations were disastrous. Once the Soviets withdrew, civil strife erupted between local Afghan warlords; and then, in the midst of the ensuing anarchy, the fanatical Taliban came to power. Although in 2001 a U.S.-led coalition came to power and overthrew the Taliban for a time, at the time of this writing a resurgence threatens the Afghan central government, causing insecurity for the population, constant internal displacement and mass migration.

Afghanistan's agriculture-dependent economy has suffered from the political and military upheavals as well as from a severe multiyear drought. Many farmers have had to resort to growing opium poppies in order to survive. Despite efforts to eradicate the opium crop, its cultivation continues to increase, supplying a thriving international underground drug market.

Afghanistan's difficulty achieving peace and some degree of welfare for its people is due in part to the fact that two-thirds of the population is illiterate—and the figure is even higher among women, who are often the main transmitters of culture.

Poverty and political confusion contrast with the great physical beauty of the country, which is crossed by the Hindu Kush, the world's second-highest mountain range, with more than one hundred peaks soaring upwards of 19,000 feet.

Kandahar and its environs ranks among the world's oldest continuously inhabited regions. The city itself, founded by Alexander the Great in the fourth century BCE, is one of the most culturally significant centers of the Pashtun people. In Kandahar's marketplace, *The Dreamer's* travelers find the storyteller who narrates the book's next story.

The Three Travelers and the Naan

This is another story that emphasizes the importance of listening to the intuitive (from the Latin word *intueri*, meaning "inward-looking, immediate-knowing") voice within us. The two travelers who employ deduction, logical reasoning and conditioned behavior get nothing, while the third traveler, who obeys his inner voice and takes direct action, gets the "food."

The tale appears in the *Masnavi*, by Jalaluddin Rumi (Book 6, Story VII), where it's entitled "The Three Travelers." Idries Shah also published two versions of the tale: one in *The Pleasantries of the Incredible Mulla Nasrudin,* where it's entitled "The Yogi, the Priest and the Sufi"; and the other in *Tales of the Dervishes*, where it's called "The Dreams and the Loaf of Bread."

Chapter 16: Indian Ocean

The Indian Ocean washes the shores of East Africa, the Middle East, South and Southeast Asia and most of Australia.

Together with the "Silk Road," an overland route linking cities from the eastern Mediterranean to the coast of China, the spice-trade routes through the Indian Ocean were major trade routes for centuries, connecting the Middle East, South Asia, China and Indonesia. When the Ottomans blocked these routes in the fifteenth century, the Europeans needed to find other sea lanes for trade, and this led to the "Age of Discovery"—when, for the first time, explorers circumnavigated Africa, journeyed to the Americas and Oceania, and made the first voyage around the world.

To reach its Antarctic island destination, *The Dreamer* had to cross the Indian Ocean. The travelers feared storms at this stage of their journey—with good reason, because storms are common across the Tropic of Cancer heading southwards.

The Book of Apolonio

This second part of the story entitled "The Book of Apolonio" (see the Notes for Chapters 9 and 10), which Zeina retells, brings us back to the first chapter, when Mirta points out that Scheherazade and her stories have the means of "saving lives." This time, however, salvation is not metaphorical but real, perhaps a reminder of how these and other wisdom tales, or teaching-stories, can have multiple effects on listeners and readers, some of them quite unexpected.

Once again, the villain of the story portrays the mental shortcoming of those who—as in the story "The Wise Man, the Merchant and the Fish" that's retold in Chapter 4—can't distinguish reality from fantasy, because their greed or fear stands in their way.

Chapter 17: Southern Hemisphere

Farooq's answer about the Infinite, "I heard that it's a sphere whose center is everywhere and whose circumference is nowhere," is attributed to the French philosopher Pascal. However, it had already been expressed much earlier in a Latin booklet by an anonymous author, and is frequently quoted and reworked by poets, philosophers and scientists in an attempt to account for concepts such as infinity, the universe and God.

To learn more about the Great Pacific Garbage Patch that's located in the North Pacific Gyre, visit https://en.wikipedia.org/wiki/Great_Pacific_garbage_patch.

For more information on the Earth's tilt and its effects, visit http://www.windows2universe.org/earth/climate/cli_seasons.html.

At the time of this writing, Antarctica is home to forty-five year-round stations and thirty summer stations, all of which are military scientific bases. Only two have permanent civilian population, with families and schools. One such station is Esperanza, which belongs to Argentina, and the other is Villa de las Estrellas, which is Chilean. For more information on these Antarctic stations, visit https://en.wikipedia.org/wiki/Esperanza_Base and https://en.wikipedia.org/wiki/Villa_Las_Estrellas.

Maruf the Cobbler

All of the stories retold in *Tales for THE DREAMER* are special to the book's author, but the tale of Maruf is one of her very favorites.

Maruf is a dreamer who imagines a caravan of riches that can save him from hardship. However, unlike most other "dreamers," Maruf is free from greed and so generous that whenever he has money, he freely distributes it to people in need. When a kindly farmer goes to fetch him some food, Maruf—quite naturally for him—immediately takes up the farmer's plough to help with tilling the soil. This action changes Maruf's circumstances entirely.

This inspiring story is part of the collection *One Thousand and One Nights*, where it's entitled "Ma'aruf the Cobbler." A version of this tale, also entitled "Maruf the Cobbler," can be found in Idries Shah's book *Tales of the Dervishes*.

In the preface to another of Shah's books, *Caravan of Dreams*, he says:

> *In one of the best tales of the* Arabian Nights, *Maruf the Cobbler found himself daydreaming his own fabulous caravan of riches.*
>
> *Destitute and almost friendless in an alien land, Maruf at first mentally conceived—and then described—an unbelievably valuable cargo on its way to him.*

Instead of leading to exposure and disgrace, this idea was the foundation of his eventual success. The imagined caravan took shape, became real for a time—and arrived.

May your caravan of dreams, too, find its way to you.

Author's Acknowledgements

I would like to express my appreciation to the many people who, with their interest, readings, suggestions and editing, made possible the publication of this book.

Special thanks go to Elena Camarillo, and to Pita Ocampo and her students at Bellevue Tillicum Middle School, as well as other young friends who read my first manuscript in Spanish and gave me their invaluable opinions on the story, especially with regard to how things might look in the year 2036. They include Andrés Vargas, Astrid Perez Otero, Carlie Stay, Carlos Garcia Jurado Moreno, Carmina Westbrook, Coco Mar, Elise Free, Emily Los, Emmanuel Spencer, EthanTampa, Fabio Vargas, Irene Vega-Hernandez, Isabela Westbrook, Jayden Kritsonis, Lucy McSherry, Marit Wineke, Mason Hogan, Naomi Kim, Samuel Mahlman, Tristan Dooly and Tyler Long.

Thanks also to my husband, Elwin Wirkala, who helped me in selecting the stories as well as in translating them from Spanish into English, and who patiently worked on the maps that show *The Dreamer's* itinerary.

Thanks to our daughter Elisa Wirkala, who extensively edited my own translation of the book's Spanish-language frame story into English, my third language. Elisa is a high-school teacher herself, and her tweaking added authenticity to the book's teen dialogue, making it lively and credible.

Thanks to Denise Nessel, Jill Barnes, Leslie Morgan and Guadalupe Rodriguez, whose careful reading and valuable suggestions greatly improved the story; to Mónica Gutierrez, for her fine illustrations; and to Shane de Haven, Dan Sperling and Stephanie Lawyer for the many hours they dedicated to the final editing of this novel. Finally, thanks to Sally Mallam of Hoopoe Books, who initiated and supervised this project from beginning to end. *Tales for THE DREAMER* would not exist without her initiative, orientation and direction.

CPSIA information can be obtained
at www.ICGtesting.com
Printed in the USA
LVHW051353110222
710784LV00010B/1124

9 781944 493905